IN HER MIND'S EYE

Hope you enjoy
the read!

Susan Gnucci

IN HER MIND'S EYE

A Novel

SUSAN GNUCCI

ISBN-13: 9781507578148

*To my good friend, Anne Gafiuk, without whom
I never would have been inspired to write*

PROLOGUE

AUGUST 2010

He was not aware of the intruder at first as the struggling girl demanded his full attention and his frenzied excitement with her was all consuming. It was only the odd sensation of being watched that finally alerted his senses. He was surprised and disturbed at the thought of an interloper, but first he had to get the girl under control and that was proving to be more difficult than he anticipated because she was stronger than she looked. Small as she was, she had been able to break free of his grip and had made a run for it, bolting headlong into the treeline. His chagrin had quickly given way to delight because a chase always added a new dimension to the kill.

It did not take him long to overtake her. Adrenaline and a head start had given her an advantage, but in her panic, she had taken off into the thickest part of woods, no doubt hoping to hide. Foolish girl. Her progress had been hampered by the dense tree cover, and the tinder dry conditions of the underbrush allowed him to track her movements. In a matter of minutes, he had been able to tackle her. And now, just as he was preoccupied in subduing her, he sensed something...someone...

SEPTEMBER

Tess trailed reluctantly after her best friend and room-mate, Leah, as they climbed the long flight of steps leading up to their local police station. "They're going to think I'm some kind of nut," she muttered with dismay, shaking her head and pausing as if unwilling to proceed any further. Crossing her arms in protest and scowling at her friend, she proceeded to worry her lower lip, a habit she always resorted to whenever she was nervous.

"Listen," Leah replied as she turned around and began walking back down the steps. "You've come this far; you may as well follow it through." She looped an arm reassuringly through that of her friend, pulling her closer to help bolster her courage. "And you're *not* some kind of nut. *Tell* them about your ability. *Tell* them about the things you've seen."

"I don't know if what I have to tell them will be of any help," Tess sighed wearily, "and I doubt they'll believe how I know what I know anyway." Leaning her head toward her friend's, Tess admitted, "To be honest, I wish I *didn't* know."

"You *need* to tell them," Leah insisted as she gently guided her friend up the remaining steps. "Maybe it'll help them find the creep who killed that poor girl."

"Alright," Tess sighed in resignation as she pulled away. "Let's get this over with." With her mind finally set, she swung open the main entrance door and strode full of purpose into the police station, leaving her best friend to catch up. Leah followed carefully behind, prepared to block Tess's retreat should she somehow lose her nerve.

As she approached the reception counter, Tess' determination quickly evaporated. Glancing back to make sure Leah was with her, she was annoyed to discover her friend's attention had been diverted by two young officers who were exiting the building. Narrowing her eyes and throwing Leah an exasperated look only prompted a shrug of the shoulders from her friend. Tess waited impatiently for Leah to catch up, elbowing her when she did so.

The clerk at the reception counter didn't even bother to glance up as the two women approached. After several awkward moments, it was Leah who boldly cleared her throat. "Excuse me. Can my friend please speak with a detective?"

When the clerk finally did look up from her paperwork, it was with reluctance, and the condescending stare she gave them set both women on edge. "A detective?" she asked, scrutinizing them over the rim of her glasses as if to say, "Now what do *you two* need to speak to a detective about?"

Tess drew in a deep breath, but before she could say anything, Leah proudly announced, "My friend has some information about that murder out at Prospect Lake."

Turning away and rolling her eyes, Tess braced herself, half expecting some bouncer of a cop to be summoned who would toss them unceremoniously out into the street, but instead, the clerk simply took their names and instructed them to take a seat in the lobby. They did as they were told, and as the minutes ticked by, Tess began to fidget nervously while Leah simply managed to look bored.

The police station of their Pacific Northwest city was an imposing granite structure built back in the days when civic buildings were constructed on a grand scale. City halls, fire stations, and libraries were all adorned with columns, clock towers, and other elaborate architectural details, and their local police station was no exception.

The massive flight of steps at the front of the building led up to impressive entrance doors that opened into a cavernous, tiled foyer. In addition to the reception counter, there were groupings of comfortable, elegant furniture situated in front of imposing portraits of local dignitaries. It was the type of building people took pride in, its restoration and upkeep lending to the quaint feel of the downtown core.

Tess heaved a sigh and wished for the umpteenth time she had never experienced her most recent 'sighting'. That's what she called her episodes because they came upon her much like visions. They were usually precipitated by a nauseous feeling and a distant humming in the back of her head that she likened to a swarm of bees. She would know then to close her eyes and await the scenes that would inevitably play out before her. Typically, they involved an event in the past, but at the time of her sightings, Tess often had no concept of time or place.

Her ability also allowed her to pick up impressions from people – these did not come to her like her sightings, for she had no conscious memory of actually acquiring them. She just *knew* things; that's all. Over the years, she had learned to trust in her ability, but she'd confided in very few people, carefully guarding her secret, intuitively understanding it branded her as different.

Tess thought back to her first experience with her sightings. She had been only ten at the time, too young to understand then, but old enough to realize the accident had fundamentally changed her. The accident. It pained her even now to recall it…

It was on a sleet driven night in the middle of winter when Tess' family was making their way home from a skiing vacation. A nor'easter descended upon them with little

3

warning that night, trapping them and many other motorists out on the highway. To make matters worse, the drifts were so heavy at that time of year, it was impossible to pull over safely to wait out the storm.

Sleeping in the back seat of the car, Tess was jolted awake by the sound of her mother's terrified scream and the glare of headlights bearing down upon them. As her eyes widened, her own scream had died in her throat.

Blessedly, the blackness engulfed her at that point, and almost a week passed before she regained consciousness in the hospital. The severity of her injuries initially led doctors to believe her chances for survival were slim at best, but over the following weeks, her young body slowly began to respond and heal. She did not have to be told her parents were dead. She knew it intuitively in the kind, sad way the nurses treated her. When she did not ask; in fact, when she did not speak at all, the doctors' concerns grew. Despite this, they finally told her of her parents' fate.

Tess remained in the hospital for almost two months, and in all that time, she never uttered a single word. Specialists and counsellors evaluated her while the police tried to locate a relative who would be willing to take her. Both of Tess' parents had been only children and because they'd conceived Tess later in life, the only close living relative was a maternal grandmother. This grandmother, however, lay in a nursing home in another province locked in the fog of Alzheimer's, blissfully unaware of Tess' condition.

When the hospital staff heard that the younger sister of Tess' paternal grandmother had come forward, they breathed a sigh of relief. They had all grown attached to the forlorn, withdrawn child, so they were thankful she had a relative to care for her. She still hadn't spoken, but the belief was she was suffering from some form of post-traumatic stress, and that given the right circumstances – a stable, loving home – she would eventually speak again.

On the day Tess was discharged from the hospital, the young surgeon who had saved her life came to her room to say goodbye. Dr. Elliott Wrightman was a rising star at the hospital – not only was he young and handsome, but his skill as a surgeon was becoming legendary. He had an ego to match, but then most of the hospital staff put up with that as a small price to pay for his talent. He was wed to an equally beautiful woman successful in her own right as a prosecutor with the district attorney's office. Both came from enormously wealthy families, and together, they were the ultimate power couple. They owned a gorgeous home, drove expensive cars, and traveled to exotic places. They led the kind of life most people can only dream about.

On the day Dr. Wrightman came to say good-bye, he found Tess sitting in a chair in her room, hands folded neatly in her lap, staring fixedly at the dreary winter landscape beyond her window. She did not stir when he entered, so he quietly took a seat, prepared to coax some type of response from her – a goodbye or perhaps even a thank you. They sat in awkward silence for a short time before Tess lifted her earnest face to his. Her eyes sought out his. It was the first time she had actually made eye contact with him, so that fact pleased him immensely. It took a few seconds though before something dawned in him – a subtle awareness – and when it did, his smile of pleasure slowly receded.

In a soft voice, hoarse from lack of use, Tess simply stated, "You shouldn't hit her."

The young doctor's face blanched, and for an instant, he stared at his patient with an odd mixture of horror and wonder. Just then, a nurse interrupted them, whisking into the room with Tess' discharge papers, prompting the doctor to stumble to his feet to scrawl a quick signature. Unable to face the child's scrutiny a moment longer, he beat a hasty retreat, red-faced and mumbling, leaving a perplexed nurse shaking her head in his wake.

Less than a year later, the eminent Dr. Wrightman's career, as well as his perfectly manicured life, was derailed by an attempted murder charge in the near-fatal beating of his lovely wife.

Tess was pulled from her reverie by the sound of a throat clearing. Standing in front of her was a very large, squat man who seemed to be squeezed into his suit in much the same way a sausage is stuffed into its casing. She had no doubt he could easily pop a button simply by flexing a muscle. In fact, he looked more like a sumo wrestler than a cop. This thought made her chuckle, for here was her bouncer cop in the flesh.

"Evening," he nodded his head curtly. "I'm Detective Baxter. I understand you have some information regarding the Katie Bishop case." His tone was matter-of-fact as he extended his hand briskly in greeting.

"Well…yes, I was hoping I could speak to someone working on her case. I'm Tessa. Tessa Walker," Tess replied as she stood up to shake his hand. Despite his size, his grip was not at all what she expected. It was firm, but not overly so, almost as if he made a conscious effort not to crush her hand. In her nervousness, she prayed he would not notice her sweaty palm.

"I'm the lead detective on that investigation. Come with me and we can speak in private," he instructed her with a terse nod of his head. Sensing Tess' hesitation, he glanced past her at Leah who sat in the next chair.

"Uh, this is my roommate. She…um…she came with me," Tess stammered as she flushed with embarrassment.

The burly detective made no further comment; instead, he simply shrugged his shoulders and stated dryly, "If you'll come with me then." Turning briskly on his heel, he proceeded down a corridor to the right without even checking to see if Tess was following him. As she hurried after him, Tess threw Leah a baleful glance over her shoulder, but her friend simply gave her the 'thumbs up' and pulled out her iPod.

Along the corridor, they passed numerous offices and cubbies on their way to the back of the building. Trailing along after the detective, Tess couldn't help but gawk at her surroundings. She was fascinated by an insider's view of an actual police station. Was that dejected man sitting at the desk of a frazzled-looking cop being booked for something? Were there any hookers being hauled in tonight? Where were the jail cells? All of these questions flooded through her mind as she took in the sights and sounds of a typical Friday night at the station. The look the detective gave her was an impatient one when she finally caught up with him at the door to what she presumed was an interrogation room. He motioned for her to enter. Taking a seat, she glanced around the small, airless space – four walls, a table, a few chairs – that was it. Detective Baxter took the opposite seat and wasted no time on pleasantries.

"So, you have some information in the Katie Bishop case, Miss Walker?" He sounded almost rote, as though he was simply going through the motions. Tess had to wonder if he was one of those over-worked cops who hung in there for his pension but whose passion for his work had ebbed away long ago. Or was it simply because it was a Friday night, and he was eager to get home to his wife and kids and enjoy some sense of normalcy from the ugliness he witnessed day-in, day-out? Their city was not a large one by any means, but it had its share of transients, and like anywhere else nowa-days, there was a growing drug culture and all the crime that goes along with it. As a result, cops undoubtedly witnessed the worst of human nature and that *had* to be hard to shake when they headed home at the end of a day.

"I'm...I'm not sure..." she hesitated.

Her response was interrupted by a second detective who entered the room and introduced himself. "Good evening," he acknowledged Tess warmly, extending his hand in greeting. "I'm Detective McLean. I'm working with Detective Baxter on the Katie Bishop case."

Tess had to crane her neck to look up at him, for at nearly six foot five, Detective McLean seemed to tower over her. His thin, almost lanky frame was such an obvious contrast to the senior detective's, Tess had to stifle a smile at the thought of their partnership. She was surprised this detective was quite a bit younger than his middle-aged partner. Tess judged him to be in his early-thirties, but then she wasn't the best at gauging peoples' ages. His handshake and smile seemed genuine enough though, and she liked him immediately.

"Hello. I'm Tessa Walker." She smiled tentatively up at him, suddenly tongue-tied.

As his partner settled into a chair, Detective Baxter continued with his line of questioning. "You're not *sure* you have any information, Miss Walker?" He managed to sound both puzzled and annoyed at the same time. Tess figured he was the type of person who didn't suffer fools lightly.

"That's not what I started to say," she corrected him. "It's just I'm not sure you're going to *believe* the information I have." She sighed heavily at this point, looking first at one detective and then the other before admitting, "Look, I'm really nervous. Could you please just call me Tess?" She found it hard to hold their gaze for any length of time, so she stared fixedly at her hands, preoccupied with a ring on her finger, spinning it distractedly. Feeling extraordinarily foolish, she tried to collect her thoughts. How was she ever going to explain something so intangible to two such rational men? After all, being detectives, surely they would expect *some* kind of concrete evidence, wouldn't they? Admittedly, she had nothing of the sort to offer them.

"No problem, Tess. Take your time. We're in no rush." Detective McLean's response was surprisingly reassuring.

Tess looked up and flashed him a weak smile. Taking a deep breath to steady her nerves, she spoke in a soft voice, "A month ago, I saw something really awful. It scared me."

Several uncomfortable seconds passed before Detective McLean gently prompted her. "And what is it you saw, exactly?"

"It's hard to explain. Can I ask you a question?" she asked tentatively.

"Of course," he assured her.

"That girl – Katie Bishop. The news made it sound like she was dumped out at Prospect Lake, but she wasn't, was she?" Without waiting for an answer, Tess continued, "She was killed out there, wasn't she?" She looked to both detectives for confirmation; however, their countenances gave nothing away.

It was Detective Baxter who answered her question. "We aren't at liberty to discuss specifics of an ongoing investigation, Miss...ah, Tess. Why do you ask?" He sounded both suspicious of her question and uncomfortable with the use of her given name. Tess could tell he was the type of investigator who preferred to keep things impersonal. He was probably one of those cops who conducted himself strictly by the books.

"Because I saw her out there." Tess squeezed her eyes shut in anticipation of their response, knowing full well the Pandora's Box she had just opened with that statement.

"You *saw* her?" both detectives exclaimed at once, their attention now riveted.

Tess held up her hands in a defensive gesture. "I need to explain what I mean when I say, I *saw* her," she was quick to add. This was a huge leap of faith for Tess because she had only confided in a trusted few about her ability. Now she would be forced to divulge her personal circumstances to those who would undoubtedly be skeptical, and she could hardly blame them. Nevertheless, she took a deep breath and forged ahead. "When I was little, I was in a car accident that changed my life in more ways than one. Since then, I've been able to..." She stopped mid-sentence, pausing as if struggling to describe something indefinable. "I've been able to *see* things others can't. I can't explain how or why. I don't even have much control over my...my sightings." She paused to let this information sink in for a second. "That's what I call them," she added sheepishly with a shrug of her shoulders, "for lack of a better word."

An awkward silence followed during which both detectives shifted uncomfortably in their seats. It was clear they were having a hard time processing what Tess had just told them. Finally, Detective Baxter spoke up. "So you *saw* Katie Bishop in your mind; is that it?" he asked her curtly, raising an eyebrow, making no attempt to hide his skepticism.

Undeterred by his partner's response, Detective McLean leaned forward to ask – "What did you see, Tess?"

It took several seconds before she could finally respond. "I saw her die," she stated flatly.

"Jesus, no wonder you were scared." Detective McLean sat back in his seat and slowly released his breath.

In contrast to his partner, Detective Baxter folded his beefy arms across his broad chest and gave her a dubious look. Tess had to wonder if this would trigger some kind of 'good-cop, bad-cop' routine in order to get to the bottom of things. Well, at least she knew who would play what role.

"You expect us to believe..." At this, Detective Baxter held up a hand toward his partner to silence any protest.

"...that you picked up on this murder *psychically?*" he asked, narrowing his eyes.

"Look, I *know* it's hard to believe. I get that, but I've had this ability for years. I *trust* it. And a girl is dead. The *same* girl I saw," Tess insisted.

"You're sure it's the same girl, Tess?" Detective McLean asked.

"I didn't at first until I saw the story of her disappearance on the news and her picture was everywhere," she confessed. "I didn't know *what* to make of my sighting at the time it actually happened. And I had no way of knowing when or where it even took place. For all I knew, it could have happened years ago," she explained.

"When you *did* realize it was the same girl, why didn't you come forward at that point?" Detective Baxter asked without mincing words.

Tess winced as though she had just been slapped in the face.

Without even giving her time to answer, the burly detective pressed, "And when her body was found, confirming it wasn't just a disappearance but a murder, why didn't you come forward then?"

"Are you *kidding* me?" Tess balked. "I've only ever confided in *two* people in my entire life about my ability. Do you know how *hard* this is for me to come forward and talk to you guys about this? I *know* what most people think of psychics. They're just like you. They think we're all a bunch of charlatans or crack pots." Humiliated and furious now, she stood up to leave. "You know, I can do without this crap."

Detective McLean rose and held his hands up in an attempt to pacify her. "Tess, please..." He motioned to her chair. "Please, sit down." He gave her such an imploring look, it made Tess regret her outburst. Despite that, she hesitated as if to weigh her options. Finally, she reluctantly lowered herself back into her seat, making a point of sitting on its edge to make it clear she was still prepared to leave. Feeling defensive, she sat with her arms crossed protectively against her chest.

"Now, let's look at this objectively," Detective McLean began.

"Listen," Tess interrupted him. "*Everything* made sense when they found her body out at Prospect Lake. My roommate and I were camping near there the weekend Katie disappeared, and that was the *same* weekend I had my sighting…" her voice trailed off.

"Oh, OK. *I* get it," Detective Baxter nodded. "So you not only picked up on this murder 'psychically', you also witnessed it *as it happened?*" Sitting back in his chair, he muttered under his breath, "*Now* I've heard everything!"

Embarrassed by his partner's reaction, the young detective turned to give Tess his full attention, almost as if in doing so, he could convince her not to leave. "For argument's sake, Tess, let's just say what you saw *was* real. Can you provide us with any details?"

It touched her that both his voice and manner were respectful. That won her over. And the simple fact he was willing to entertain the idea calmed her, but before she was willing to answer, she shot his partner a withering glare. Then she purposely took her time collecting her thoughts. "Well, it was dark…" she began. Shifting in her seat so as to direct her explanation solely at Detective McLean, she continued, "At first, I saw only her. I saw 'flashes' of her running through the woods. My sightings are usually like that," she explained. "It's…it's kind of like a strobe light going on and off in the pitch dark, so you only catch images for a split second."

"Go on, Tess," Detective McLean encouraged her.

"She was frantic...and disorientated...and utterly terrified. I could actually *feel* her fear." Tess exhaled deeply and closed her eyes, massaging her temples in a vain attempt to erase not only the image but the feelings it evoked as well. She did *not* want to remember that poor girl's agony.

Detective McLean waited patiently for her to collect herself before he gently asked, "What happened to her, Tess? What did you see?"

A look of anguish washed over Tess' face as she continued, "He tackled her from behind." At this admission, she buried her face in her hands, and several more seconds passed before she could regain her composure. The detectives waited in awkward silence, one of them clearly intrigued, the other just as clearly unconvinced. "She fought *so* hard," Tess looked up with a tortured expression. "But her hands were bound behind her, and she couldn't even scream because of the duct tape covering her mouth." The mere thought of that dreadful image made Tess wince and look away.

Leaning his bulk over the tabletop, Detective Baxter posed a simple, direct question. "*How* did he kill her, Tess?" He waited expectantly for her answer as this information had not yet been released to the public.

Turning to face him, she replied with equal directness, tears now coursing down her face, "He strangled her."

"*How?*"

Eyes brimming with resentment that he would so clinically tease the gruesome details from her, she finally admitted, "With his bare hands." Having said that, Tess lowered her head and wiped at her eyes with the back of her hand, knowing she was likely smearing her mascara.

Detective Baxter leaned back and shrugged his shoulders, his body language making it clear he considered her answer to be nothing more than a lucky guess.

Sympathetic to her discomfort, Detective McLean rose from his seat. "Let me get you a glass of water," he offered. He left the room only briefly and reappeared with a tall glass of cold water and a box of tissues that he placed in front of her. Tess threw him a grateful half-smile and took several sips from the glass while dabbing at her eyes, mortified with the knowledge she always looked so gross when she cried. No doubt her nose was swollen and red; her skin was blotchy; and her eyes were puffy.

"Look, I *know* how difficult it must be to believe something like this," she finally told them. "Trust me, I can appreciate that. Why do you think I've waited this long to come in? But I *know* what he did to her," she stated defiantly. "He never raped her, you know. That's not what excites him. It's the kill. That's why he strangled her with his bare hands. *That's* what he gets off on, the sick SOB."

Both detectives seemed taken aback at her outburst. It was obvious this woman believed wholeheartedly in what she was telling them, however implausible it might seem.

"I'm sure this has been awful for you, Tess," Detective McLean's voice was soothing, "but is there any chance you would be able to identify this guy?" He asked the question tentatively, afraid of upsetting her further.

"It was dark, but yeah, I got a look at him," she admitted warily.

"Good enough to work with one of our police artists?"

"Oh, I don't know if I'd be any good at that…" her voice trailed off. When she witnessed the disappointment clouding the young detective's face, however, she was quick to add, "…but I guess I could give it a try."

"That's great, Tess." Detective McLean brightened. "Let's see what comes out of a session and we'll go from there."

"But you don't understand!" She grew suddenly irritated. "He *knew* I was there."

"What do you mean, Tess?" Detective McLean frowned.

"He's like *me*. He *saw* me!"

"What makes you think that?"

"Because he smiled at me."

"**H**e *smiled* at you?" Detective McLean repeated, at once perplexed and transfixed.

"Yeah, I think he knew I was there all along," she sighed. With this statement, Tess leaned over the table and lowered her voice as though afraid the killer could somehow hear her even now. "And do you know what?" she paused, shaking her head solemnly. "It didn't bother him *in the least.*"

Detective Baxter braced his elbows on the table at that point and lowered his head into his hands, making it clear he wanted no part of the farce he saw unfolding. He felt a headache coming on.

For the moment, the young detective was rendered speechless. He didn't quite know what to make of the intense young woman who sat before him, but he wasn't willing to let her go until he'd heard everything she had to say. It certainly couldn't hurt. Besides, they had no other leads right now anyway. "What happened *after* he smiled at you?" he asked, his voice low.

Tess paused briefly and then sank back against her seat. "He took a *souvenir,*" she muttered, pronouncing the last word slowly as if to emphasize her disgust.

"A souvenir? And what was that?"

"Her hair," she replied numbly.

Detective Baxter slowly raised his head with that comment and shot his partner a bewildered look. "Her hair?" he repeated, straightening in his seat and clearing his throat as though he had something stuck in it. Leaning his bulk over the table once again, he asked in a guarded tone, "And just *how* did he do that?"

Tess looked up with a flat expression on her face. "He twisted it into a ponytail and sliced it off with a knife he had with him," she explained, all emotion seemingly drained from her voice.

A moment of silence ensued while both detectives absorbed this information, the senior detective looking more puzzled than ever, the younger detective even more engrossed. "And afterwards, Tess?" McLean eagerly asked.

"I came out of it. Just like that." She snapped her finger to emphasize the suddenness of it.

"Is that usual?"

"To end like that – yes, but to feel what I felt – no," she admitted.

"And what was that?"

"Like I'd been hit by lightning." Leaning forward in her seat, she confessed, "I don't know if it was the power of our connection, or...the power of *his* ability."

For a moment, no one spoke. Finally, Tess broke the silence by expressing her biggest concern. "It occurred to me he might be able to track me, you know. What if he can do that?" She turned to them, half expecting an answer, but in reality, knowing neither of them could provide her with one.

"Even if what you think is true, Tess, this is a city of 300,000 people. The odds of this guy finding you are pretty remote," Detective McLean assured her. "And in our experience, these perpetrators are often transient. In all likelihood, he has moved on by now, especially if he thinks someone can ID him."

"I guess you're right. It's been weeks and I haven't had any more sightings; maybe he hasn't either. I just hope he isn't able to control his ability..." her voice trailed off.

"Then it's important we get his sketch out there as soon as possible," Detective McLean informed her. "Can you come back in the morning to work with our police artist?"

"Sure. I usually go up to the university on Saturdays, but I can always do that afterwards."

"Are you a student?" Detective McLean asked, the curiosity in his voice was something Tess in her innocence didn't pick up on.

"Yes, I'm an Astronomy graduate student. I'm finishing my Master's degree this year," she replied, suddenly self-conscious he would find her bookish, suddenly caring if he did.

"Well, hopefully, we won't keep you too long in the morning. Can you stay a while longer tonight while we go over things one more time?" Detective McLean seemed to tread lightly, almost as if he was afraid Tess would be eager to be on her way after having unloaded her burden. "We need to make some notes."

The senior detective raised his eyebrows with that statement but made no comment.

"I guess so. My roommate is waiting for me in the lobby though. I need to tell her how long I'm going to be." Tess worried her lower lip.

"If she can't stay, we can have someone drive you home."

"OK, let me check with her." With that, Tess returned to the lobby in the company of young detective where it was decided Leah would head home. As she turned to leave, her friend playfully winked at Tess, clearly supportive of leaving her best friend in the company of the tall, clean-cut officer.

It was a good two hours later before they finally finished questioning her. Detective Baxter had been relentless. Did she see his car? Did he wear gloves? How did he bind the girl's wrists? Were any items of clothing removed? Did he take anything else? By the end, she was exhausted from the effort of trying to remember every little detail. Rising stiffly from her chair, she stood on tiptoe and stretched her arms high over her head in an attempt to relieve her aching muscles. All she wanted to do was go home.

Detective McLean suppressed a grin. "OK, I think that's all for tonight. Let's make sure we have your contact information and then you can be on your way. We'll have one of our units drive you home."

As she was guided back out into the hallway, Tess had to temper her disappointment that the young detective had not offered to drive her home himself.

As they parted ways, he thrust a business card in her hand. "Here's my card, Tess. If you have any more sightings, be sure to contact me, OK? My cell number is on there as well as my office number. It doesn't matter what time of day or night," he advised her.

She winced inwardly with the knowledge that this was the first time she had ever received a man's phone number, and sadly, it was only because she was a witness in a murder investigation. 'Great. Leah will have a field day with that one,' she thought dryly to herself.

"Thank you detective." The corners of her mouth lifted in a tentative smile. "I know your partner doesn't buy any of this, but I do appreciate *your* willingness to consider my information. Not a lot of people are open-minded when it comes to psychics."

"Oh, don't mind him," the young detective assured her with a wave of his hand. "He didn't mean any disrespect. He's just old school, I'm afraid."

Tess nodded and turned to leave but then seemed to think better of it. She stood pensively for a second as if reluctant to say anything further. Finally, she cautioned the young detective – "The man who killed that girl has done this before, you know."

"What makes you think so, Tess?"
"Because he enjoyed it so much."

After arranging a courtesy ride for Tess with a patrol unit that was heading out, Detective McLean made his way to his partner's office, and as he did so, he prepared himself for the reaction he knew he was sure to encounter. It was the first time he'd taken the lead with a witness, but it had been without his partner's consent or direction. Testing the waters, he stuck his head in the door and braced himself.

He was met with a frown and a stern look. "You actually bought all that mumbo-jumbo?" grumbled the senior detective who sat back in his chair and crossed his beefy arms, indicating with a nod of his head for his partner to take a seat.

Detective McLean entered the office reluctantly and silently folded his lanky frame into a chair, after which he leaned forward, elbows resting on his knees. He knew this would not be an easy conversation. He knew he would have to tread carefully. His senior partner had very definite ideas on things, *and* he was not easy to convince if his mind was made up. Nevertheless, in their three years together, he had always encouraged his young partner to speak up. If it was one thing Detective Baxter loathed, it was a 'yes' man. He *liked* a partner who could stand up to him – 'chew his ass out', so to speak.

And so, Detective McLean spoke his mind. "She came across as totally believable to me, Ed. Besides, how else can you explain all the things she knew? She knew just about everything. We both know that only comes from being an eye witness."

"Maybe she *was* there, Jay." Detective Baxter arched an eyebrow at him. "And I don't mean 'psychically'."

"And just how does a woman her size abduct a teenage girl and strangle her with her bare hands?" Detective

McLean asked, trying to keep the tone of his voice respectful while getting his point across.

"Maybe she had help," the senior detective said with a shrug. "Maybe she and a boyfriend abducted the girl and they killed her, or maybe the boyfriend did the killing and she just witnessed it."

At that, the young detective became animated, rising from his seat to walk over to the window where he began to pace, running his hand repeatedly through his cropped hair. "So you think she and some boyfriend were driving around and just decided on a whim to pick up a teenage girl to kill? Come on, Ed. She's a well-educated woman. She's on a career track."

"We both know plenty of professional people commit serious crimes, Jay," Detective Baxter retorted, "*including* murder."

"I know. I know," Detective McLean admitted reluctantly. "But I seriously can't picture her involved in this, Ed, not in the way you mean. And if she was, why come forward? Isn't that shooting herself in the foot?"

Detective Baxter shrugged nonchalantly. "Maybe her conscience got the better of her." Suddenly irritated, he added, "How the hell am I supposed to know, for Christ's sake?"

"*Or*, maybe she did witness the murder just like she said she did." Detective McLean held up his hands to defend his point of view. "I *know* it sounds implausible, but we both know some psychics are legit." Witnessing the annoyed look on his partner's face, he was quick to add, "Not many, I grant you, but *some*. And we both know police departments occasionally bring them in on tough cases, so why don't we just give Tess the benefit of the doubt and circulate her sketch simply as a person of interest? What harm is it going to do? If the guy isn't real, we won't get any hits anyway."

"Listen, Jay. If you wanna waste your time on this psychic thing, be my guest. Fill your boots. I've got better things to do." The senior detective made a point of rifling through the mound of paperwork on his desk, a more than subtle hint that their conversation was at an end. Before allowing the young detective to leave; however, he added, "But I want her story checked out, Jay. If she says she was camping the weekend of the murder, I want that confirmed. Bring in the friend."

Pausing at the door, Detective McLean turned around. Despite the risk of annoying his partner further, he advised, "I've got a gut feeling about this woman, Ed. She's the real thing."

He needed to clear his head. He had been thinking about the witness for weeks now. At first, he wasn't even sure if she really existed. He speculated she was someone from his past whom he had simply conjured up in a moment of frenzy, but he trusted his ability implicitly. It had never failed him. Oh, yes – he knew she was real alright. And she was obviously psychic. Like him.

He stood in the cool, crisp air at the top of a popular lookout that evening gazing out over the lights of the city, lost deep in thought. It was a cloudless, windless night; the stars scattered above him like diamonds on black velvet; the muted traffic noises far below. It was a perfect vantage point from which to contemplate and strategize.

She was out there somewhere. He could *feel* it. What a job it would be to find her! Almost impossible, really. But then he was not one to shy away from a challenge. In fact, despite the complication, he hadn't felt this energized in years. Moving here had indeed been a fortuitous decision as it would offer him perhaps his greatest challenge.

He knew what she looked like. He had that much to go on. She was young, no more than mid-twenties. Long dark hair framed a delicately boned face. He smiled knowingly when he remembered her eyes; they had been enormous as they'd taken in his handiwork.

But how to find her? He was at a disadvantage because his search would undoubtedly be hampered by his pathological fear of public places. What else did that leave? He felt certain their connection had been the result of proximity, so he reasoned he could attempt to track her that way. He was fortunate his job entailed shift work as it would leave plenty of time to conduct his search.

And if he found her? He had to be careful, for surely she knew what he looked like as well. He had to admit at first he had been concerned, especially when the girl's body had been found so quickly, but from the nightly news coverage, it appeared as if that had been by accident. Hikers had apparently stumbled across the body. So the witness obviously hadn't gone to the police. Why not? Did that mean she was frightened? He had to admit that thought delighted him.

And what of her ability? How developed was it? Could she *see* him without his knowing? He didn't think so, but couldn't be certain. Had she always been this way? Could she control it? What was she capable of *seeing*? She was fast becoming an obsession with him as he had never met anyone like her before. Oh, of course, he knew other psychics existed, but to actually meet someone as extraordinary as himself...

After the car accident when she was ten in which her parents perished, Tess moved to Victoria, a picturesque city on the southern coast of Vancouver Island in the Pacific Northwest. It was the home of her guardian, Emily, or more simply as she came to be known – Emmy. Tess had only met Emmy on the odd family occasion, for Tess' paternal grandmother and Emmy were sisters who lived on different coasts. At a time in Tess' life though when her whole world had changed so drastically, Emmy's familiar face was a godsend. To a frightened, traumatized child, she represented a safe haven. Her warmth and sincerity were genuine, and she lived in a wonderful old house close to the ocean. Tess was given her own room under the eaves, and in time, she grew to love and trust her guardian, this woman who had willingly put aside her own retirement plans to care for a broken-hearted child.

Tess woke bewildered that first morning in a strange house in a strange city. The unfamiliar, eerie bellow of a fog horn echoing off the water had roused her. It was still dark, not the pitch-black darkness of the night, but the soft darkness of the early morning when the air is tinged with the gentle colours of the rising sun. Tess lay cocooned under her comforter and took stock of her room. 'Her room.' It felt odd to consider this *her* room. Until yesterday, she had never even laid eyes upon it.

The furniture, like everything else in Emmy's house, was from another era – large, ornately carved pieces fashioned from rich, dark wood dominated the rooms, and Tess' bedroom was no exception. Her bed was so massive a footstool was needed to climb onto it. It was a canopy bed complete with draw curtains, and Tess was enthralled with it, for she had only seen such a bed in story books. In one corner of the room, there was a large dresser in which Tess placed the few items of clothing she'd brought with her. Stubbornly, she had refused to bring many of her things, including much of her clothing, almost as though they carried with them all the pain and sadness of the past few months. Along one wall, there stood an old fashioned vanity with an elaborately carved mirror and a stool. On its surface, Emmy had thoughtfully laid out a vintage ivory comb and brush set for her use. Next to the vanity, there sat an ancient looking rocking chair, its leather seat cover faded and worn. Tess had reached out a hand to set it in motion, wondering at the generations that had undoubtedly taken pleasure in its use.

But it was the window seat that had charmed her from the moment she set eyes upon it. It was situated on the west side of the house, and as a result, it was bathed in late afternoon sunshine. The seat cushions were sewn from a soft floral print, and three old-fashioned, well-loved teddy bears made it their home. Tess would come to know it as a perfect perch upon which to spend many an idle hour simply watching the clouds drift along or the sea birds in their aerial play. A blustery day would provide added entertainment in the form of a multitude of colourful, fanciful kites that soared and swooped or hung on currents of air on the bluffs overlooking the ocean, their tails streaming out behind them, the laughter and shrieks from excited children trailing along after them.

Tess was at the police station bright and early the morning after her initial session with the detectives. She was mildly annoyed neither detective was there to greet her; instead, she was escorted by a young officer to the second floor after giving her name at the reception desk. At least the clerk there treated her with more respect than she had the day before. Climbing the stairs, Tess tried to shake off her irritation, feeling guilty for having experienced it.

The police sketch artist was a likeable, middle-aged woman named Sue. Her most remarkable feature was a crop of wild looking red hair. Perched atop a stool at her easel, she reminded Tess of some exotic tropical bird. Conversation was easy while Sue readied herself.

As the minutes passed, Tess grew pensive. The thought of giving life to the image in her mind frankly unnerved her. It was bad enough it was locked away inside of her head, but to actually put it to paper disturbed her more than she cared to admit. She did not want this killer to be real, and yet, she knew with certainty he was. He was no figment of her imagination, however much she wished him to be. Never one for hiding her emotions well, Tess flashed Sue a weak smile as their session got under way.

"It's alright, Tess. Most of the people I work with don't *want* to remember the face of their perpetrator. That's natural. But trust me; once a sketch is done, you'll feel relieved. It's like all of that fear, and much of the emotional baggage that goes along with it, is transferred to the paper, you know?"

With this assurance, Tess felt somewhat better. She was still unconvinced though about her ability to direct Sue to reproduce any kind of likeness, let alone an accurate one. She needn't have worried, however, because the process, although slow, wasn't nearly as difficult as she'd imagined.

29

Under Sue's expert guidance, a face slowly began to take shape – the long, thin chin; the deeply set eyes topped by bushy eyebrows; the rather large ears visible through thinning, wispy hair. They took a break a few times when it was evident Tess was getting tired or frustrated. It was on one of these breaks when Detective McLean stopped by to see how things were going. He came up behind Tess and leaned across her shoulder in order to better view the sketch.

"Ah, I see the sketch is coming along nicely," he remarked.

"Morning, Detective McLean. Yeah, it's getting there," she agreed. "Sue is great to work with." Tess tried to sound casual despite the fact her pulse had quickened from the mere smell of his cologne.

"Yes. Yes, she is," he agreed. "She's been at this a long time." He flashed Sue a brilliant smile that served to squelch any objection she might have had as to his comment having anything to do with her age. Turning his attention back to Tess, he said, "I was hoping I could speak with you some more about your… "

He seemed at a loss for words, so Tess graciously came to his aid. "About my ability?"

He gave her a grateful, lopsided grin that set her insides fluttering. "Yes, your ability."

"Sure. When I'm done here." She smiled up at him, hoping her voice didn't sound *too* eager.

"Great, thanks. I'm down the hall, last door on your right," he replied. As he left the room, she noticed he practically had to bend down to go through the doorway.

After he left, Tess found herself anxious to finish the sketch, and she secretly hoped Sue wasn't able to pick up on that fact. They were close to being done anyway, but it seemed to take forever with the finishing touches. When the sketch was at last completed, Tess sat back in her seat and studied the likeness. It was not an entirely accurate one to be sure, but the general likeness was there, enough that it unnerved her.

Sue noted her reaction. "I'm sure *that's* a face you'd hoped never to see again," she mused.

Tess could only nod her head solemnly in agreement.

"Hopefully, we'll get some tips from this," Sue speculated as she vigorously massaged life back into her cramped hands.

Tess thanked her profusely and proceeded to head down the hallway to Detective McLean's office. Although his door was closed, she became aware of a heated argument from within as she approached. Not wanting to eavesdrop, she knocked conspicuously. The angry voices instantly ceased, followed by the scraping of chairs, after which Detective McLean swung open the door. Upon seeing her, his frustrated look quickly evaporated to be replaced by one of embarrassment. Standing awkwardly aside, he ushered her in. Tess could see the source of his annoyance – Detective Baxter stood at the window, his arms folded sternly across his broad chest. As she entered, he mumbled an excuse and took his leave.

Detective McLean gave her an apologetic look before explaining, "I'm sorry, Tess. Sometimes my partner and I disagree on things. As the lead detective on this case, he has pretty definite ideas on how to conduct the investigation..."

"And you have other ideas?" she finished for him.

"Let's just say I'm a little more 'open-minded' as you called it," he replied while trying to suppress a grin. "Please, sit down. Can I get you anything? A coffee?" he offered.

"No thanks. I'm fine."

"I was hoping to talk to you some more about your ability. I know you said you don't have much control over it, but I was just wondering..." he hesitated as if uncertain about proceeding.

"You were wondering what?" Tess asked, at once both curious and cautious.

"I was wondering if you might be able to pick up on anything from handling something of the victim's," he finished quickly, as if laying all of his cards out on the table at once was the best course of action. He seemed unsure of her reaction, afraid that having merely proposed the notion, he would scare her off.

Tess hesitated before she admitted, "I really don't know. I have had impressions, even sightings in similar circumstances, but they more or less just happened. I've never sat down and actually tried to conjure one up before," she said with a frown. "I don't know if I even could. I suppose I could give it a try." She shrugged her shoulders to indicate her agreement.

"Good then. Let me set something up." Detective McLean was obviously pleased with her willingness. "Do you have some time to go through a couple of things? There are a few more questions I'd like to ask you…"

It was after lunch before Tess emerged from the police station and made her way up to the university. She felt a keen sense of disappointment at not being able to provide any further information for the police to go on. If she was honest with herself, she wasn't entirely sure her disappointment stemmed from not being able to further the investigation so much as not being able to help Detective McLean specifically. She shook her head in order to clear it – 'Come on, Tess. That's the *last* thing you need right now'. At least he believed in her. She could tell that much. His support was obviously creating friction with his partner, but she was secretly thrilled by it nonetheless.

Tess was so incensed her hand literally shook as she punched in Detective McLean's number on her cell phone the next afternoon.

He answered on the very first ring. "Detective McLean here."

"You brought in Leah for questioning about our camping trip?" She tried but failed to keep the accusatory tone out of her voice.

There was a long pause before the young detective answered in a calm, measured voice. "It's routine, Tess. We needed to rule you out."

"Rule me out from *what*?" Her voice rose not only in pitch but in volume. When there was no immediate response, she groaned, "You've *got* to be kidding! You think *I* had something to do with this? Are you *serious*?"

"You knew things you shouldn't know, Tess," the young detective attempted to explain, keeping his voice carefully controlled. "We have an obligation to find out the reason for that." What Tess couldn't see, of course, was the way in which the young detective rose from his desk and began to pace his office, one hand riffling repeatedly through his hair.

"I *told* you the reason!" she insisted angrily.

"I *know* you did, and you were very credible, but we *have* to do due diligence and check out your alibi," he advised her as he stood in front of his window bracing himself for her reaction.

"Jesus. *My alibi*? You make me sound like some kind of criminal," she muttered.

"Not at all, Tess. Leah was able to produce a receipt from the campground booking, and she gave us the names of several of your friends who have verified your story," he informed her.

"Story?" she repeated forlornly. "I've done nothing but tell you the truth."

The vulnerability of her voice tugged sorely at his conscience. "For what it's worth, Tess, *I* believe you," he confessed in an attempt to console her. "It's just that your ability…well, it's hard for most people to accept. You must understand that," he added gently.

"Yeah, I know," she sighed resignedly.

"Listen, I *want* to work with you. I hope you're still willing to do a session with something of the victim's."

The anticipation in his voice did not escape her notice, and with that, Tess' spirits suddenly lifted. "And your partner?" she asked dryly.

"Don't worry about Detective Baxter," he assured her.

"You're going to go against his wishes?" Tess asked, clearly surprised.

"Let's just say I'm confident I can elicit his cooperation," he chuckled. "Well, maybe not with bells on or anything," he admitted.

"Hey, I don't want to get you into any trouble," her voice softened.

"Like I said; don't worry about it. I have thick skin. I'll call you when I have something set up. OK?"

"Yeah, I'll be there…with bells on."

He burst out laughing at her jest and returned to his desk to sit back in his chair, his mood now much lighter. "Thanks, Tess. Let's hope something comes of it."

"Yeah, no pressure or anything."

It was an appallingly bad likeness. The nose was entirely too long, giving the face a thin, pinched look and the ears were grotesquely large. He felt shock and indignation as he stared at it. So she *had* gone to the police after all. Well, she would pay dearly for that he vowed.

The evening news had featured his sketch in its updated coverage of the Bishop murder. No sooner had he settled himself in front of the TV with his supper than there it was staring out at him – his own likeness. A poor likeness, true, but it was his all the same. Thankfully, she had missed the scar; it had probably been too dark to see it. Absent mind-edly, he lightly traced his fingers over it as he sat there. At the age of seven, a large mole had been surgically removed leaving an angry red scar that had faded over the years but had nevertheless left him marked. He had been painfully self-conscious about it when he was younger because many of the children at school had teased him relentlessly, calling him names like 'Frankenstein' and 'monster'. Even his own mother had been embarrassed by it, always applying some of her makeup to cover it. But now he was almost relieved to have it, because with the scar, he differed significantly from the sketch.

As the consequences of the sketch sunk in, he grew annoyed with the thought of having to alter his appearance. He'd never encountered this problem before. He had *always* been so careful. Meticulously careful. It was something he prided himself on. But how could he have foreseen something like this? Someone like her?

In his annoyance, he vowed not to change anything, but as the evening wore on, he began to feel uneasy. He was ill-equipped to handle such emotions. Finally, he was forced to admit the sketch bore a *slight* resemblance to him, so in the end, he decided to err on the side of caution and trim his hair. It was an amateurish job, and he knew it, and that only served to irritate him further. Perhaps he should grow a beard? Dye his hair? Shave it all off? He had to be careful he reasoned, for too radical a change might only serve to draw attention, would it not?

He went to bed that night puzzled and unsettled by an entirely new feeling – fear. He did not like it. Not at all.

He *had* to find her.

Tess lay in her bed so keyed up from having seen her sketch on the evening news, she was unable to sleep, her mind awash with fears and worries. It was at times like this she sorely missed the simple comfort of her dog, Bailey. Bailey had actually been Emmy's dog, a beautiful, gentle golden retriever, but from the day Tess entered their lives, he had also bonded with her. It was like that dog knew instinctively what a motherless, traumatized child needed, and he provided unconditional love and devotion from the first moment they met. Tess smiled as she recalled meeting Bailey for the very first time…

After breakfast on their first morning together, Emmy made a simple announcement – they had an important errand to run. On the drive out to the boarding kennel, Tess was preoccupied with her new surroundings. There was so much to take in – from the quaint rows of heritage homes, to the enormous cedar trees with their massive trunks, to the smell in the air that was both salty and pungent. Upon arriving at the kennel, Tess found it hard to suppress her curiosity. She could not know it, of course, but her reaction delighted Emmy who was encouraged to see her ward interested in something.

At first, Emmy had been worried about Tess, but before leaving the hospital, she had been briefed as to her ward's prognosis. Physically, Tess had healed remarkably well, and even her muteness, which was deemed to be psychological, was not expected to last. The doctors had assured Emmy that in time, and with the aid of therapy, Tess would surely speak again. Emmy wisely wanted to give her charge some time to settle in first before she enlisted the aid of therapists, and her beloved dog was a first step in that process.

Bailey had come into Emmy's life five years earlier as a retirement present to herself, and she loved him dearly.

And now, her hope was Tess would be able to bond with him as well. And indeed, when Tess first laid eyes on that dog, it had been both an unexpected joy and love at first sight. Never having had a pet of any kind, she was thrilled beyond measure, especially with one who would not mind her muteness. Sinking to her knees, she wrapped her arms around the dog's neck and buried her face in the softness of his fur. The unabashed contentment on her young face when she looked up was profoundly moving, her eyes expressing everything she could not say, a ghost of a smile playing across her lips.

Tess didn't think it possible to be more nervous than the first time she was interviewed by the police, but she felt doubly so today. She had no idea what to expect in her session this morning in which she would handle something belonging to Katie Bishop. She did not doubt the accuracy of her ability, that wasn't it at all, but she did not feel confident about being able to summon it at will. Usually, it came upon her of its own accord. It was never really anything she had ever tried to force before, so trying to conjure it up, especially in such an artificial setting, was daunting to say the least. But she had agreed to this session of her own free will, so she was determined to see it through.

If she was honest with herself, she had to admit a simple truth – in addition to aiding the investigation, she was just as eager to please Detective McLean. She knew she was being foolish. Although he wore no wedding ring, he could be married, or at the very least have a girlfriend. Even if he was unattached, she had no idea if he was at all attracted to her. She was so inexperienced in these matters, and that fact only made her more anxious. By the time the two detectives entered the room, she was downright jumpy.

"Good morning, Tess. Thank you for coming in today." Detective McLean took the lead and sat down across from her. Although his tone was formal, he smiled warmly at her.

"Sure, no problem." She tried to sound casual while making a concerted effort to push aside the giddiness she was experiencing in his presence.

"Detective Baxter and I have discussed what we would like to try today."

Tess glanced up at the senior detective who took a seat somewhat grudgingly and then proceeded to type away on his cell phone. She marvelled how his beefy fingers were able to work the small keypad so easily.

Tess' attention was drawn back to the task at hand by Detective McLean who subtly cleared his throat. "We have an item of the victim's and we're hoping you might be able to..." He seemed at a loss for words.

"Channel?" she suggested helpfully. Her insides fluttered when he grinned back at her.

"Yes, channel," he said with a nod.

It was then that Tess noted the clear plastic evidence bag in his hand. Inside was a woman's ring. She cocked her head and looked at it in wonder.

Detective McLean studied her gaze for a moment before proceeding to place the bag on the table between them. He then slid it gently towards her. "Go ahead, Tess. Open it," he encouraged her.

She looked over at Detective Baxter as if to also seek his permission, and he nodded his head curtly, his face expressionless.

Reaching out tentatively, she suddenly hesitated, her arm pausing in mid-air. Her hand visibly shook, indicating with glaring clarity her lack of composure. Humiliated, she quickly snatched it back. "Oh, God. I'm so nervous," she confessed, letting out a long sigh.

"What would make you more comfortable, Tess?" Detective McLean's question rang with sincerity. "Would you prefer to spend some time alone with the ring?"

She was thankful for his suggestion and the look she flashed him expressed her gratitude. She nodded her head vigorously.

"No problem. Take your time." He pushed his chair back from the table and stood up, prompting his partner to do the same. "And feel free to handle the ring if you think it will help. We'll check back with you in a while."

Tess did not catch the annoyed look the senior detective threw his partner as they left the room. That was just as well because she was nervous enough. Left by herself, Tess had no doubt she was far from *alone*. After all, she'd seen enough movies and cop shows to know the glass she was staring at was likely the two-way kind and that behind it, they were probably gathered around watching her like some kind of zoo exhibit. All the same, she did feel better not having people right in the room with her, especially one whose silence was so indicative of his skepticism. Sighing heavily, she moved her chair around the table to face away from the glass, essentially sitting with her back to them, knowing that in doing so, she was rudely making a point, but she needed to concentrate.

At first, she could not even bring herself to touch the evidence bag; instead, she simply stared at it, lost deep in thought. It was fascinating, albeit morbid, to know the ring in front of her had been on the hand of that poor girl as she'd fought so desperately for her life. It was a simple ring, a thin silver band with a single blue stone. She had to wonder if it was the girl's birthstone. Who had given it to her? Was it a favourite? Finally, Tess reached out and pulled the bag slowly towards her. She lightly placed her hands on top of it, hoping to pick up on something without actually having to handle the ring itself, for to do so seemed almost sacrilegious, like she would somehow dishonour the girl.

As the minutes ticked by and the seriousness of the situation hit home, the expectations placed upon her weighed heavily. She sincerely wanted to help find this killer and bring the victim's family some measure of justice and closure. She just didn't know if she could.

Lowering her head, Tess squeezed her eyes shut in a vain attempt to concentrate. Trying to clear her mind, she focused solely on the ring...and yet...nothing. After several more attempts, she knew she needed to touch it. Hesitating only briefly, she opened the bag. The ring slipped out and fell with a soft clank onto the surface of the metal tabletop. It looked so innocuous lying there. If Tess had seen it in a store, she wouldn't have given it a second glance.

Almost as if to get the moment over with, she snatched it up. Clasping the ring in one hand, she closed her eyes and leaned back in her chair. Several minutes passed marked only by her deep, rhythmic breathing. And then...tipping her head back, she seemed to wince slightly, and her brows knitted together in confusion. Upon opening her eyes, she looked down at her closed hand and frowned. Turning her hand palm-side up, she slowly uncurled her fingers and studied the ring intensely for several seconds, turning her hand this way and that.

Finally, she gingerly set the ring back on the table in a deliberate, careful movement. With an exasperated sigh, she slid her chair back forcefully and stood up from the table. Slipping her arm through her book bag, she yanked open the door and stormed out of the room. Once out into the hall, she ran headlong into Detective McLean.

"Tess? Is everything alright?" he asked, his expression one of puzzled concern.

"No, everything is *not* alright," she replied defiantly, crossing her arms against her chest.

"I don't understand. Did you pick up on something about Katie?"

"As a matter of fact, no. But I *do* know one thing for certain." Her anger was mounting.

"What's that?"

"*That*," she declared as she pointed back to the room she'd just left, "is *not* her ring."

"*What?*" Detective McLean sounded genuinely shocked. "What do you *mean* it's not her ring? Of course it is. We retrieved it from the evidence locker this morning."

"*No*, it isn't," she corrected him as she glared up at him. "And I don't appreciate being played for a fool, Detective."

He held his hands up in front of her, effectively blocking her way, and yet, he was careful not to make any physical contact. "Wait. Please wait." He tried in vain to calm her. "If you're telling me that's not her ring, then whose is it?"

"Ask your partner," she replied angrily as she brushed past him and stormed off down the hall.

He was greatly relieved the sketch did not appear to have raised any suspicions at work, not that he had much contact with anyone there anyway. By the time he started his shift, the only person left in the building was a woman who did the books, and occasionally, his employer stayed late if there was an emergency to attend to.

Even during his shift, he kept to himself in the back of the building and simply did his job. But now with the release of the sketch, he felt as though the tables had been turned – the hunter felt like the hunted. That did not sit well with him. It had taken all of his willpower and all of his focus to appear normal, to concentrate, however distractedly, on his work in the days after the sketch's release.

She'd noticed his hair cut, had actually complimented him on it – the stupid woman who did the books. He avoided her like the plague, for she was truly the most annoying creature he had ever run across, and he did not want to encourage her in the least. He doubted she possessed the intellectual capacity to put two and two together even if he were to walk around with the sketch plastered on his forehead. By her own admission, she was addicted to sappy romance novels and to the care of her menagerie of pets. That was the only redeeming quality about her as far as he was concerned – the fact she loved animals. Had she been less annoying, that shared interest may have created some common ground. Even had that been the case, he had a cardinal rule about personal relationships. He didn't engage in them. Period. He was a loner through and through, and that suited his purposes just fine.

When he first started his job, the 'pest' (as he dubbed her) had flirted outrageously with him, hoping no doubt to strike up some sort of romance. She was grossly overweight and had a needy, almost clingy, air about her. If she only knew how much he would have loved to wrap his hands around her fleshy neck and squeeze. Despite the fact she knew she didn't stand a chance with him, she always hurried into the back whenever he came on shift. He would hear her heavy breathing as she laboured down the long corridor to greet him.

"Just making sure it's you," she'd natter upon seeing him. "You never know these days. A woman alone is fair game for any psycho or crook."

He would acknowledge her with a dismissive nod of the head while hanging up his coat and then make a quick escape to his work area. He knew only too well that anything more, anything as slight as a simple "hello", would set her off on a tangent. Given the slightest encouragement, she would drone on and on about whatever nonsense had caught her fancy that day. Once he started his shift, she would drift back to the front desk, no doubt to read her trashy novels when she was supposed to be doing the books.

Since launching the search for his witness, his life had taken on a new routine. When his evening shifts were finished, he would spend several hours driving methodically through the different neighbourhoods in the city. He meticulously organized his search on a grid-like basis using a large city map he tacked up on the wall of his kitchen. Each night, he would keep track of every street, cul-de-sac, and back road which he would then mark off on the map. He felt certain he would be able to pick up on *something* at *some* point. Their connection had been that strong. He believed it would be akin to picking up on a scent, much like the lingering smell of a woman's perfume long after she had passed by.

Although he did not feel the need to disguise himself at work as such a measure would have only have drawn attention anyway, he made a point of altering his appearance whenever he had to go out in public, even while cruising in the evenings. He would take the time at the end of his shift to apply a disguise, becoming quite adept at using make-up, wigs, facial hair – anything to render him less conspicuous in terms of his sketch. At first, he found it most inconvenient, but there was always the possibility someone would recognize him. Despite his initial reluctance, he actually came to pride himself on the many different looks he could achieve from products he found online. It was never anything he'd had to do before, of course, as none of his victims had ever lived to provide the police with anything, but given the situation he had been forced to contend with, he was really quite pleased at his resourcefulness.

But he was *most* annoyed that to err on the side of caution, he would have to go farther afield to hunt, possibly up island or over to the mainland in order to keep the police at bay. And yet, he would find his witness; of that, he had no doubt. He knew it would take time, but he was a *very* patient man. After all, the hunt was almost as sweet as the kill.

When Tess arrived home after the ring incident, she unloaded on her friend Leah. They had been roommates for several years now, and their friendship had developed to the point where they were as close as sisters. After stomping around the kitchen unleashing a torrent of obscenities, Tess stopped and hugged herself, taking several deep breaths in an attempt to calm down.

Leah just sat there. Finally, she simply sneered, "Ah, screw'em."

This comment sent Tess into a fit of laughter, effectively deflating her anger. She shook her head and plopped down on the chair beside Leah, bringing her knees up to her chin and resting her head there. It never failed to amaze her how different they were. She had immediately kicked into overdrive while Leah had remained collected, simply summing up the situation with that simple phrase.

Their temperaments were the complete opposite in every respect. Leah was the outgoing one, always up for trying something new, always quick to volunteer. Tess, on the other hand, always hung back, never seeking attention of any kind. Leah had been a track and field athlete throughout high school while Tess had stuck to her books.

The two women not only differed in temperament, but in looks as well. Whereas Leah was tall and blond, Tess was small and dark. Leah was a 'knock-out' and it was a fact she could have had her pick of any guy she wanted, but she was in no rush to settle down with anyone. She dated half-heartedly, always having to be the one to ease out of a relationship if it proceeded too quickly. Although Tess wasn't unattractive, she simply never drew much male attention. She certainly never courted any, preferring instead to stick to her studies, particularly when she entered graduate school.

Throughout her childhood, it wasn't as if Tess *longed* for companions. Her life was stable and safe with Emmy, and that had been enough. When she entered high school; however, she suddenly became self-conscious about her lack of friends. Then everything changed when she met Leah. Assigned as Biology lab partners, Tess was enthralled with Leah from the very start. Leah had everything – looks, athletic ability, and brains, but in addition to all of this, it was her compassion Tess was drawn to.

As to what drew Leah to her, Tess could only speculate. She was more than surprised when Leah would seek her out to walk home together or sit with her at lunch break. Tess began to wonder if she was some kind of pet project, someone Leah wanted to mentor along, but Leah never made any attempt to change her. That was the funny thing. She never tried to mould Tess into something she wasn't, and for that, Tess was grateful. Years later, when Tess asked Leah about the start of their friendship, she received a characteristically simple response – "You looked like you needed a friend."

Emmy was delighted when Tess brought Leah home. She approved whole-heartedly of their friendship and did everything in her power to foster it. Even Bailey seemed to take to Leah, sidling up to her whenever she came to the house, fully expecting to receive some extra attention. And so their friendship had grown over the years despite their very apparent differences. It was the strongest relationship in Tess' life next to that of her guardian.

"Tess, please open the door," Detective McLean sighed heavily as he rang the doorbell for the third time. He felt foolish standing out there on her front porch imploring her to answer. When she did not, he glanced self-consciously over his shoulder at the neighboring houses, hoping anyone witnessing his actions would not misconstrue this as some sort of lovers' spat. After a long pause, he knocked loudly against the screen door. "Come on, Tess. I know you're home. There's a car in your driveway."

Still no answer.

"Tess, I need to speak with you. I had *nothing* to do with what happened the other day," he pleaded.

When there was still no response, he hung his head, flipped up the collar of his coat against the wind and turned to leave. All of a sudden, he heard the latch. Turning back around, he spied a blonde woman half hidden behind the screen door, her arms crossed tightly against her chest, her look defiant.

Hope sprung into his voice. "Hello, Leah. Is Tess at home?"

"She won't see you. She says to leave her alone," Leah retorted haughtily.

"Please tell her it's me. Detective McLean," he implored.

"She knows it's you. You guys should be ashamed of yourselves. If I was Tess, I wouldn't give you the time of day. She was just trying to help, you know, and you guys go and do that to her." The tone of her voice was full of contempt causing the young detective to wince at her tongue lashing.

"Look, I need to explain things to her. I had nothing whatsoever to do with what happened," he declared. "It was my partner. He retrieved the ring from lockup. He's got some issues with this whole psychic thing…" his voice trailed off. When he saw his explanation was getting him nowhere, he sighed wearily and slowly backed down the steps, raising his hands in a defensive gesture. "Just tell her that, please."

He was halfway to his car when he heard the screen door open. As he turned around, Tess stepped out onto the porch, her face unreadable. She too had her arms folded across her chest. He suppressed a smile of relief that threatened to show itself, tugging at the corners of his mouth as he walked resolutely back towards the house. Stopping at the base of the steps to the porch, he was careful not to go any farther; after all, he didn't want to press his luck. "Thanks, Tess. I really appreciate you seeing me. Can we talk?" he asked with delicate care.

She frowned at him, gave a huff as if to resign herself to such an unpleasant task, and disappeared back inside the house, leaving the screen door banging in her wake. He meekly followed her lead. Once inside, he noted her house wasn't at all what he would have expected of a young woman. It was like walking into an antique shop. Tess noted his interest, but she was far too annoyed with him to make any comment. For the time being, she was enjoying his discomfort. Leading him into the sitting room, she motioned for him to take a seat. He sat down on a large armchair, sitting tentatively on its edge so as not to disturb the plethora of pillows placed there. Tess settled in the opposite chair and folded her hands neatly in her lap, prepared to hear him out.

The young detective wasted no time. "Thanks for seeing me, Tess. I really appreciate it. Listen, I *know* you're upset, and I don't blame you one bit, but you need to know I had *nothing* to do with what happened. Ed...I mean, Detective Baxter, retrieved the ring from the evidence locker." He paused at this point, suddenly aware of the fact he'd had been talking to the rug because he couldn't bear to witness the glaring mistrust in her eyes. Finally though, he looked up, made eye contact, and forged ahead. "Detective Baxter is having trouble with all this…psychic stuff. He figured one way to verify it would be to switch out the ring, so I'm afraid he swapped it for one of his daughter's." McLean winced when he witnessed the sour look Tess threw him. "But I guess you already know that, don't you?" He shrugged sheepishly.

She did not answer but simply regarded him haughtily.

The young detective stood up at this point and ran his hand through his hair as he paced the width of the room. "Look, I *know* it was a lousy thing to do. Believe me, I told him so. And he's pretty ashamed; I can assure you. But the fact of the matter is we still have an investigation to do. There's still a grieving family looking to us for answers, and there's still a killer on the loose out there. I *believe* in you, Tess. I have from the very beginning. I think the gift you have is genuine, *and* I think you can help us catch this guy. Please don't let your anger stand in the way of that." The pleading look he gave her took the edge off her indignation. She believed he would have gotten down on his knees if he thought it would help.

Almost as if his speech had drained him, he dropped back into the armchair and hung his head.

Several moments of uncomfortable silence followed before Tess finally cleared her throat. "Fine. Apology accepted," she announced dryly.

He gave her an incredulous look. "Alright, then. That's… that's great." He placed his hands on his knees and nodded his head vigorously, smiling broadly. "Can we try again?"

She raised an eyebrow at him.

"I mean, with the ring. Can we try with the real ring?" he added.

"Yes, but we do it here. You bring the ring here where I am comfortable, and I'll see what I can do." She gave him her terms.

"No problem. No problem at all, Tess." He was quick to assure her.

She stood up from her chair, indicating their conversation was at an end.

He took the hint and rose from his seat. "Can I bring it over today?" he asked tentatively. He was worried that might be pushing it, but he asked anyway.

"Alright. I'll be home by about 7:00 tonight. You can bring it over then," she replied, leading him to the front door. "And as a matter of fact," she added, "be sure to bring Baxter along. He can apologize in person."

"Ah, yeah…sure. No problem."

Tess followed the young detective out on to the porch to see him off.

"Thanks, Tess. Thanks again." He nodded his gratitude and headed to his car, his step much lighter now that they were on speaking terms once again. The wind had picked up, tugging at the tails of his overcoat.

Tess stepped to the porch railing, hugging herself against the chill and called after him, "Hey McLean…"

He stopped at his car and turned to face her.

"Baxter and his wife should have had 'the talk' with their daughter a lot sooner." She paused in order to let her comment sink in. Witnessing his puzzled look, she added – "She's pregnant."

A look of astonishment passed over the young detective's face before he broke out into a huge grin.

"It gets better," she added wickedly. "It's twins.

❧   ❧   ❧

He was a methodical hunter. Years of practice had allowed him to hone his skill such that he took very few risks, and as a result, he had been very 'successful'. Only rarely did he ever chance upon a victim. In most cases, the hunt took days or weeks or even months to come to fruition. Those were the ones he enjoyed the most, for the reward when it came was all the sweeter.

Sometimes it was the location he settled on first – an isolated parking lot or a deserted back road that he would then proceed to stake out. His keen eye missed nothing, and of course, he trusted his instincts implicitly. If he picked up on anything, even the slightest thing, he moved on. Once in wait for a victim, he had the cunning and acumen of a true hunter with the uncanny ability to spot the most vulnerable, the least suspecting. Like a spider, he waited patiently to ensnare some hapless prey in the web he had carefully crafted.

Perhaps his greatest attribute as a hunter was the simple fact he appeared to pose no threat. He was not a large man by any means; in fact, he was rather slim and bookish in appearance. This seemed to set most women immediately at ease. And his manner wasn't at all offensive; quite the opposite – it was polite, almost apologetic. Again, that drew no warning flags for most women, and so they were easily drawn in. By the time they had any inkling of the true danger they were in, it was always too late – the trap had been sprung; their fate sealed.

Sometimes rather than settling on a location first, he would concentrate instead on selecting a potential victim. This type of hunt invariably took longer, for he had to be extremely careful. He had to stalk his victim, and yet, not give himself away in the process. This meant weeks, sometimes even months, of learning her habits and routines in order to spot her vulnerabilities. He needed to find her 'Achilles heel', so to speak. He needed to know what situation she would trust, when that was likely to occur, and what approach would lure her in.

In choosing his victim, he was immediately attracted by a woman's hair; it drew him like a moth to a flame. Blonde, red, black, brown (and every shade in between), straight, curly, wavy – his hair fetish encompassed *everything*. Well, that wasn't entirely true. The only thing he could not abide was a poor dye job. And of course, a woman's hair *had* to be long and flowing; the longer, the better.

In addition to hair, it was a must for a woman to be small in stature because he was not a large man. He'd made a mistake once (although he was loathe to admit it) in selecting a larger woman, and she had almost cost him everything. *Almost.* No, he wouldn't make that mistake again. He was strong for his size, very strong in fact, but he had a cardinal rule about his victim's size, and he took no chances whatsoever when it came to that.

But this hunt, this one was different. He *had* to find her. She was a loose end he could ill afford. Even more than that though, more than *needing* to find her, he *wanted* to find her. He had never shared his ability with anyone, never told a soul. And yet, here was a complete stranger who, by virtue of her ability, had shared something incredibly intimate with him – his latest kill. He marvelled at their connection. She was a kindred soul.

It was a pity she had to die.

Tess could still recall the first real conversation she ever had with Emmy all those years ago. After their first few weeks together as Tess began to feel some sense of security in her new life, she started to respond with one-word answers. Wisely, Emmy never pressed for more than that. Instead, she simply worked around that fact, talking to Tess, stimulating her, but never actually requiring or expecting much of an answer in return. It was amazing Emmy intuitively understood how to parent such a fragile child when she`d never had any children of her own.

As the weeks turned into months during their first spring together, Emmy and Tess spent their time at the public library indulging in their mutual love of reading, or down at the beach combing for shells and other sea creatures in the warm tidal pools, or wandering the numerous antique shops in their city in search of vintage treasures. Emmy was a passionate patron of the arts, so Tess benefited from days spent wandering local art galleries and museums through which she learned all about the rich cultural heritage of the Pacific Northwest. While other girls her age were watching TV and listening to pop music, Tess attended concerts, plays, and festivals, all of which served to stimulate her senses.

Slowly, Tess began to emerge from her self-imposed isolation under her guardian's gentle care, but she still remained a naturally quiet, thoughtful child. On one particular day in late spring while taking advantage of a stretch of gloriously fine weather, Emmy took Tess down to the beach. They spent their entire day searching for shells, building sand castles, and playing with Bailey in the surf. Afterwards, they sat in companionable silence with their backs against a massive log, one of many to wash ashore during a particularly stormy winter season that year.

It was late in the day and they had just spread out a tasty picnic supper. Bailey stood obediently at the foot of their blanket waiting patiently for some tidbit should it happen to fall his way. As they relaxed, Tess turned to Emmy, squinting up at her in the fading afternoon light and asked in a manner seemingly far older than her years, "Why didn't you marry him?"

Emmy didn't register surprise, not at the question being asked, or at the fact Tess had actually *asked* a question. She simply replied, "Marry who, dear?"

"The man in the picture on your dresser."

"Ah, yes. Well, things were a lot more complicated back then," Emmy sighed. After a moment's hesitation in which she seemed to collect her thoughts, Emmy proceeded to explain things further. "That was back in 1941. We were young and in love and *very, very* headstrong, I'm afraid." Glancing down at her charge, she chuckled, "Oh, my. I'm sure it's hard for you to believe – that someone as old as me was young once." She leaned over with a conspiratorial wink and whispered, "But I *was!*"

"Now where was I?" she checked herself. "Oh, yes. Back in those days," she explained, "the type of family you were born into mattered a great deal. If a boy's family didn't – how shall I put it? – travel in the same social circles…" Without waiting for Tess to question the meaning of this phrase, she continued, "I know. I know. It's ridiculous to judge someone based on that, but times were different back then. Oh, it never meant anything at all to me, but my parents – now *they* were another matter entirely." Her voice suddenly sounded very weary, and she sighed heavily. "And then he went off to war as so many young men did in those days. He wasn't afraid at all. Thought it was some grand adventure, the silly fool. We'd agreed to run away together as soon as he returned, but like so many others, he never did. It was some time before I learned he had been killed in France."

Tess nodded her head as if satisfied with the explanation given to her, and a minute or so passed before she thoughtfully asked, "But why didn't you ever marry somebody else?"

"Well, I suppose because I never found anyone I liked quite so much," Emmy replied with a wistful smile.

Tess seemed satisfied with such a simple answer, so Emmy left it at that. They soon packed up their picnic basket, called to Bailey who was off chasing sea gulls, and headed back along the steep path leading up from the beach. That night as Emmy tucked her in, Tess responded with a fierce hug. When the tears finally came, it was as if they could not be stopped. Emmy gently placed a hand on either side of the little girl's pixie face to tilt it up to her own and simply advised, "You cry it out child."

Later in the evening as she prepared for bed, Emmy stood beside her dresser gazing at the faded photograph of her first and only love, the wisp of a smile softening the lines of her wizened face. "Now don't you get *me* crying," she muttered affectionately as she turned out the light.

Tess was home in plenty of time to change her clothes and refresh her makeup before the detectives were due to arrive with the real ring. As she did so, her thoughts drifted back to the fact Detective McLean had actually come to her home to apologize. Granted, she wouldn't answer any of his phone calls so that had left him little choice, but she'd been secretly thrilled to see him nevertheless. And he believed in her. He believed in her, *and* he had asked for her help. She knew she would do whatever she could to help him.

Leah was sorely disappointed to learn the detectives were to return after dinner as she had a dance class to attend. Flying out of the house with her gym bag just as the two detectives pulled up, she made a point of openly scowling at them as she got into her car. She wasn't nearly as forgiving as Tess, and she wanted them to know that.

The two men made their way up to the front door, the taller of the two striding purposefully, the larger lagging reluctantly behind. It was McLean who rang the doorbell. Beside him, his partner shifted nervously on his feet and ran a finger under his collar in an attempt to loosen it. McLean turned aside to suppress a grin, thankful it wouldn't be him in the 'hot seat'.

Tess greeted them coolly and led them both into the sitting room.

"Thanks for agreeing to try this again, Tess." McLean's voice was conciliatory.

She simply acknowledged his comment with a curt nod of her head and turned her full attention to his partner. She had to admit she was enjoying the senior detective's obvious discomfort, for he would not make eye contact with her, but rather stood like a truant schoolboy about to be disciplined – hands clasped firmly behind his back, feet braced apart, head hung down. When he finally had the nerve to steel a glance at her, he was met with raised eyebrows.

"So whose ring do we have today, Baxter? One of your wife's perhaps?" She witnessed the look of embarrassment on his face turn to one of pain which made her realize her sarcasm had hit a nerve. She immediately felt remorseful for allowing her anger to get the better of her.

With his face a brilliant shade of red and with genuine contriteness in his voice, he replied, "No, Miss Walker. I can assure you; it's the victim's." He hesitated and glanced at his partner who gave him a look as if to say, "Go on…"

"I owe you an apology, Miss Walker. It was a stupid thing to do, and I'm sorry it caused you distress."

"Thank you, Baxter. Apology accepted." Tess' tone softened for a moment, and then she switched gears. "I do want to make one thing clear from now on though. If you want my help, you will treat me with respect. That means no games, no tricks, no lying." She crossed her arms against her chest and looked to both detectives for their agreement.

"I understand, Miss Walker," Baxter answered solemnly.

"Yes, of course," McLean also assured her, nodding earnestly.

"Good then. Now, Baxter, please loosen up and call me Tess," she smiled tentatively at him, glad the air had been cleared. "Let's have a look at that ring, shall we?"

They brought the ring out in its evidence bag and handed it to her. She held it up to her face in order to examine it more closely. This ring was a simple silver band engraved with a delicate scroll pattern. She was immediately drawn to it. Several moments passed before she suddenly announced, "I want you to leave it with me for a few days." The challenging look she gave them was meant to squelch any objection. "I don't want to feel like some kind of lab animal expected to perform on command," she explained. "It just doesn't work that way."

"That's against p…" began Baxter before he was cut off.

"I'll take full responsibility for the ring, Ed," McLean reassured him.

"Good then," Tess said. "I'll let you know if I come up with anything."

He loved the city after dark. He loved the sense of freedom and the anonymity it afforded him. He could come and go as he pleased without the press of traffic or the bother of people. Nestled in his car in the evenings after his shift work, he cruised the streets at will with only the dim light of his dashboard and the soft play of classical music from his radio. So far, the search for his witness had not produced any result, but by his own calculations, he had only covered a fraction of the city. He'd started his search in the university area on the off-chance his witness was a student, but so far, he had come up empty.

In contrast to the sprawling metropolis of Vancouver just across the Strait of Georgia, the city of Victoria had a reputation as a sleepy community; its populace was a unique mix of winter weary retirees from other parts of Canada and young, active families drawn to the outdoor west coast lifestyle. The city had its share of bars and clubs, of course, but it was better known for its many parks and walkways and was often referred to as the 'garden city' because of its proliferation of hanging flower baskets and manicured gardens.

It never ceased to amaze him that despite Victoria's quiet reputation, a world unto itself sprang up when the majority of its residents were safely tucked in their beds. Wayward street people shuffled along with their overloaded grocery carts in their nightly quest for shelter; groups of rowdy, intoxicated teens made their presence known by their loud, obnoxious banter; and women of the evening plied their trade with tourists in the lower streets of the harbour. With virtually no effort on his part, he felt part of something – connected somehow to this nightly realm. It was the closest he had ever come to feeling like he belonged anywhere.

It was hard, however, not to get distracted, particularly when he came across a lone female because his hunting instinct would automatically kick in. It was only by virtue of his superior willpower that he managed to stay focused. He simply could not afford distractions at the moment. He knew at some point he would have to feed the need within him to keep it at bay, but for now, his witness was his top priority. And he knew the reward when he found her would be far sweeter than any he had experienced yet.

Oh, yes. This one was worth the wait.

Looking back, there was really no way Tess could have kept her ability hidden from Emmy. Without a doubt, her guardian had to be one of the most perceptive people she knew. At first, Tess wondered if Emmy could be psychic as well, but she soon ruled out such a notion. To her credit, Emmy was just extraordinarily observant. If Tess was quiet or upset, it didn't take Emmy long to deduce why. It was probably due to the simple fact she noticed things most people didn't; she paid attention to the little things.

Tess recalled it had been during their first fall together when Emmy figured things out. Tess had just started at school, one carefully chosen by Emmy – a small, private school that would provide a well-rounded education. In addition to personalized instruction, there was a strong music and arts program. Although Emmy had misgivings about sending Tess to school at all, she knew the importance of being around other children. After all, it wasn't healthy for a young girl to be spending all of her time in the company of an old, eccentric spinster!

Emmy had been delighted with the news of a social studies project requiring Tess to work with a partner. However, it was just Tess' luck her partner was another misfit, the result of everyone else pairing up. Tess and Amber Bolen had been left staring at one another, their blank expressions hiding the humiliation they both felt deep inside. However, they soon made the best of things as they were both conscientious students.

One rainy Sunday afternoon, Emmy invited the girls to work on their project while she baked them some cookies. If it was one thing Emmy believed in, it was that good food made just about any situation tolerable. On this particular afternoon, the two girls were bent over their masterpiece at the kitchen table – a map of Canada on which fur trading forts and routes were intricately laid out. Lost in her own thoughts while colouring, Tess began to feel vaguely nauseous. At first, she chided herself for having eaten too many of Emmy's cookies, but she soon realized it had nothing to do with that. When the soft buzzing commenced in the back of her head, she knew for certain what was coming. Hanging her head, she closed her eyes and waited, oblivious to everything else save the blackness and the rhythm of the sound in her head. Alerted by some sixth sense many animals seem to possess, Bailey rose from lounging underneath the kitchen table to rest his head on his young mistress' lap, emitting a soft whimper of concern. Tess stroked him absent-mindedly.

The first image slashed through the blackness much like lightning. It flashed and was gone in the same instant. Tess cocked her head, not understanding at first. When subsequent images unfolded in rapid succession, she began to piece together their meaning. Slowly she turned her head, and upon opening her eyes, she caught Amber staring at her. Even if Tess had wanted to, there was simply *no way* she could have hidden the horror written all across her own face. She was too young to fully understand what she had seen, of course, but what little she *did* know told her intuitively it was *very, very* wrong.

Amber, looking equally aghast, stood up from the kitchen table and stumbled backwards, never breaking eye contact while her hands desperately sought out the handle of the door to the mud room. Upon finding it, she spun around and yanked the door open, scooping up her coat and backpack in the process. She thrust her feet into her gum boots and literally burst out of the back door. Startled, Emmy looked up from her dishes at the sink to see Amber clattering down the porch steps. That poor child tore off across the lawn and down the street like she had the very devil at her heels. Emmy frowned and turned a puzzled eye towards Tess who simply hung her head.

For the next several days, Amber was not at school. When Tess inquired, her teacher paled and simply mumbled something about a family emergency. When days turned into weeks and still Amber did not return, people began to gossip. Tess caught wind of several rumours – Amber's father, a prominent local businessman, had been arrested; Amber's mother had been hospitalized; the Bolen house was up for sale. Because of all this turmoil, Tess felt a heavy burden of responsibility for whatever had befallen Amber's family.

One night while she lay reading in bed, Tess looked up at the sound of Bailey's whimper to see Emmy standing in the doorway, arms clasped behind her back, a gentle but concerned look on her weathered face. For a long moment, her guardian never said anything. When she finally did enter the room, she paused to pat Bailey affectionately on the head and then sat carefully on the edge of the bed. Once seated, it was obvious she needed to say something, but it was equally obvious she didn't quite know *how* to say it. Finally, she began, "Tess, I've learned something about Amber Bolen."

Tess tensed, praying her partner (she couldn't exactly call her a friend) was alright.

"Amber's mother has taken her and her little sister away."

"Where?" Tess' question came out like a croak.

"I believe to her mother's in Toronto."

"Why?"

"I think you know why, Tess. I think you knew weeks ago. I just can't figure out *how* you knew," Emmy said gently. Her uncharacteristic bluntness caught Tess off guard, and as a result, an awkward silence hung in the air between them. Emmy's face was full of concern as she gently pressed, "How did you know her secret, Tess? You knew it that day in the kitchen, didn't you? Without her even saying anything. Am I right?"

With that question, Tess flopped onto her side to face the wall, purposely turning her back to her guardian. There was a long pause during which Emmy heaved a weary sigh. "I know you feel bad about what has happened to Amber, but you *must* understand you are *not* to blame, Tess. What her father was doing was very wrong, and I can assure you, someday, Amber is going to thank you."

When Tess still did not respond, Emmy rose from the bed and gave Bailey a good night pat as she headed for the door. Once there, she turned around and spoke to her ward's huddled form. "I believe you have the gift of sight, Tess. I believe that's how you knew."

Again, Tess said nothing but her body tensed and that did not escape Emmy's notice.

"Oh, I won't bother you with any more questions tonight, but please don't be afraid. I hope you can talk to me about it when you're ready." She turned to leave the room and then seemed to think better of it. Standing in the doorway, she added, "You may feel very alone with this, Tess, but please know I understand. I understand because my own mother had the very same gift." And with that, she gently closed the door.

OCTOBER

A utumn in the Pacific Northwest was a glorious season. Unlike the rest of Canada where the long, lazy days of summer came to an abrupt halt with the onset of cooler temperatures and frost warnings as early as the beginning of September, the city of Victoria typically continued to enjoy fine weather. It wasn't unusual to tend gardens and mow lawns right through to the end of October, sometimes even longer. When the temperatures finally did dip, the leaves on the trees that were green one day turned into a tapestry of blazing golds, oranges, and reds the next.

It was on one such warm fall day when Tess took a seat in Detective McLean's office and sighed in exasperation. "How is it I spend a few minutes with a ring *not* belonging to the victim and I have a sighting, and yet now, when it's so important I have one with the real ring, I can't?" she sighed in disgust.

"You're too hard on yourself, Tess." Detective McLean came around to the front of his desk and leaned against it, arms folded. "It's only been a week," he added gently.

She looked up at him with such frustration and hopelessness, he experienced a pang of guilt for asking her to channel with the ring in the first place.

"I should never have asked you to try this," he muttered, shaking his head.

She reached out to place her hand on his arm. "I agreed to try this. You didn't force me."

He smiled down at her, and for a second, she thought he would say something; instead, he rose and went around

SUSAN GNUCCI

to sit behind his desk as if to purposely put some distance between them.

Awkwardly, she placed her hand back in her lap.

Finally, he spoke, "Do you think your lack of sightings has anything to do with your fear of this guy, Tess?"

His question broke the tension, and Tess gave it some thought. "I never thought of that, but I suppose it could be a factor." She could not bring herself to confess her real fear – that the likely problem was her infatuation with the young detective himself. And unfortunately, she knew the possible consequences of such an attachment – she never had sightings when she was emotionally involved with someone. Take Emmy and Leah, for instance. Never in all their years together had Tess ever experienced a sighting involving either one of them. What a cruel twist of irony to be unable to help with the case simply because of her feelings for the young detective.

"In which case, we have to be prepared for the fact you may never have any more," he advised.

"I guess that's a possibility," she admitted, sinking back in her chair. In a disheartened voice, she asked him, "I guess I'm not much help, am I?"

"You've been a big help, Tess, regardless of any more sightings," he was quick to assure her. The seriousness in his voice made her look up, and for a long moment their eyes locked; however, the intensity of his gaze soon forced her to break eye contact. Not knowing what else to do, she changed the subject.

"Hey, I really put my foot in my mouth with Baxter, didn't I?" she said staring at her hands in her lap. "I know my comment struck a nerve."

"You couldn't have known." The young detective reclined in his chair. "It's been hard on him this last year with his wife leaving."

"Yeah, I figured that was the case. And now with his daughter and everything."

"You know, in a strange way, their situation has actually pulled all of them together as a family," he mused.

"I'm glad," she smiled. Her sincerity seemed to puzzle him. "What?" she finally asked.

"You're…refreshing," he smiled broadly at her and her heart soared.

The shrill ringing of the phone interrupted them, and McLean reluctantly turned to answer it. Tess felt so flustered, she signalled her intention to leave by gesturing toward the door. Seeing her head out, McLean placed his hand over the receiver and called after her, "Thanks, Tess. And don't worry. Give it some more time. Let's see what happens."

She nodded at him and smiled half-heartedly. Once out into the hallway, she shut the door and leaned heavily against it, closing her eyes and letting out a long sigh. She needed to collect her thoughts; her head was swimming. It wasn't long before she heard a conspicuous cough. Upon opening her eyes, she spied Baxter standing there, one eyebrow raised. Mortified to be caught 'mooning' outside McLean's door, she summoned what little dignity she had left and greeted him with as much cheer as she could muster.

"Hey, Baxter. How's it going?"

"Fine. Everything alright?" he assessed her quizzically.

"Yeah, I'm fine. Thanks. Just checked in with McLean. No sightings yet, but I'm trying," she said as she smiled weakly at him. An awkward moment passed between them before Tess screwed up the courage to broach what was on her mind. "Hey, my comment about your wife…" she began.

"Don't worry about it." The dismissiveness in his voice was an obvious indication he was uncomfortable discussing his personal life. She figured as much.

Despite that, Tess felt compelled to apologize. "No, I was really out of line. It was hurtful, and I regret saying it. I...I hope you guys can work things out. I really do."

A look of genuine appreciation crossed his face. "Thanks," he mumbled.

She turned to leave and was half-way down the corridor before he called to her in a resolute voice, "We're going to catch this guy, Tess."

She nodded in agreement, smiling inwardly at the way he'd said it, for he made it clear the '*we*' included her.

It had only been a few months since the Bishop girl, and yet, the hunger ate away at him as it always inevitably did. Although he usually went much longer between kills, he had been experiencing a mounting need, one that would not leave him, one that gnawed at his gut day and night, giving him no peace. Even his faithful tabby cat had been a poor distraction, for she had been giving him the cold shoulder these days, almost as if displeased with his absences, she chose to punish him with her lack of affection. At first, he'd been hurt by her indifference, yet he was so consumed with the search for his witness, he hadn't had much time to think about anything else. Stimulating as the search was, it was proving to be a daunting task, one even he was beginning to find taxing, although he would never admit it.

To distract himself, he had been making quick trips over to Vancouver on the mainland where he had been stalking a young prostitute. Although she plied her trade on any number of streets within a ten block radius, she was always dropped off in the same deserted alleyway in the wee hours of the morning. She was very young – he estimated sixteen or seventeen at most. And she was a scrappy little thing, able to hold her own against the hardened, street-wise dregs she hung out with. Her manner of dress offended him – cheap, skin-tight dresses; gaudy jewellery; knee-high black boots; and a ratty coat tossed carelessly across her shoulders like an after-thought, despite the chilly weather. Her lithe body, although on full display, held no appeal for him. It was her hair he had been drawn to – it was long and blonde. She wore it in a high pony-tail that swayed hypnotically to and fro with her constant scanning of the intersection in which she stood. He wondered briefly if it was a hair extension. He had yet to encounter one and would be most disappointed to do so.

He did not know Vancouver well at all, but he knew enough to select the east end, a derelict, decaying neighborhood of rundown rooming houses, sketchy bars, and dingy 'mom and pop' establishments. It was notorious as a haven for drug dealers, prostitutes, and street people – anyone down on their luck. It was the type of place where people minded their own business, for to mind anyone else's was foolhardy. It was not the type of neighborhood he frequented as a rule, and yet it afforded him the anonymity he needed. Crime was a way of life on these mean streets, so the disappearance of one more runaway teenage prostitute would hardly make the news. Yes, it was the perfect hunting ground.

He'd thought his plan through very carefully. Because Vancouver was a sprawling metropolis of more than two million people, it posed a problem when it came to…disposal. At first, this concerned him because he was used to the luxury of the woods; however, he soon came up with a solution. The mighty Fraser River ran right through the heart of the city, and people drowned in its waters all the time – bridge jumpers, careless swimmers, boating accident victims. Undoubtedly, it had also seen its share of murder victims. In places, its churning waters and strong current could carry a body far downstream, and after such a journey, there would be little physical evidence left. Yes, it would suit his purposes just fine.

It was while he was hunting in 'East Van' as the locals called it that he first happened upon the girl. Parked on a deserted side street well after midnight one night, he noticed a dark sedan swing into an adjacent alleyway and pull up to an abrupt stop, at which point a young woman unceremoniously exited the vehicle. Or rather, the passenger door opened and she was shoved out, cursing and flailing into the street. Even though the driver quickly slammed the door shut in her face, she fired off a round of colourful obscenities, and to make her displeasure even more apparent, she spat on the window. The driver, obviously unimpressed with her tirade, made a point of roaring away in a squeal of tires, leaving the poor girl coughing and choking on his exhaust. She kicked at the air as if the car was still there then turned abruptly on her heels and disappeared down the alley, staggering and swaying as she went.

He was thoroughly amused at her spunk. Obviously, she had not received payment for her services. Whereas some teenage girls wouldn't have risked angering a John over such a turn of events, she had 'expressed' her displeasure loud and clear. He chuckled. Although he had only seen her briefly in the dimly lit alley, he'd been intrigued. He vowed to stay another night on the off-chance she would be 'dropped off' again at the same location. His instincts proved right, for the next evening at a similar hour, she exited a Jeep in a much more dignified manner this time and leaned over to flirt with her John before sashaying down the alley, her long, blonde ponytail bobbing and swaying with every step. It was like a beacon to him, stirring the hunger from deep within him.

Once Tess found out about Emmy's own mother being psychic, her curiosity got the better of her. "Emmy, what was your mother's name?" she asked quietly as she sat at the kitchen table swinging her short, little legs rhythmically, petting her faithful companion who had come to sit beside her chair. The smell of freshly brewed coffee hung heavily in the air of their cosy kitchen.

Emmy, who was busy serving up bowls of steaming porridge, smiled knowingly to herself. "Let's let this cool a minute," she said as she set the bowls down on the table. "There's something I want to show you." With that, she took Tess by the hand and led her down the hallway into the sitting room. The 'parlour', as Emmy often referred to it, was the one room in the house in which Tess was not allowed to play. It was considered off-limits for the most part as it was where Emmy received her guests. The dark wood panelling lent the room a somber air, and the formal antique furniture faced a massive stone hearth.

As they entered the parlour this morning, Emmy motioned for Tess to take a seat on the settee by the window while she retrieved something from a cabinet. Tess, whose curiosity was piqued by this point, sat expectantly on the edge of her seat. In the meantime, Bailey had joined them, circling once before flopping down rather dramatically onto the plush rug in front of the fireplace.

"Now you know you're not allowed in here," Emmy fussed half-heartedly. She looked disapprovingly at the dog, but if she thought she could shame him into leaving, she was sorely mistaken. He merely gave her a baleful look and stretched out on his side facing away from them, almost as if he could better ignore her displeasure that way. Emmy sighed in resignation and took a seat next to Tess. As she did so, she placed a weathered photo album on their laps.

"I'm glad you asked about my mother, Tess, because she was very special to me, just like you are." She smiled warmly at her charge. "Her name was Lida."

"That's a funny name," Tess spoke with the guileless honesty only young children possess.

"Oh, it's an old fashioned name these days, I suppose, but back then it was common enough. But my mother was far from common, Tess. Far from it." With that, she opened the album and pointed to several faded photographs of a diminutive, attractive woman. Tess was intrigued and stared at the photos with rapt attention. It wasn't just the unfamiliar style of clothing or the old fashioned cars that held her attention. All of that was interesting enough, but more importantly, it was the simple fact there had been someone (and a relative, no less) who was like *her*. As young as she was, Tess felt an incredible kinship with the woman who stared out at her from the pages of the faded album.

After several minutes of careful examination, Tess looked up at her guardian whom she now entrusted with her secret and asked, "She was just like *me*, Emmy?"

The question was asked so tentatively, Emmy was reminded once again of the fragility of this child. She knew in her heart she would do anything to protect her. She marvelled with the realization that such a wee little thing had changed her life so completely, had given it a purpose and a richness she never knew were missing from it.

"Yes, Tess. Yes, she was. People didn't understand back in those days like they do now, so my mother rarely ever talked about her ability outside of the family. But I know first-hand of her gift."

"Gift?" Tess pronounced the word as though the very sound and feel of it was strange on her tongue.

"Why, yes. Her gift. That's what it is, you know. *Everyone* has a gift. Some gifts are obvious like being able to play a musical instrument or being able to write stores and books. Other gifts aren't so obvious like being able to make people laugh or being a good listener. And still others are even less tangible; in fact, they are very rare indeed, like my mother's and yours."

"Did your mother get her gift from an accident?" Tess asked thoughtfully.

"Well, no. She always had it as far as I can remember. Do you want me to tell you the story of when I first learned of it?"

Tess nodded her head vigorously, and she and Emmy settled back together on their seat. Their movement stirred Bailey from his slumber, who after assessing nothing was amiss, laid his head back down on his paws with a contented huff.

"Back when I was a little girl, probably no older than you are now, I was terrified of a boy in our neighbourhood named Billy Thompson. He was a few years older, and all the neighbourhood children were frightened of him because he was such a bully. We excluded him from our play which only seemed to make him even meaner whenever we crossed paths with him. Oh, I look back on it now, of course, and I can see a lonely little boy who just wanted to fit in, but back then, his actions only served to drive all of us further away."

Emmy paused briefly to see if Tess was following her and then continued with her story. "One day while we were play-ing out in our front yard, Billy came along on his bicycle. When we caught sight of him, we all scattered faster than you could say 'Jack Rabbit'." Emmy chuckled and shook her head as if the memory of that was still fresh in her mind. "Instead of continuing on his way, Billy climbed down off his bicycle and marched over to the base of the large apple tree that stood in our front yard. He boasted to all of us within earshot that he was going to climb to the very top and give the tree a good shake to loosen all of the apples. Now my mother loved her apple tree and the crisp, juicy apples it always produced every year, but there was *no way* I was going to come out of my hiding place to alert her to the impending calamity with her tree. There was no need, however, for my mother was standing at the parlour window, and when she saw what Billy Thompson was up to, she stormed out of the house madder than a hornet."

At this, Emmy tried but failed to suppress a grin. "I can still see her at the base of that tree, hands on hips, ordering him to come down '*right this minute*'! When he wouldn't, she took off her apron and proceeded to climb up after him."

Tess started giggling at this point.

"My mother grabbed that boy by the ankle and literally hauled him down out of that tree. He fell the last few feet and landed in a heap, but honestly, I think he was more astonished than hurt or humiliated. Afraid he would run off before she could scold him properly, my mother grabbed hold of one of his arms as he was struggling to his feet. It was then, quite suddenly, when the wind went right out of her sails, and a strange look came over her face. She stared at Billy with a look I didn't understand at the time, but one I now know was full of anguish. Billy shook off her hand as though he'd been scalded, and without saying another word, he grabbed his bicycle, hopped onto it and pedalled like a madman down the street. My mother composed herself and dusted off her dress before heading back into the house. The very next morning on our round of errands, my mother and I stopped in at the druggist's. There were only a few family-owned drug stores in town back in those days, and one of them was owned by a big bull of a man named Mr. Thompson. Yes, one and the same – Billy Thompson's father. I had heard talk on occasion that Mr. Thompson was a drinker, but he was a God-fearing church-goer, so most people never believed such rumours about him. He was bold and brash though, and my mother sorely detested him. You knew my mother disliked someone when she wasted no time on pleasantries. Well, that morning was no exception. My mother marched right into Mr. Thompson's shop, which she never normally frequented, and without so much as a 'How do you do?' or a 'Good morning', she announced to him that if he ever so much as raised a hand to his son again, she would ruin him. She vowed to broadcast the fact he was a drunkard who took his frustrations out on an innocent child. *And* she threatened to initiate a petition amongst all of her friends and neighbours to boycott his store. Without another word, she spun around and ushered me towards the door. As I turned around to catch a parting glance at Mr. Thompson, who stood with his mouth agape by the way, I caught sight of Billy cowering in the back of the shop. Billy made all of the prescription deliveries on his bicycle, and that morning no doubt, he was just heading off on his route. He looked after my departing mother with something akin to awe."

Tess glanced up at Emmy, a look of fascinated pleasure on her face. "What happened to Billy after that, Emmy? Did his father treat him any better?"

"Oh, yes. Yes, he did."

"How do you *know*?" Tess was anxious for confirmation of a happy ending to the story.

"I know because he came to see my mother not long afterwards."

"To thank her?"

"Yes. And do you know, for years afterwards, he would often visit my mother, and on those occasions, he would always bring her a bag of apples."

That night, after Emmy tucked Tess into bed and turned out the light, she paused in the doorway for a moment and looked around her ward's bedroom that by now was bathed in a sliver of moonlight slipping through the curtains. "I'm glad I chose this bedroom for you, Tess. It used to be my mother's."

November

October slipped quietly into November, the brilliant fusion of fall colors fading as the wind stripped the trees bare of their leaves. The November winds on the west coast could often reach gale force, and that, combined with the notoriously damp climate, created a penetrating chill even in the absence of sub-zero temperatures. So although Victoria's climate in the fall and winter months was deemed 'mild' compared with the rest of Canada, it still packed a bite.

On a particularly brisk evening, Tess and Leah decided to take a walk, both of them bundled up against the biting wind, strolling with their arms linked as they often did, a companionable silence between them. As a reward for having ventured out on such an inhospitable night, they ducked into a local coffee house that was still open. After ordering mugs of steaming tea and the obligatory pastry, they settled into a booth, both of them chuckling over each other's 'hat hair'. Leah suddenly stopped laughing, however, when Tess stripped off her gloves.

"OK, Tess, now that's just plain morbid."

Tess immediately retracted her hands and tucked them in her lap. With a sheepish grin, she tried to defend herself. "I know. I know. I just thought it might help to wear it."

Leah made a face to indicate what she obviously thought of that idea. "I thought it creeped you out."

"It did, at first," Tess admitted sheepishly, "but then I thought it might help to wear it." When she witnessed her friend's disapproving look, she added, "I don't wear it to school or anything…" Her voice trailed off as though she was having a hard time convincing even herself. Leaning forward across the table, she lowered her voice, "They're *counting* on me, Leah."

"Look, Tess, you're trying too hard. I've never seen you like this before, and I get the feeling it's not just a matter of wanting to solve this case...even though I know you'd like to help that girl's family," she added.

"Is it that obvious?" Tess sighed, giving up all pretence.

"To me it is. And I bet McLean knows as well if you act like this around him." Leah rolled her eyes.

A nervous giggle erupted from Tess before she could restrain herself. "Do you really think so?" She looked at her friend in earnest.

"Tess, you know I tell it like it is. But even if he is interested, I don't think he'd do anything about it. He's too professional. Besides, he'd probably get in trouble. You know – conflict of interest and all that."

Tess slowly sank back against her seat, frowning in displeasure.

Leah continued, "You need to face it, Tess – you're not going to channel anything because you're focusing on him. And from the looks of it, that isn't going to change anytime soon," she grinned mischievously.

Tess gave her friend an exasperated look and leaned forward to rest her chin on her hands. "I guess you're right," she sighed heavily. Knowing what she needed to do but disheartened all the same at the necessity of having to do it, she admitted, "I suppose I need to return the ring, don't I?"

The very next day, Tess made a point of returning the ring to McLean before she could change her mind. It pained her to see the expression on his face when she did so. He seemed reluctant to accept it back.

"You OK?" he asked softly.

"Yeah, I'm fine," she answered without looking up. "I just can't force anything, you know. It's been weeks now, and I'm not picking up on anything, and I don't think that's going to change." She couldn't look him in the eye, but rather sat talking to her hands in her lap.

He leaned back against the desk in his office and folded his arms across his chest, studying her intently. Finally, he broke the silence. "It's OK, Tess. Don't worry. It was good of you to try." He hid his disappointment behind a kind smile. She admired that about him – you could lash out at him, no doubt, and he would probably *still* be considerate.

All of a sudden, she needed to escape, or she feared she would burst into tears. Scooping up her book bag from the floor by her chair, she headed for the door.

"Tess," he called after her, causing her to pause in the doorway. "Do you think we could try something else?" he asked carefully.

Turning around, she eyed him warily, not at all sure where this was heading.

"I've been *really* loathe to ask you this. I didn't want to stress you out any more than you already were with the ring," he began. "But maybe you'd have more luck if you met Katie's parents," he suggested tentatively. When she did not respond, he took her silence as a positive sign and continued, "For some time now, Katie's parents, particularly her mom, have wanted to meet with you. They asked about the sketch, and at the time, all we told them was a psychic had produced it. They have no idea of the extent of your sighting the night of the murder, and I don't think that's something you'd ever want to tell them, frankly. But they do want to meet you."

Tess appeared deep in thought as she shifted uncomfortably on her feet. Finally, she spoke – "I can see why you didn't talk to me earlier about this." As she continued, she sighed wearily and her voice took on a pleading quality. "Please understand. It's not that I don't *want* to meet them..." At this point, she took a deep breath and released it slowly. "Look, I have to be honest with you. I've never been able to have sightings when I get...emotionally involved. It's like there's this...this mental block or something. I'm afraid that's what's happening in this case." Looking up, she tried to gauge if he was following her. "And besides that, I just don't think I could handle their disappointment on top of everything else, you know? I already feel like a failure with you guys, and that's bad enough, but what if I fail *them*?" Although she had only confessed a half-truth, she was desperately afraid he would now be able to put two and two together and deduce the real reason for her failure to channel with the ring. This thought made her blush furiously, forcing her to hang her head.

If he did suspect anything, he gave no indication; instead, he moved to stand in front of her, taking her gently by the shoulders and waited for her to tilt her head up to his. "I understand, Tess. I *know* you want to help. Believe me, I know that. And I *know* you feel bad about not picking up on anything from the ring. But even if you don't have a sighting after meeting her parents, they're really no worse off. They have *nothing* to lose at this point. Yes, they're looking for answers, but if you can't provide them with any, they're not going to hold that against you."

Tess dropped her gaze because his nearness was making her weak in the knees. She was frightened her own body would betray her, that it would somehow reveal her biggest fear lay in disappointing *him*. She stepped back to put some distance between them, effectively forcing him to drop his hands from her shoulders. Immediately, she sensed his embarrassment. Feeling guilty about his discomfort and unable to concentrate a moment longer in his presence, she stammered a hasty reply, "I'll…I'll think about it. I promise." Turning quickly on her heels, she bumped squarely into Detective Baxter as he entered the room. Bouncing off his massive frame, she was made to feel even more self-conscious at her less than graceful exit. Mumbling an apology, she fled the room, leaving the senior detective staring blankly after her.

He felt ready to make his move. The young prostitute he had been stalking in Vancouver would make an easy target. She was dropped off in the same deserted alleyway every night, and invariably, she was inebriated or high. All he had to do was lure her into his car with the promise of more drugs. He had scored some weed (or 'BC bud' as the locals called it) earlier in the day, and now as he lay in wait for her, he fantasized at the pleasure the next few hours would afford him.

As the hours ticked by with no sign of his victim, he began to feel uneasy. Refusing to accept the obvious, he sat stone-faced and chilled in his car, listening to the incessant drumming of rain on the roof, the silence broken only occasionally by the shrill blare of an ambulance siren as it sped to its destination.

It was the pale glow of the pre-dawn sky that finally alerted him to the fact it would soon be light. He could not believe she had not shown. Tonight of all nights, she had altered her routine. He frowned and shifted uncomfortably in his seat in an attempt to relieve his cramped muscles, trying to decide how much longer he should wait. After another half hour, he finally accepted the fact there was nothing to be done, and so sighing in disgust, he started his car, vowing to return the next night. A second night of lying in wait, however, proved fruitless as well – the girl did not show. Now after all his work, he was to be denied his pleasure. That did not sit well with him. Not at all.

Although it had been a relief to return the ring, Tess now struggled with McLean's request to meet with Katie Bishop's family. She wanted to help them, of course, and she also wanted very much to please McLean. She couldn`t deny that fact. And yet, she knew the chances of successfully channeling were slim. As she sat sorely conflicted on the bus ride up to the university on a particularly dreary November morning, she was taken back to a similar bus ride a few years earlier...

She remembered with clarity how it had been a comparable day – gusts of wind buffeted the bus, and heavy raindrops splattered noisily against the fogged up windows sounding like tiny glass beads being hurled against the panes. Thirty damp people stuffed into an enclosed space created a humid, uncomfortable ride, so most people tended to keep to themselves. Unable to find a seat on the crowded bus, Tess stood in the aisle battling against claustrophobia from the press of so many patrons. She was so preoccupied with that and with trying to keep her balance despite the constant lurching of the bus, she failed to notice at first the middle-aged woman who sat before her.

The woman stared fixedly at her hands in her lap and gently rocked herself to and fro, mumbling incoherently, seemingly oblivious to her surroundings. Tess tried to shield her from the curious stares of some of the less sensitive passengers who snickered or openly gawked at the poor woman, no doubt expecting some type of outburst from her.

Several minutes into the trip, someone rang for a stop, and for a brief second, the woman lifted her head and made eye contact with Tess. Her stricken face was tear-stained. What would normally have been an awkward moment wasn't, as it was readily apparent the woman was entirely lost in her own thoughts. Tess dropped her gaze in an attempt to allow her some privacy anyway. Afraid the lurching of the bus was bringing on nausea, Tess planted her feet wider apart in order to stabilize herself. She quickly realized, however, it wasn't the movement of the bus causing her queasiness; it was something else. And then the humming began...

When the bus pulled to a stop at the next corner, the woman rose quickly from her seat and made her way to the exit doors, many of the other passengers giving her a wide berth. It was not Tess' stop – hers was still several blocks away, but she felt compelled to get off the bus as well, so she ducked through the open doors at the last minute. Stepping abruptly into the wind and rain, she was momentarily disorientated. Several patrons who had exited the bus at that particular stop had quickly opened their umbrellas, so it took a few seconds to spot which way the woman had headed. As Tess hurried after her, she called out, "Excuse me, ma'am. Ma'am. Please wait."

Once she caught up with the woman; however, she suddenly grew self-conscious. "I'm sorry. I...I don't mean to pry. I just couldn't help but notice on the bus...you were crying. You've had some bad news."

The woman stared at her blankly before turning to resume her way, muttering, "I'm sorry. I have to get home. I *have* to get home."

Tess gently took her by the arm and led her a few steps to the relative shelter of a store awning so they were both out of the wind and rain. "I won't keep you; I promise," she assured the woman, who by now was eyeing her warily. "I just need you to know something. Your son..."

The woman gasped and clapped her hands to her mouth.

"Please, it's alright." Tess held up her hand. "Your son is alright. Well...he's hurt. It's his leg, but he's alright," she blurted out.

The panicked woman grabbed Tess by the arms, the force of her grip so strong, it was painful. "You've heard from my son? Are you a friend of my son's?" The desperation in her voice made Tess wince.

Gently, Tess pried the woman's hands off her arms and held them in her own. "No, I don't know your son; I'm sorry." Quickly realizing she was in trouble, Tess replied sheepishly, "I...um...I just know he's alright."

"But how could *you* know? The crash just happened. His fiancé just phoned me at work from the airport. We haven't heard anything from the police or the airline. I don't understand. How can you know *anything?*" The woman's voice rose higher and higher such that people standing around them were beginning to take notice.

"I...uh," Tess stammered. "I can't explain. I just *know.* And I couldn't let you suffer in agony not knowing." She knew she sounded ludicrous.

The woman took a step backwards, shaking her head in confusion. "I lost my husband this time last year. I watched him waste away from cancer. I *cannot* lose my son on top of that. Do you hear me? I just *can't!!*" Stifling a sob, she ran headlong into the storm, leaving several passersby staring blankly at Tess who, by now, had turned a brilliant shade of red.

On the national news later in the evening, Tess listened to the story she knew would be featured. A commuter jet had crash landed in Edmonton that morning killing 29 passengers and crew. There were 27 survivors, and Tess knew with certainty the son of the woman on the bus was among them. She just prayed by now his mother knew as well.

It pained her to remember the sound of McLean's voice – an odd mixture of relief and disappointment – when she told him she would meet with Katie's parents, but she needed to do so by herself. Ever the professional, he thanked her profusely and attempted to hide his disappointment behind that. She knew her decision brought him relief in that he didn't have to stall any longer about such a meeting, but she also knew he naturally wanted to be involved. She was certain he was puzzled at the fact she was effectively shutting him out, and she worried he would take it the wrong way, but she simply *could not* have him present. It was hard enough to focus on *anything* when she was around him, let alone try to channel. In reality, she was quite sure of the futility of such an attempt anyway, but she couldn't bring herself to refuse the request. And so, she found herself driving up the peninsula on this blustery, gray November afternoon.

Katie's family lived on a hobby farm half-way up the peninsula among a pastoral setting of acreages making up the Agricultural Land Belt. Driving through fields and farmhouses that looked like they were straight out of a Norman Rockwell painting, Tess passed numerous road-side stands selling everything from freshly cut flowers and organic vegetables to home-spun crafts. It was easy to get distracted, but she tried instead to focus on the purpose of her trip this afternoon. Stopping only once to check her directions, she backtracked and took a right turn onto a smaller road that wound its way steeply up the back side of Observatory Hill, aptly named for the astronomical dome at its peak.

When the dome was constructed in the early 1900s, it had been built on a hilltop well outside the city limits. Despite increasing light pollution from the ever expanding city, its telescope was still used on a regular basis. In fact, it was one of only a few federal observing facilities in Canada.

Tess had worked there several summers as a tour guide during her undergraduate degree, and now in graduate school, she collaborated with several of the researchers stationed there, but she had always accessed the facility from the other side of the hill. She did not know there were acreages on the back side.

Pulling to a stop at the end of a long driveway next to a dilapidated old barn, Tess turned off the car engine and tried to collect her thoughts. It was going to be hard to witness the hope on their faces. If she was in their shoes, she knew without a doubt she would grasp at everything and anything for answers. She desperately wished she could provide them with some.

Gathering her courage, she stepped out of the car and made her way up to the front door of a modest rancher, noting it was painted a deep shade of green such that it blended naturally into the surrounding hillside. As she steeled herself to ring the doorbell, she looked around at the front yard. It gave her the impression of a neatly tended garden, albeit one that had been left to its own devices for several months. Although carefully laid out, it was a mess of overgrown plantings that had long since reached their peak but had not been cut back or pulled out. It had the air of something sad and neglected. She tried to imagine it in its prime in mid-summer, understanding the comfort and pleasure such a lovely place would undoubtedly provide.

Unable to stall any longer, she rang the doorbell, her hand shaking visibly as she did so. The door was opened almost immediately by a young boy who couldn't have been more than five, but before he could say anything, a man placed his hand on the boy's shoulders and gently moved him aside. Extending his other hand toward her, the man greeted Tess. "Hello, you must be Miss Walker. I'm George

Bishop, and this is our son, Brett," he explained, patting the little boy affectionately.

"Hello. Pleased to meet you both." Tess shook the hand offered to her and smiled warmly at the young boy as she entered the foyer. She was a firm believer in what handshakes told you about a person and was therefore impressed that Mr. Bishop's had been strong and genial. It said something about his character. "Please, call me Tess," she advised him, wanting to set an informal tone for their meeting.

"Of course. And please call me George," he replied. "Come in. Come in." He took her coat and waved her into the living room, indicating a comfortable chair for her to sit in. "My wife is a bit…under the weather today, but I'll get her." As he turned to do so, a woman entered the room of her own accord. She needed no introduction. In comparison to her husband's composed demeanor, she wore her grief like a mantle. It was visible in every line of her face; in the slow, deliberate manner in which she carried herself as though every movement required a colossal effort; and in the deep, sad recesses of her sunken eyes. From her own family history, Tess thought she knew grief well, but her experience seemed to pale in comparison to the raw, shattered look of this woman. Surely the loss of a child, and a loss such as one under these circumstances, had to leave a mother gutted. Tess wondered briefly if the woman was medicated.

"Tess, this is my wife, Sandra." George made the introduction as he carefully guided his wife to the sofa, taking great care as one would with an invalid.

Tess stood up from the seat she had taken, unsure if another handshake was in order, but then thought better of it when none was offered. The woman simply nodded at her blankly like she had no real comprehension of what this meeting was all about. Tess was left with little choice but to sit back down.

After an uncomfortable silence, George motioned to his son who had also settled himself on the sofa beside his mother. "Now, Brett. You've got your chores out back to finish. That rabbit cage isn't going to clean itself."

The boy threw his father a petulant look, the kind only a young child can who knows the futility of protesting but does so anyway. Slipping off the sofa and crossing his arms defiantly against his chest, he marched across the room. "But I want to talk to the sidekick too!" he wailed.

George threw Tess an apologetic look as he rose from the couch and gently steered his son out of the room. "*Psychic*, son. The word is psychic."

If the circumstances had been different, the little boy's comment would have amused her no end, but as it was, she was profoundly moved by his dogged determination to find out more about his big sister's murder. 'Great,' she thought. 'So much for staying detached.'

"Sorry about that. He's overheard Sandra and me," George attempted to explain as he resumed his seat next to his wife and placed her hand lovingly in his. Such a gesture elicited a sad smile from her, and she leaned in to her husband for support. There was such a fragility about this woman, and it tugged sorely at Tess' heartstrings.

"No worries," Tess replied. Seizing the moment, she thought it best to explain something. "I just want you to know I'm not the kind of psychic who can...commune with spirits. I'm afraid I can't help you there." Her comment drew some interest from the mother who looked up with a flicker of hope lighting her otherwise dull eyes. Witnessing the poor woman's face, Tess would have given *anything* to have been able to say *something* of comfort. Instead, all she could do was offer a suggestion. "There are people like that, you know. If you think it would bring you some peace of mind."

"Thank you for the clarification, Tess." George seemed genuinely touched. "The police have told us very little, and we understand that's often the case in an open investigation, but I'm sure you can understand, we'd just like answers. All we've been told is you produced a sketch of the suspect. Do you work often with the police?"

"No, this is my first time," Tess admitted. Her mind was racing as she realized how difficult it was going to be to keep the true nature of her sighting from these people as Mclean had recommended. For one thing, George was obviously very astute. And besides, didn't they deserve to know? But what comfort would the knowledge of their daughter's last anguished moments bring them anyway? Despite her inner turmoil, Tess tried to appear calm as she continued, "I...um...sought out the police after seeing your daughter's story on the news." At least that was not a lie.

If George picked up on Tess' inner conflict, he gave no indication. "Oh, so you had some kind of vision after seeing the story?" he asked.

"Yes, that's right," she nodded vigorously. "An image of this guy just popped into my head, and I knew it had to be the ki...um...the suspect." She winced as she corrected herself, knowing the pain the more accurate term would undoubtedly inflict. OK – so she had just stretched the truth a little. "You see, I've had this ability since I was a little girl, and it has never failed me," Tess assured them. "That's how I know my sighting is accurate. Oh, I know the sketch is pretty generic, but it does resemble him. I'm hoping it's close enough to produce a tip."

SUSAN GNUCCI

"So are we, Tess. So are we," George replied solemnly. After a moment's hesitation, he delicately asked the question she had been prepared for. "So there's nothing else you can tell us?"

"I'm afraid not. Not right now, but maybe I can ask you something."

"Of course. Anything. Anything at all." George leaned forward, eager to be of some assistance.

"The ring Katie had on – the band with the scroll pattern. Was it special to her?" Her question sparked an immediate response from the mother who gripped her husband's arm and closed her eyes as though to steel herself against something inordinately painful. Tess winced, mortified with the knowledge she had provoked such an anguished response.

George flashed a kind, sad smile to assure her he knew she meant no offence. "No, not really. Sandra and Katie went to a flea market back in the summer and Katie bought it then. That was only a few weeks before…" Turning his attention to his wife, he whispered into her hair, "It's OK, dear. It's OK." He rubbed his wife's hand vigorously in a vain attempt to transfer some of his strength to her.

Tess knew she was pushing it, but she forged ahead anyway. "I know this is asking a lot, but maybe it would help if I saw Katie's room."

At Tess' suggestion, Sandra rose abruptly off the couch and stifling a sob rushed from the room, leaving her husband to heave a weary sigh. "Would you excuse me for a minute?" He seemed anxious to go after his wife, but not before turning to Tess. "Please don't go. Of course you can see her room. Just give me a minute."

Tess heaved a heavy sigh herself, for her heart went out to this poor man. Surely, he must be struggling with his

94

own grief, and yet, circumstances dictated he shelve it right now in order to stay strong for his wife. And what of the little boy? What do you tell a child so young? What a way to lose your innocence. Tess' musings were interrupted when George returned several minutes later. Although flustered, he appeared resolute.

"Sorry about that. My wife simply hasn't been able to set foot in Katie's room since this all happened. And she won't let any of us touch anything in it either, so it's hard for her to let a..." he paused and corrected himself, "to let someone she doesn't know go in it."

"I understand. I don't want to upset her. Maybe I should come back another time."

"No, no. If she was in her right mind, she would want this; I can assure you," he said with a sad smile. "Please come with me, and I'll show you to Katie's room." He led her down a long hallway and opened a door into a sunlit room on the west side of the house. Pausing at the threshold as if unsure of entering himself, he stepped aside to allow Tess access. "Please take your time. And please handle anything you like. If there's anything you want to ask about, just come and get me. I'll be out back with Brett."

Tess thanked him and tentatively entered the bedroom. As she did so, she experienced the strangest feeling, a momentary sense of guilt – not at the thought of violating someone's privacy, but more like the uneasiness of walking over someone's grave. Shaking off the feeling, she slowly circled the room and came to stand at the window that overlooked the back yard. Out on the patio, Katie's little brother stood beside a rather large wooden hutch holding a flop-eared rabbit, his face buried in its fur. Almost as though he sensed her staring at him, the little boy lifted his head and made eye contact.

His open, guileless expression unnerved her, so much so, she flinched and moved out of his line of sight.

Tess tried to concentrate on the room before her. It was painted a bold purple colour – obviously the girl had wanted to make a statement. A single bed stood against one wall, and a large closet occupied the entire length of the opposite wall. Gently prying open one of the doors, Tess took note of the assortment of shoes, sneakers, sandals, and boots. She was amazed at how many pairs there were. It put Leah to shame. The other side of the closet was knee-deep in a teenage girl's wardrobe – tank tops, sweaters, jeans, T-shirts, belts, etc. Inside an alcove opposite the window, a custom-built desk was strewn with a wild display of note-books, sticky notes, make-up, jewellery, and an assortment of other knickknacks.

One thing Tess did find surprising was that the room lacked any of the typical teenage posters of boy bands and tween heartthrobs. Instead, the posters adorning the walls depicted horses, many of them fanciful creatures with long flowing manes galloping through fantasy worlds. A large table stood in the middle of the room neatly laid out with all manner of craft supplies meticulously organized into jars and baskets. Tess traced her hand lightly over the items and closed her eyes…nothing.

'Please let me help you, Katie,' she thought desperately. 'Let me give your family some closure.'

Some twenty minutes later, Tess stood at the front door saying her goodbyes, promising she would help in any way she could with the investigation. As she turned to leave, she hesitated. Part of her simply wanted to walk out the door and not assume any further responsibility for this family's anguish, and yet, another part of her wanted to be able to offer *some* hope, however false. And so, she asked,

"Mr. Bishop. I mean, George. Do you have anything of Katie's that was special to her? Anything you could lend to me for a while?" Tess felt like a fraud asking such a question when she knew in her heart it was not likely to yield any result. Not only was she emotionally attached to McLean, she was now emotionally connected to this family as well. Once out of her mouth, however, the words could not be taken back.

Comprehension dawned on George, and when it did, his whole face lit up. "Of course. No problem. Please wait here. I've got to go down to the basement, but I'll only be a minute."

While waiting for him to return, Tess struggled with a myriad of conflicting emotions. To have witnessed his smile was worth it, but she knew she was only prolonging their pain in the long run. She waited several minutes in silence pondering her predicament before she spied Katie's little brother peering at her from around the corner of the living room. His unsophisticated attempt to catch her attention was not only amusing, it was endearing.

"Goodbye, Brett. It was nice to meet you," she called out to him.

Considering her acknowledgement an invitation, he entered the foyer and scrambled up onto the bench seat by the front door where he sat assessing her from his perch. Finally, he asked her a simple question – "Can you catch the bad man who hurted Katie?"

His question caught her off guard, causing her to wince and look away. In doing so, she discovered George standing at the top of the basement stairs, slightly out of breath. She could not discern whether he was embarrassed by his son's pointed question or whether he needed to hear an answer himself, for he simply stood staring at her. Tess felt torn.

She didn't want to lie, but neither could she tell the whole truth. Kneeling down in front of the little boy, she replied, "I don't know if I can, Brett, but I want you to know I will really, really try. OK?"

Nodding solemnly, he seemed satisfied with her answer. George cleared his throat conspicuously and stepped forward to place a small white box in Tess' hand. She naturally assumed it would contain a piece of jewellery, but when she opened it, she gasped at the delicate beauty of the object inside. Lifting it carefully by its pink ribbon, she held it up in front of her. It was a hand blown glass angel, the type of ornament that typically adorned a Christmas tree.

"We have two other children besides Katie and Brett," George explained. "There's Jake who is ten, and Amanda who just turned twelve. We've had a Christmas tradition in our family from the time the kids were born where we buy them a special ornament to hang on the tree on Christmas morning. Sandra puts a lot of thought into finding something unique for each child every year. We figured once they were out on their own, they would have a whole set of ornaments to decorate *their* first Christmas tree."

He pointed to the glass angel in her hand. "This was Katie's first ornament on her first Christmas morning." Turning the angel over to reveal a small sticker on the underside, he proceeded to explain, "See – the 'K' stands for Katie and '1994' was the year she was born." He was smiling broadly now with the simple pleasure of that memory.

"Thank you, George. Thank you very much. I *promise* I'll keep it safe," Tess assured him, incredibly touched he would entrust it to her care.

"I know you will," he replied, gently taking the ornament and setting it back in its box. As he guided her out onto the front porch, his voice took on an apologetic tone. "Sandra's been so insistent about seeing you, but when the time actually came today, I'm afraid she just kind of...fell apart."

"It's OK. I understand."

He reached out to gently touch her arm. "I want to thank you for coming, and more importantly, I want to thank you for sparing her what I'm sure you know. I'm...I'm sorry you have to live with that." He regarded her sadly, and she was humbled beyond measure by the fact he would worry about any burden she might be carrying when his own was so monstrously heavy.

DECEMBER

As winter settled in, it brought with it the seasonal wind and rain storms that often lashed the coast for days on end. Being on the southern tip of Vancouver Island, Victoria's climate was similar to that of its close neighbor – Seattle, Washington. Winters were inundated with rain, punctuated only occasionally by clearing skies. Snow was a rarity, and as a result, the city virtually shut down when there was any accumulation as it was ill-equipped to deal with plowing and sanding. Children were always delighted at such a turn of events because it usually resulted in a snow day (or two) from school. A snowfall rarely lasted more than a few days; however, so despite the inconvenience and calamity it brought, it was tolerated by most Victorians with good humour as a temporary predicament.

By mid-December, it had been weeks since Tess' visit with Katie's family, weeks of sitting and staring at Katie's glass angel, of meditating in order to relax herself, of staring at the police sketch; all to no avail. And Tess had purposely kept her distance from McLean during all of that time in order to concentrate. It saddened her to keep putting off his phone calls and updates, but she simply couldn't bring herself to confide the complete truth to him.

Despite her lack of success, Katie's father insisted she keep the glass angel for the time being on the off-chance it could produce something at some point. Tess was surprised the Bishops hadn't pressed for another meeting, particularly since the mother had been so out of it at the previous one. What she didn't know, of course, was Mrs. Bishop had suffered a nervous breakdown and was now in the care of her sister on the mainland.

On stormy nights, Tess would sometimes bundle up and walk out to the breakwater, Leah often accompanying her in companionable silence. Staring out at the angry waves, Tess had to wonder how Katie's family would cope with the approaching holiday season. That had to be hard. That first Christmas. What on earth was there to celebrate? How did you ever make such occasions normal again? Sadly, she surmised a family never really could.

Rather than head down east for Christmas to visit her parents as she sometimes did, Leah chose to stay instead with Tess, attempting to distract her with delicious meals and treats, and Tess loved her all the more for her effort. All the same, it was a strained, sad holiday as there didn't seem to be much cause for celebration.

And so the Christmas season passed, and Tess was frankly relieved to be done with it. By month's end, her involvement in the case had all but died down, and without many other leads, the investigation gradually stalled. Tess was sorely depressed, not only at her failure to channel, but also at effectively driving McLean away, for she knew he had gotten the wrong idea about her lack of contact. It pained her, the thought of not being able to get to know him better. She'd never felt this way about any man before – it baffled her to discover her feelings were both thrilling and frightening at the same time.

As the New Year approached, Tess could only pray it would somehow bring resolution to a case that was haunting them all.

❧ ❧ ❧

It always puzzled Tess why she never had any sightings with those closest to her. Never once was she able to pick up any kind of impression from either Emmy or Leah. She finally chalked it up to her emotional connection with them as there didn't seem to be any other explanation. And because of this, she never knew about Emmy's cancer until it was too late. Tess had been only nineteen at the time, having just finished her first semester of university.

Emmy had been a smoker for many years, starting in her youth when it was considered fashionable, but she'd kicked the habit upon retiring, choosing at that point to live a healthier lifestyle. It was a shock, therefore, when a nagging cough in the fall of her 79th year was diagnosed as lung cancer. She chose not to tell Tess right away, preferring instead to allow her ward time to adjust to the start of her first year of university. Both Tess and Leah had moved on to university together – Tess pursued Astronomy while Leah chased her dream of being a writer. After high school graduation, Leah's parents moved back east, but Leah had been adamant about staying in Victoria. It had become her home. So it only made sense to invite her to move in.

At first, it wasn't difficult for Emmy to explain away her condition because she often came down with colds. Having had pneumonia as a child in the days before antibiotics, she was prone to chest problems (although even that had not dissuaded her from smoking for many years). And both Tess and Leah were so busy with their university courses, it was only natural they were less attentive than usual. It wasn't until Leah made a comment about Emmy's weight one night at dinner when Emmy realized she couldn't hide her condition much longer. But she brushed off the comment all the same, declaring she was simply attempting to shed some unwanted pounds.

The fatigue was hardest to hide as everything tired Emmy out. On many occasions, she was caught napping when the girls came home from classes. She tried to make light of the situation, simply chalking it up to her age, saying, "Wait until you're turning eighty, my dear. We'll just see how spry you are then!"

When her fatigue worsened, Emmy was forced to break the news. Above all else, above all the worry and fear over her own imminent demise, was the overriding anguish of having to leave Tess. They had been blessed with nine wonderful years together. Emmy remembered all too well the fragile child who had come to her all those years ago. If she closed her eyes, she could still see the poor wee thing curled up in bed as though to protect herself, her little face locked in a pained expression even in sleep. More than anything else, Emmy wanted to spare her any more grief. And so, instead of telling Tess first, she confided in Leah and enlisted her help.

It was perhaps the most difficult thing Emmy ever had to do – to tell Tess about her condition. In some ways, it was even harder than receiving the news of her diagnosis. One night after dinner when all three women were sitting around the kitchen table enjoying a glass of wine, Emmy chose her moment. Bracing herself, knowing the devastation her news would undoubtedly impart, she simply stated, "Tess, I haven't been completely honest with you about something. I'm afraid I'm sicker than I've led you to believe."

Tess looked at her with a quizzical expression.

"There's no easy way of saying this…" Emmy seemed fixated on her hands, wringing them like a nervous child. "I have lung cancer." Tess immediately looked over at Leah, as though willing her to deny what had just been said, but her good friend simply hung her head. Struggling to digest the news, Tess shook her own head slowly back and forth and moaned in disbelief. "*No! No!*"

Leah rose quietly to stand behind Tess, gently rubbing her friend's shoulders in an attempt to massage the pain away.

"How long have you known?" Tess finally spoke.

"A few months," Emmy confessed.

"A few *months*? But why didn't you *tell* me?" Tess asked in an anguished voice, one that sounded years younger than her age.

"I couldn't, Tess. I just couldn't. You were so excited about university. You were just starting your life. How could I tell you something like that? You're nineteen, and yet, you've gone through more pain than most people experience in a lifetime." Emmy regarded her with a sad smile.

"But have you *done* anything? Chemo? Radiation?" Tess fought to keep her emotions in check.

"Tess, it's terminal. I have no intention of prolonging the inevitable or of putting you girls through a protracted illness where I would just become a burden," Emmy declared. Witnessing the anguished look on her ward's face, she gently added, "I *need* you to respect my decision on this."

Tess reached out to clasp Emmy's hands in her own, pulling them up to her face and rubbing them against her cheek. "I can't lose you, Emmy. I just can't." She began to weep.

"Now you listen to me, young lady." Emmy waited for her ward to calm down and then extricated her hands so she could pat Tess' lovingly. "You're going to be just fine. You're all grown up now. You're strong, Tess. I know you are. And Leah is going to help you. She'll be here for you."

Leah bent down to wrap her arms protectively around her friend. "That's right, Tess. You won't have to go through this by yourself. I'll be here with you."

The look Tess gave her best friend was one of sincere appreciation. Stoically, she then turned her attention to the problem at hand. "How long?" she asked bluntly.

Before Emmy could respond, she launched into a coughing fit that forced her to double over, prompting both women to rush to her aid. They patted her back soothingly and talked her through the worst of it. Several minutes later, after she had finally caught her breath, Emmy admitted, "It's advanced. The doctor said six months at the most." She hadn't sugar-coated her response, knowing instead that laying out the honest truth was the cleanest, easiest thing to do.

Tess gasped and leaned into Leah. "Oh, Emmy. I'm *so* sorry. I don't know how I could have failed to notice. I've been so busy with school and everything…" There was a long moment of silence before Tess knelt down before her guardian, settling herself on her knees in much the same way she did when she was a child. Smiling sadly, but determined to put on a brave face, she spoke in a resolute voice, "Here I am being selfish and you've got to face this…this terrible thing. We'll be here for you, Emmy. Me and Leah. We're going to help you through this. And I'm going to be OK. I don't want you to worry about me. Promise?"

APRIL

He had been able to tamper his need over the long winter months after his failed attempt to abduct the young prostitute the previous fall, but by the time spring rolled around, he was restless with agitation. Although he was confident the police sketch had not produced a link to him, he still felt compelled to hunt afield. And so, he returned to the mainland on his days off to search for a potential victim. Although he was an extremely careful hunter, he was beginning to chide himself that he was perhaps being *too* picky.

He sighed in frustration as he reclined in the driver's seat of his car on the ferry ride back to Victoria after yet another unsuccessful hunt in Vancouver on a particularly warm spring day. During the hour and half ride to and from Vancouver, he always remained in his car on the car deck, preferring the dark solitude of its confines to the hustle and bustle of the crowds up on the passenger decks. Drivers were allowed to stay in their cars during sailings, so some people took the opportunity to catch a quick nap or sit with an anxious pet.

Closing his eyes, he fell easily into a light sleep, lulled by the sway of the ship as it entered the rough waters of the strait. Only moments later, he was jolted awake. At first, he couldn't quite believe it. He could sense *her*. This knowledge – that she was on the very same ferry sailing with him – so unexpected and so thrilling as it was, left him feeling almost faint. He had to close his eyes and take several slow, deep breaths in order to calm his racing pulse.

And then he *saw* her. She was out on the front deck of the ferry, the wind whipping in lusty gusts through her luxurious hair. And she was laughing. He watched her throw back her head in a delightfully unselfconscious manner. She was obviously very comfortable with whoever was making her laugh. He experienced a fleeting twinge of jealousy for which he chided himself. And then she was gone...

Opening his eyes slowly, reluctant to let go of the image still lingering in his mind, he faced a dilemma. He desperately wanted to see her in the flesh, but to do so, he would have to leave the sanctuary of his car. He was not worried about anyone being able to ID him, for he disguised himself as a matter of course any time he was out in public; it was more the fact he would have to mingle with the other passengers. He *hated* crowds, detested them in fact – the press of sweaty bodies, the dreadful yowling of red-faced babies, the incessant drone of idle chatter. But what choice did he have?

He knew he had to be very careful. Despite his disguise, he had no idea if she was capable of sensing him. That would not do. If the ship was boarded for a search, there was no way off. Yes, he would have to be very careful indeed.

After much deliberation, he finally decided to risk it. After all, he was confident in his ability to sense danger, and thus far, his senses had not been alerted in any way. But what was he to do? He could follow her down to her car on the lower decks, but then what? Even if he could get her license plate number, what good would it do him anyway? He had no way of tracking it. As he tried to brainstorm, his frustration mounted to a level that was almost painful. To be so close to her after all this time, and yet to lose her when the ferry docked was almost more than he could bear. All these months of fruitless effort searching for her, and now she had landed right in his lap! And to think she would slip away again. He had to think of something, and he had to do it quickly – the ferry would dock in under an hour.

He formulated the only plan he could think of under the circumstances. He would follow her to her car and note the make and colour. If his car unloaded first, he would drive slowly in order to allow her to catch up. If she unloaded first, he would simply try to catch up with her. There really wasn't anything else he could do under the circumstances. She was not alone. He was certain of that, so there was no hope of taking her. Such an attempt would be too difficult anyway with the hundreds of people on board.

Reluctantly leaving the sanctuary of his car, he cautiously made his way up to the first passenger deck, pulling his hat lower in order to shade his face. He broke out in a cold sweat at the noise and smells that hit him squarely in the face as he came up the stairwell. Steeling himself, he continued. As the ferry had been under way for over thirty minutes, most passengers had already grabbed a bite to eat in the cafeteria and made their way to the front seating lounge in the bow of the ship. A quick scan of the cafeteria confirmed this fact, so he continued on his way, searching restlessly for her face among the crowd.

Over the next half hour, he toured the entire deck, both inside and out with no luck, necessitating a climb to the second level of the ship. Whereas the first deck was designed for business travelers and for those who just wanted to work or read quietly after a meal, the second deck of the ferry was designed for families. In addition to a large seating lounge with tables where passengers could play cards or games, this deck was equipped with a bright, colourful playroom and a video arcade, both of which immediately set him even more ill at ease than he already was.

Rounding a corner in search of a washroom where he could escape for a minute, he was jostled by several young children who brushed excitedly past him in their game of tag. His nerves frayed, he took refuge in the forward lounge, finding a seat near the back where he would be less conspicuous. As he caught his breath and fought to quell his anxiety, he attempted to focus on scanning the room. His seat not only enabled him to peruse the lounge, it also afforded him a panoramic view of the front deck of the ferry. He found it impossible to concentrate, however, as the noise was simply intolerable, prompting him to sit with his fingers in his ears.

Despite a lack of success in spotting his witness, he had no doubt she was on board. Oh, she was here alright, and his inability to locate her left him aggravated and perplexed. Had she somehow sensed him and was even now hiding from him? Had she alerted the crew? But how could that be? *Surely*, he would have known. He *had* to find somewhere quiet where he could think.

Just as he rose from his seat – he spotted her. She was still there as she had been in his vision standing on the deck in front of the main bank of windows, out of the wind now that the ship had turned. She was dressed casually in a windbreaker and jeans with a tote bag slung across one shoulder, talking animatedly to someone on her left who was out of his line of sight. Again, he experienced a stab of annoyance.

He had to admit she enthralled him. Even without her ability, he was still attracted to her. For one thing, her hair was the deepest sheen of black he had ever seen, reminding him of a sleek raven's wing. And she was petite, just as he preferred.

His ruminations were interrupted by a movement in his peripheral vision as a second woman came into view. He was immediately struck by her beauty. Not only was she statuesque and blonde – she was a stunner. She looped her arm companionably through that of his witness, and together, they turned to make their way back along the side of the deck. He frowned upon seeing this other woman, for he experienced the oddest sensation he had seen her somewhere before. But of course he couldn't have, for surely he would have remembered someone so striking. He had no time to dwell on it, however, as an announcement came over the loud speaker – passengers were advised to return to their vehicles in preparation for docking.

A surge of passengers headed for the stairwells, and for a moment, he feared he would lose sight of the two women. His height, however, gave him an advantage, allowing him to keep their blonde and raven heads in view as they bobbed in and out of the congested crowd. The press of so many bodies squeezed into the narrow stairwells was making him sick to his stomach, and he began to sweat profusely. He hung back at what he hoped was a safe distance, apprehensive and hyper-alert.

When he saw the two women turn off on the lowest car deck, it dawned on him *his* car was a deck above. He watched anxiously as they picked their way over to an old, white Volvo station wagon. At least that was distinctive – it would be easy to track. He realized with dismay, however, it was parked in an inner lane, and as such, it would be one of the first to unload. Satisfied only when they were seated inside, he raced up to his own car.

Unloading seemed to take forever, and as a result, his agitation soared to new heights. He realized he had a virtual death grip on his steering wheel, so he had to force himself to sit back, release his hold, and flex his whitened knuckles. At least he could breathe easier now that he was back in the familiar confines of his car and not wedged in that repulsive glut of humanity, but he was stuck in an outer row of cars and could only watch helplessly as the inner rows were unloaded first. Once his turn came, his car almost leapt forth from the bowels of the ship, so anxious was he to get out onto the highway.

His witness had a head start, but it was a good half hour into town, so he was hopeful he could catch up with her. He sped along in the fast lane trying to keep reasonably close to the speed limit, all the while keeping his eyes peeled for her white Volvo. Despite the adrenaline coursing through him, he knew the *last* thing he needed was to be pulled over for speeding.

"Turn off the highway," Tess ordered as she closed her eyes and leaned forward to lower her head to her knees, grabbing onto the car's dashboard for support.

"What's wrong? Are you alright?" Leah gave her a concerned look and reached over to place a hand on Tess' back, worried her friend was suffering from a sudden bout of motion sickness triggered by the ferry ride.

"Get off the highway *now*, Leah!" Tess barked. The urgency in her voice bordered on panic.

"OK. OK. The airport exit is coming up. I'll take that." Fearing her passenger was about to be sick in the car, Leah cracked her window as she sped up.

"Oh, my God! Oh, my God!" moaned Tess as she rocked herself back and forth.

"It's OK, Tess. It's gonna be OK. Just hang in there. We're almost there." Leah was thankful she sounded a lot calmer than she felt. In her haste, she took the airport exit faster than was prudent, and as a result, had to ride the brakes forcefully in order to handle the turn. It had been raining heavily earlier in the day, so taking the exit at that rate of speed wasn't the smartest thing to do. For a split second, Leah feared she would lose control. Something in her friend's voice unnerved her. Tess was not one for dramatics. Once off the highway and onto the airport feeder road, Leah signaled her intention to pull over onto the shoulder, but Tess shook her head vehemently.

"*No! No!* Don't stop. *Keep going! Keep going!*" she croaked.

Leah threw her a puzzled look but shut off her signal indicator and sped back up.

"Are you going to throw up?"

"No, no. Give me a minute. We've *got* to get off this road. It's too obvious. Take the next side street."

"OK, now you're scaring me, Tess."

"Just *do* it!!"

Leah took the next left and silently wound her way up a hill into a newer subdivision of exclusive homes. She drove aimlessly for several minutes, winding ever farther up the hill and then down the other side before she slowed and finally stopped. She waited a moment for any protest before she shut off the engine and leaned back in her seat, letting out a long sigh.

"OK, are you going to tell me what all this is about?" She turned her attention to her passenger, who by this time was also leaning back in her seat, one arm draped over her eyes.

"I think we lost him," Tess turned slowly to face her friend, the strain and fear of the last few minutes etched deeply on her face.

"Lost who?"

"*Him.*"

It took a minute for that to register with Leah. "You mean…*him?*" she asked incredulously.

Tess simply nodded.

"How…how do you know? Are you *sure?*"

Tess nodded again. "He was right behind us, Leah! In fact, I think he was on the ferry." Tess shuddered and shook her head vigorously in a vain attempt to somehow dislodge such a notion entirely from her mind, as if by dislodging it, it couldn't possibly be true.

"You mean to tell me we've been on the *same* ship with him for the last hour and a half?" At this, Leah's composure broke. "You've *got* to be fucking joking."

"You *know* what that means, Leah? It means he lives here. He's *not* some transient. He was coming home tonight, just like we were." Tess began to shake uncontrollably.

"Alright. Alright." Leah reached over to hug her friend.

"It's *not* alright, Leah!" Tess angrily pulled away. "The only way I've gotten through all these months is by trying to convince myself he was some psycho drifter, that he was probably halfway across the country by now. But he's been *here* all along. What if we'd actually run into him on the ferry? Or on the street? Or wherever he works?"

"OK, you're probably right," Leah admitted. "He probably *does* live here. But you just said he was trying to catch up with us right now. Why would he risk chasing us if he already knew where we lived?"

"I'm scared, Leah. He must know my car. How many white Volvo wagons do you think are in a city this size? And what if I hadn't channeled him and he'd followed us home…" her voice trailed off.

Leah shifted in her seat so she was able to take her friend firmly by the shoulders. "You've *got* to calm down, Tess. This isn't helping. Can you tell where he is now?"

That stopped Tess dead in her tracks. She knitted her brows in concentration for a few seconds then sighed heavily and shook her head. "I don't think he's nearby, but I can't be sure."

"You need to phone McLean," Leah advised resolutely.

It had been weeks since Tess last spoke with McLean. She'd tried to put him out of her mind only to be disturbed by the odd phone call he made to check in with her. It was hard to hear his voice during those calls, and she feared he could somehow detect the longing in hers. Now they would be thrown together again.

Tess bit her lip and began to rummage through her tote bag.

Leah watched her for several seconds before asking, "What are you doing, Tess?"

"I can't find my damn phone!" Tess began to panic.

"Here, give me that." Leah reached over and gently pried the tote bag from her friend's grasp. She quickly located the phone stuffed in a side pocket and handed it over with a gentle smile.

Tess fought back tears as she scrolled through her contacts. "He said to call any time, day or night…"

The year of Emmy's passing had been bittersweet, for it was in Emmy's gentle care, Tess had come to life again, and now when the tables were turned, she wished she could do the same in return. It seemed a cruel twist of fate for a person as sweet and as loving as Emmy to be dealt such a cruel blow. In her private moments, Tess railed against such an unfair turn of events.

Being only nineteen that year, Tess was legally an adult in the eyes of the law, but she was still thoroughly unprepared to face the impending death of a loved one. Of course, she was old enough to know there were no guarantees in life – of anyone, she knew that. She knew she should be thankful for the nine wonderful years she'd been given with Emmy and not chafe at the years to come, but Emmy had filled the gaping hole left by her parents' death, and now Tess feared another loss. She sighed heavily at what the future would hold and prayed for strength in the coming months. She knew she would need it.

As winter gave way to spring that year, Emmy outlived her doctor's predictions; however, her condition steadily declined. Her coughing fits came on with more frequency often overwhelming her frail frame, leaving her weak and exhausted.

When Tess finished her university classes, she decided to take the summer term off – no work, no school – in order to spend whatever precious time she had left with her guardian. Although Emmy was too frail to go down to the beach anymore, Tess often pushed her in a wheelchair along the footpaths that laced the bluffs overlooking the water. It was unseasonably warm, so they were able to spend long, lazy days together much like they had when Tess first arrived all those years ago. Their time was spent reading or chit-chatting or simply people-watching. Bailey, who always accompanied them, seemed more attached than ever to his mistress, preferring to sit at her feet rather than romp and play. Granted, he was old and arthritic, but that dog always came alive whenever he was by the water. He never tired of investigating everyone and everything. These days, however, he was quite content to stay by Emmy's side. Every once in a while he would rouse from sleep and raise his head to look up as if checking on her. She would look down at him then over the top of her book and satisfy him with an – "I'm fine, you old fool. Go back to sleep."

It was on one such outing when Emmy made a prophetic announcement, "I'm afraid I shan't be here for your birthday at the end of the month, Tess. I'm sorry I will miss it." She looked over her shoulder with a nostalgic smile.

Tess patted her guardian's shoulder lovingly and marvelled at the fact she was capable of feeling such fierce devotion to this woman who, although a blood relative, was once almost a stranger to her. She did not doubt Emmy's ability to sense her own imminent demise, but the simple bluntness of her guardian's statement threw her. As she moved around to the front of the wheelchair, she cupped Emmy's face in her hands.

"Are you sure?" she asked gently.

Emmy simply nodded.

Tess bent to kiss her tenderly on the cheek, marveling at the soft warmth she encountered there. "Then I shall miss you more than I can say."

The end came as Emmy knew it would only weeks later when she took a sudden turn for the worst. Confined to her bed, she was comforted by both Tess and Leah who took turns sitting with her day and night so she was never alone. Her pain was well controlled with a pain pump, and a Hospice nurse visited daily. Bailey lay on the floor at the foot of the bed subdued along with everyone else, able to sense the seriousness of the situation as many animals somehow do, refusing to leave his mistress except when Tess coaxed him outside now and then for a few minutes of much needed exercise.

On the day of Emmy's passing, Tess woke early having spent another fitful night of sleep in the chaise lounge she had moved alongside Emmy's bed. The subtle awareness of movement had woken her, and she squinted in the early morning darkness at Emmy's frail figure in the bed. Bailey rose stiffly and padded softly over to the chaise lounge, resting his head there, his doleful eyes expressing his concern. Tess stroked him distractedly, transfixed as she was by what she saw before her.

Emmy lay in her bed with one arm outstretched in mid-air, a look of pure joy on her face. Tess rose quickly to the side of the bed, thinking that in a more lucid moment, Emmy wanted to hold her. She quickly realized, however, Emmy wasn't even aware of her presence. Instead, her guardian's gaze seemed focused on something or someone only she could see. Laughing softly, she spoke only one word – "Charles". And then her arm slowly lowered to the bed covers, and sighing softly, she closed her eyes.

Tess waited in vain for another breath, holding her own for several seconds before she could actually accept the fact that Emmy was gone. Bailey began to whine softly and nudge his nose against Tess' arm, prompting her to kneel down and embrace him. She buried her face in the soft fur of his neck and released the tears that welled up with sudden fierceness from deep within her. It wasn't yet daybreak, so she lay down beside Emmy for a last time and tenderly stroked her face, thanking her guardian for breathing life back into a child who had all but died.

Arthritic as he was, Bailey managed to jump up on the bed and gingerly pick his way across the comforter where he lay down between his mistress and Tess, almost as if he needed some closeness in order to grieve as well. And that's how Leah found them both when she came to relieve Tess a short time later.

The rest of the morning was a blur of phone calls and arrangements, most of which Leah handled. It was weeks before Tess could even bear to enter Emmy's room. Every time she stood on the threshold, her arms folded across her chest, her head resting against the door frame, she was overcome by an intense wave of grief. Leah offered to go through Emmy's things and box them up, but Tess insisted she needed to do that in her own time.

When she finally summoned up the strength to sort through Emmy's personal possessions, Tess closed her eyes and drew comfort from the familiar smell in her guardian's bedroom. She was pleased it still smelled like Emmy – the delicate scent of lavender was everywhere. Crossing over to the dresser in the far corner of the room, Tess picked up the framed picture of Emmy's beau who had died back in the war. The photo showed a handsome young man sitting on a picnic blanket on the bluff overlooking the ocean, knees drawn up, arms resting casually around them. She wondered if he had been staring out at the water when someone had called his name to take the photo, for it captured a faint smile on his lips and a wistful expression on his face. What had he been thinking? Had Emmy taken the picture? Tess gave in to a strong desire to remove the photo from its frame. As she did so and turned it over, she found a name and date written in Emmy's fluid handwriting –

My dearest Charles
August 1941

✤ ✤ ✤

Halfway into town from the ferry, a sinking feeling settled over him as it dawned on him he had somehow lost his witness. He pulled off the highway at the next exit and parked on a side street, trying to collect his racing thoughts. Had she stopped for gas? Had she turned off the highway? He had only passed a few exits – should he retrace his route and search those?

It suddenly occurred to him she could have channeled him, and with such a possibility, came the very real fear the police could be setting up a road block for him this very minute. He was sorely disappointed to give up the chase, but now that his sixth sense had been alerted, he trusted it implicitly. Carefully winding his way over to a secondary road in order to connect to the one he needed to take, he reluctantly made his way home.

It took another forty minutes to reach his rented farmhouse, for it was situated on a large acreage southwest of the city. Located in a sparsely populated rural area, it was perfect for his needs. He had few neighbors, and the ones he did have were hard working farmers who had little time for socializing. That suited him just fine.

Entering his bedroom this evening, he threw himself dramatically onto his bed landing on his back, the bedsprings squeaking loudly in protest. His faithful tabby cat jumped gracefully onto the mattress with him, circling lazily before settling down beside him, purring in contentment and seeking a greeting. No longer annoyed with his absences now that she was used to them, she was back to being her affectionate self. He lay for a long time staring vacantly at the ceiling with one hand clasped behind his head, the other stroking his beloved cat. He chided himself at his lack of control over his emotions. How uncharacteristic of him. *She* did this to him.

Finally, he rose with a sigh and set about fixing his cat something to eat. Making her needs clear, the tabby paced the countertop, her tail swishing to and fro with avid interest at the meal being laid out before her. "There you go, my pet," he drawled as he set the dish of cat food down onto the linoleum. "I've neglected you all weekend, haven't I? No matter. I'm back now, and we shall visit just as soon as you've had your supper."

Settling into his armchair in the living room, he flipped on the television, annoyed at having missed the late news. As he sat there half listening, a fleeting recollection came over him. Like a leaf swirling in the wind, it danced tantalizingly close, and then at the last second, it whirled just out of reach. Knowing if he chased it, it would elude him, he closed his eyes and sat back in his chair to clear his mind.

After several minutes of quiet meditation, the memory fluttered and gently settled, and as it did so, a slow, lazy smile crept over his face. He *had* seen her before – the blond woman. A memory of her replayed in his mind. She was a reporter. He was certain of it. He had seen her on several local news features. Why hadn't he remembered that? He was very good with faces, but he realized she looked quite different in person from her broadcast persona – she was even lovelier. He vowed to watch the early news tomorrow in the hope of catching one of her pieces, but he already knew he was right. And he knew with equal certainty she would be the key to finding his witness.

Tess was thrilled to hear the obvious concern in McLean's voice when she phoned him from the cul-de-sac in which she and Leah were parked after fleeing from the killer off the ferry. Although surprised to hear from her, he immediately took charge of the situation, calmly directing her to backtrack towards the ferry in order to cross over the highway so they could take the scenic waterfront route into town. It was precautionary, he said, and he stayed on the phone with her the whole time, putting her on hold only once to call Baxter.

It was late by the time they arrived home, almost 11:30 p.m., but both McLean and Baxter were there waiting for them. Despite the hour and the interruption to their own lives, they were both anxious to hear the details of the girls' encounter with the killer. Before entering the house, however, Tess and Leah were made to wait at the front door while the two detectives checked out every room from top to bottom. Only once they were satisfied all was clear did they allow everyone to settle into the parlour.

It was hard for Tess to concentrate on relating the events of their ferry ride because she was positively giddy in McLean's presence. It was *so* good to see him again. She was badly shaken by her brush with the killer, which in itself would have made it hard to focus on anything, but on top of that, Tess was also distracted by the worry written all over McLean's face. That, combined with the late hour, virtually made her head spin. It was Leah who kept having to prompt Tess on specifics and keep her on track as the detectives busily made notes.

Tess was keenly disappointed with the fact her sighting had taken place in the interior of the killer's car because it meant she was unable to describe the make or model. The only things she had 'seen' were his grimly determined face behind the steering wheel and a mobile of sorts dangling from the rear view mirror. She *was* able to describe his changed appearance – darker hair stuffed under a woollen hat and a thick, bushy beard.

Grudgingly, Tess agreed to surveillance on her house at McLean's insistence, hopeful he would be the first to volunteer. She had to temper her disappointment when he did not. No doubt, routine stuff like that was assigned to junior officers. Never one to hide her feelings very well, especially when she was stressed, she grew suddenly quiet, prompting McLean to throw her a quizzical look.

"I'm sorry. I'm really tired," she smiled weakly. She looked over at Leah, who by now was curled up on one end of the settee dozing, an exhausted, worried expression marring her otherwise lovely face.

"Sure. We understand, Tess. I think that's enough for tonight anyway," McLean informed her. As if on cue, both men rose to leave.

"Tess, even though it's a long shot he knows who you are or where you live, we could forget the surveillance and you could consider…"

Baxter didn't have time to finish his sentence before Tess interrupted him. "I'm not going anywhere, Baxter. You can't get rid of me so easily." She shoved her hands in the pockets of her jeans and smiled bravely at him. "Besides, I'm helping with the investigation, aren't I?"

"Yes, of course. You've been a big help, Tess," McLean assured her, laying a hand on her shoulder as if to convince her.

From that simple touch, she was surprised by the vulnerability of her voice when she found it. "Besides, I have nowhere to go."

"No family? No friends? Nowhere out of town?" McLean asked gently.

"No, and anyway, I can't just leave my program. I have labs to teach and my supervisor is counting on me to help with his research."

"What about Leah?" Baxter nodded to her sleeping form.

Tess' head snapped up. "What about her? You don't think...?"

"Does she have anywhere to go?"

"Her parents live down east. I suppose she could go there for a while, but I doubt she would leave me. We're like sisters." Tess worried her lower lip and frowned. "But I couldn't live with myself if anything were to happen to her."

"Does she have a boyfriend she could stay with then?" Baxter asked.

"None that I know of," she replied dryly, mildly annoyed he hadn't asked the same question of her.

"We don't have to decide this right now, Tess. It's late. Talk to Leah in the morning." McLean headed for the front door. "I'm going to place some calls to get a surveillance team over here tonight. They'll be in an unmarked car so as not to alert your neighbours."

"Are you *kidding* me? This is Oak Bay." She shook her head and chuckled. "I'll place bets old Mrs. Peterson will be over here first thing in the morning." Her remark served to break the tension.

By the time the surveillance team arrived, it was almost 2:00 a.m. and Tess was utterly exhausted. Noting that Leah hadn't budged, she threw a blanket over her friend and left her in peace. At the front door, Baxter gave Tess a curt nod in passing and went out to give the surveillance team their instructions for the night. Left standing in the foyer, Tess massaged her temples, her expression pensive.

"Are you OK?" McLean came up behind her.

"I don't know," she frowned. "I sense something with this guy, McLean. I haven't been able to put my finger on it until just now," she replied wearily.

"What do you mean?"

"The mobile in his car. It was a mobile of a cat. I get the distinct feeling there's some connection with this guy and animals." Tess shook her head as though annoyed with herself. "I can't pick up on more than that, but I definitely sense *some* connection." She looked up at him and frowned again.

"OK, Tess. Good to know. It's hard to believe this psycho could be an animal lover when he thinks nothing of snuffing out someone's life."

"Yeah, I thought these guys start out by torturing or killing animals." Tess seemed to be thinking out loud. "McLean..."

"Yes."

Her composure suddenly broke and she looked up at him with an imploring look. "I'm *so* afraid..." Her voice was disarmingly child-like and it took the young detective close to the breaking point.

Moving closer to her than was prudent, he lowered his head toward her, his voice low and intimate. "Hang in there, Tess. We're *going* to get this guy." Despite his apparent confidence, he winced inwardly, knowing how hollow his reassurance really sounded.

Looking up at him, she slowly shook her head. "He's going to hunt again, McLean. I just *know* he is. And I don't think I can handle seeing that, let alone have it on my conscience."

Taking her by the shoulders, his voice tight with emotion, the young detective assured her, "Hey, listen. You are *not* to blame for what that maniac does."

"I *know*, but I'm tied to him all the same," she attempted to explain. "It's like being bound together with a length of rope. There's just enough lead that I'm able to stay out of his way, but it's awful being tethered to him. I feel...I feel tainted," she confessed. Looking up into his handsome face, Tess battled against a strong desire to lean against him, to feel his solid presence against her. There were times in her life like tonight when she would have given anything just to be held.

"You're the key to nabbing this guy, Tess. I *know* it. And we're going to keep you safe; you hear me? He's not going to get that close to you again." McLean struggled to keep his voice from wavering.

"You don't understand," she replied despairingly, "He already is."

Just then, Baxter returned for his partner, forcing McLean to release his hold on Tess, which in turn prompted raised eyebrows from the senior detective. McLean ignored the look and brushed past, his head down.

Losing Emmy had not only been incredibly hard on Tess, it had been equally hard on Bailey. Although he loved Tess and was fiercely protective of her, his mistress was and always had been, Emmy. Without her, he just seemed to lose all interest in things. For years, he'd slept on the floor by Tess' bed and he still did so most nights, but now in the wee hours of the morning, he would rise stiffly from sleep and trot into Emmy's room. Tess would find him there, curled up on Emmy's bed. Somehow that poor arthritic dog could still make it up onto the bed. Tess was at a loss as to how to ease his grief when she could barely deal with her own.

Leave it to Leah to see the humour in the situation. She commented dryly how Emmy would have thrown a fit to see a dog up on the bed. Tess agreed, but she just didn't have the heart to discipline the poor thing when it was abundantly clear he only sought closeness with his mistress, and so she left him there, respectful of his need, feeling it keenly herself. Sometimes he would open his eyes at her as she stood in the doorway – he wouldn't raise his head at all, but would just stare at her with his big, sad eyes and whimper softly. In response, Tess would curl up beside him and stroke him lovingly, offering what simple comfort she could.

As the days passed, Tess and Leah tried to coax Bailey out of his depression with delicious little tidbits and treats, and although he never failed to gobble them up, he simply wasn't the same dog anymore. Granted, he was almost fifteen years old, but up until Emmy's passing, he had always been an active, healthy animal. With her death, it was as if he had aged overnight, and no amount of pampering was going to restore his zest for living.

To cope with Emmy's loss, Tess spent countless hours down at the beach. Sometimes Leah accompanied her, but more often than not she headed there alone, unable to coax Bailey to go with her. She thought it ironic the weather was so glorious, almost as though Emmy had a hand in it in order to cheer her. It was therapeutic for Tess to sit on the beach with the cool sand between her toes and the warm ocean breeze wafting through her hair. Rather than distress her, her memories of days spent at the beach gave her comfort. It was the place she felt closest to Emmy.

One night, Tess woke from a deep slumber, rising to consciousness slowly as if from a great depth. Gradually, she took in her surroundings – the moonlight streaming through her thin curtains, the familiar contours of the furniture in her room, the door ajar just as she'd left it. She was chilled. Had that woken her? Pulling the covers up to her chin, she burrowed deeper into the warmth of her bed. She could not relax, however, as a nagging feeling would not leave her. An uneasiness she could not name settled over her, and she finally leaned over the edge of her mattress in an attempt to gain a view of the rug at the foot of her bed. It was empty. She frowned and lay back against her pillow.

Sighing heavily, she threw back the covers and climbed out of bed, muttering at her foolishness in chasing after an old dog who just wanted to be alone anyway. Tiptoeing down the hallway, she turned to enter Emmy's room, fully expecting to see Bailey curled up as he often was on the bed. When she noted he wasn't there, she was puzzled. He wouldn't be in with Leah, would he? Stepping quietly across the hall, she peered into Leah's bedroom. It took a minute for her eyes to scan the room, but she soon came to realize Bailey wasn't there either.

Awareness dawned slowly, and with it, a sense of utter despair flooded through her. Retracing her steps, she returned to Emmy's room and stood for several minutes in the doorway, struggling to find the courage she needed. She contemplated waking Leah so at least she would have some support, but something held her back. Instead, she entered Emmy's room and quietly closed the door behind her, leaning heavily against it for support. After a full minute, she took a deep, steadying breath and moved into the room to stand beside the bed. Dropping down on all fours and squeezing her eyes shut, she carefully lifted the bed skirt and lowered her head. She didn't even have to look, for she instantly knew the smell of him – that sweet mixture of fur and mustiness. Hanging her head, she sank to her stomach and gave in to her anguish.

She was brought back to reality some moments later by the cold hardness of the floorboards. Once again, she reached out to lift the bed skirt, this time tucking it up under the mattress. Steeling herself against the inevitable, she looked under the bed – there lay Bailey barely a hand's breadth away, still and silent.

Tess reached out, her hand shaking visibly, to touch his paw. As she did so, she groaned at the lack of warmth she found there. For several minutes, she stroked his fur and whispered words of endearment to him. She knew, of course, he could no longer hear her, but she felt compelled to say them anyway. And she thanked him, for he, like his mistress, had been instrumental in saving her life.

Later that week, Tess and Leah held a solemn ceremony for the cremated remains of their faithful companion and spread his ashes off the bluff overlooking the ocean as they had done for his mistress only months before.

It wasn't until several days after the ferry incident when his suspicions were actually confirmed. The blonde woman reported on a local bike race on the evening news. She did indeed look quite different than she had on the ferry. Her hair was swept up in a stylish bun, and she sported a professional-looking skirt and blazer. Leah. Her name was Leah McKinnon. A smile broke over him as a feeling of triumph washed over him. He leaned back in his recliner and savored the exquisite feeling for several minutes before setting his mind to planning.

What to do? What to do? If he abducted this Leah, he was certain she would tell him where to find his witness, but her disappearance would only alert the police who would undoubtedly step up their campaign to find him. They would also probably place his witness under protective custody at that point, effectively blocking his access to her. He had to wonder if they already had her under any kind of surveillance.

But surely he didn't need to snatch this Leah when sooner or later she would simply *lead* him to his witness, now wouldn't she? Such a course of action, although less complicated, had its drawbacks as well. Either one of the women could potentially ID him. And he had no idea if his witness would be able to sense *him*. Oh, yes, he had to be extremely careful. He had to think this through *very* carefully. To rush now would be foolhardy. After all, he'd already waited so long – another few weeks or even another few months hardly mattered now.

The lure of a hunt in which he would stalk one woman in order to find another, all the while eluding the police, excited him beyond measure. He *knew* he was more than capable. He just had to be thorough in his planning. But he was no fool. He also knew that sooner or later the police would catch up with him...but he planned to be long gone before they did.

"I'm going to take this coffee out to the surveillance team, Leah," Tess shouted up the stairs as she put on her shoes. It was late, almost midnight, and Tess was about ready to turn in. Grabbing her coat from the closet by the door, she slipped it on and pulled out an umbrella from the stand in the hallway. Once out onto the porch, she frowned at the virtual downpour that had settled over the city earlier in the evening. Setting her tray of coffee and cookies down on one of the porch lounge chairs, she sighed in exasperation as she fought to open the stiff umbrella. A damp chill quickly settled through her and she shivered.

'What a lousy job,' she thought to herself as she headed down the walkway, concentrating on balancing both the tray and her large umbrella, 'having to pull a surveillance shift, sitting all night in a car in the pitch dark.' As she approached the vehicle parked across the street, she slowed her step when it dawned on her it was different from the SUV she had grown accustomed to seeing. This was peculiar in itself, but even more alarming was the fact there was a lone occupant...

Her eyes widened in terror. Almost as if in slow motion, she released her hold on the tray, and before it even hit the ground, she had spun around and made a break for the house, ditching the umbrella as she ran.

The lone occupant struggled to get out of his car and leaned across its roof shouting, "Tess! Tess! It's me, McLean."

Instantly recognizing his voice, she stopped dead in her tracks and slowly turned to face him, her laboured breathing creating soft clouds of steam that encircled her head. Cautiously retracing her steps as if still unsure, she squinted to see him through the downpour.

"What the bloody hell..." she cursed as she approached the car.

"Get in, Tess." McLean gestured. "You're getting soaked." He ducked back into the shelter of his vehicle.

Tess did as he bade her, pulling open the passenger door and settling in beside him. Now that she was over her shock and fright, she was thrilled to see him, but cautious and confused as to his presence at this late hour. "Is anything wrong? Where are your regular guys?" she asked.

McLean sat with his hands braced against the steering wheel almost as if he needed something with which to steady himself. "No, nothing's wrong," he replied in a strangled voice, clearly mortified to be caught parked outside her house. "I...um...I took over for the regular team tonight. Sometimes when I have a free night..."

An awkward silence followed before Tess blurted out, "*You're* taking a shift?"

Sinking back in his seat now that all pretence was basically gone, the young detective confessed in a quiet, halting voice, "I was...I mean, I've been...thinking about you, Tess." He winced as he turned away from her, almost as if unburdening himself was painful. "*A lot.*"

Tess sucked in her breath. Could this really be happening? Was this man whom she had been fantasizing about for months now confessing his interest in her? Oh, God. Where was Leah when she needed her? As the seconds passed, Tess chastised herself – '*Say* something, you idiot!!'

"Um...I..." She simply couldn't collect her thoughts or force her mouth to form any intelligible words.

McLean, whose face was flushed crimson by now, spoke in a slow, tortured voice, "You've avoided me all winter, Tess." He shifted in his seat to face her. "Is it anything I've said or anything I've done?"

The look on his face almost undid her, prompting her to finally speak. "No! No! Not at all!" she blurted out, reaching instinctively to lay a hand on his arm.

The relief on his face was palpable, and he let out a long sigh as he moved his hand to cover hers. "But I'm not imagining it – you *have* been avoiding me, haven't you?" he asked gently.

She hung her head. "Yes. But it's not what you think," she was quick to add, her gaze glued to the floorboard because she was too shy to look up. "Do you remember why I was anxious about meeting with the Bishops? That I can't channel when I'm emotionally involved?"

He nodded, remembering their conversation.

"Well, I can't channel when you're around either; that's probably why I had no luck with the ring." When she finally found the courage to look up at him, she discovered a huge grin had replaced the worried strain on his handsome face.

He slowly brought her hand up to his lips and held it there. His warm breath against her skin turned her insides to jelly, prompting her head to fall back against the head rest as she closed her eyes.

Lowering their hands, McLean sighed heavily and admitted, "It's totally inappropriate for me to see you, Tess. Ed would kill me."

Opening her eyes slowly, she nodded her understanding. "I know."

"I can live with that...for now," he grinned at her, "now I know how you feel."

She smiled warmly at him.

"Even if we just talk on the phone or you come down to the station." His voice took on a vulnerable quality.

Unable to calm her racing thoughts, Tess simply nodded.

Looking past her out the passenger window, McLean nodded at the abandoned tray and the spilt coffee cups and cookies littering the street. "What's that all about?" "Oh…um, Mrs. Petersen's away so I promised her I'd take coffee out to your officers," she admitted rather sheepishly. "She sometimes takes them out a morning coffee, but I'm not exactly a morning kind of person."

"Mrs. Petersen?" he asked, cocking his head.

"My neighbour. She…uh…she's visiting her daughter in Calgary this week."

McLean burst out laughing. "Well, I'll be damned. That's a first." He arched an eyebrow and smiled broadly.

Just then, the front door to Tess' house opened, spilling light into the street, and Leah stepped out onto the porch. Dressed only in her pyjamas and bathrobe and hugging herself against the chill, she moved toward the railing and scanned the street. "Tess?" she called out, a worried edge to her voice.

Tess rolled down her window in order to answer. "It's alright, Leah," she called out. "I'll be right in." Turning to face McLean, she giggled, "I'd better get in. I'm gonna get a grilling."

MAY

Spring arrived in typical fashion in Victoria, bursting forth in a profusion of colour and fragrance as the cherry trees lining many of the city's streets threw out their blossoms at the slightest hint of warm weather. Sidewalks and roadways were showered with their white and pink flower heads, forming a thick, downy carpet of petals. Famous for its annual 'flower count', Victorians were encouraged to report all manner of bulbs – daffodils, crocuses, hyacinths, and snowdrops, much to the chagrin of other cities in Canada that were still suffering under freezing temperatures. By the time May rolled around, trees and shrubs were in full bloom – rhododendrons with flower bundles the size of dinner plates, richly coloured camellias in shades of pink and red, and stately magnolias with their exotic, showy flower heads – all combined to create a striking display. Victoria was a beautiful city, but never more so than in the spring when nature came to life with a vengeance.

One night in early May, he made his weekly call from a pay phone in town. He was always careful to vary the phones he used, sometimes driving far afield to find one. It disgusted him to use a public phone, but he really had no choice, so he always held it gingerly even after sanitizing it with a cleaning wipe.

She couldn't speak with him, of course, but he always received an update on her status from the care home. The staff was puzzled at first why he would not provide a contact phone number, but he told them he travelled a great deal, so it was best if he was the one to contact them. He scoffed at the idea of a cell phone and said he couldn't afford one anyway. He called the care home faithfully once a week, always on Sunday nights. She had been in the nursing home for more than a year after being struck down in the prime of life by the early onset of a form of dementia akin to Alzheimer's. Why he called her at all was something even he was at a loss to understand. For years, he had had no contact with her, but now at the end of her life, did he feel some responsibility for her? In some ways, it was easier that she did not know him. There was a freedom in that, but still, he could not help himself – maybe, just maybe, this would be the week she would remember her son. Could he ever wrestle a blessing from her? Would she ever give him one?

When his mother's care attendant came to the phone, he immediately sensed something was wrong. He was informed his mother had suffered a stroke and was not expected to pull through. He felt nothing with this news, of course; it was more the cold, hard reality he had never been worthy of her acceptance, her approval, or her love. Their relationship had soured long ago, but now he would truly be alone.

He wrestled with conflicting emotions. He should attend her funeral, if only for appearances sake. After all, it wouldn't do to be seen as heartless, now would it? And then there was the matter of her estate. He already had a little money put by, but why should he not lay claim to what was rightfully his? It suddenly occurred to him she may not have willed him anything. He grew indignant at that thought. He didn't know if he could handle more rejection from her. Besides, who else would she leave it to? There *was* no one else. For this reason alone, he had to go. But her impending death was most inconvenient. It would mean a halt to the search for his witness.

As he made his plans, he decided to drive down east because it was less of a risk than flying. A road trip, however, would require several days, and he would still need to be careful for he had no idea how far his police sketch had been circulated. He hated the thought of days on the road, but there was one benefit – he would have the freedom to hunt.

She hummed quietly to herself, giggling occasionally as she staggered along the side of the dirt road. The soft puffs made by her breath in the chilly night air were illuminated in the pale moonlight, dissipating like thin wisps of smoke.

He had not planned to stop in this small prairie community on his way east; however, he was finding the road trip more grueling than expected, so he had pulled in for some much needed rest. As on previous nights, he'd found a suitably isolated location in which he could bed down for the night in his car rather than take a chance with a motel. Just as he was settling down, bundled up against the chill, she had passed by on the other side of the road. He'd been more than startled to see someone wandering along a deserted back road at this time of night, let alone a woman. It was clear she was inebriated, however, from her unsteady gait and from the fact she hadn't even noticed his car. Nor did she seem to be aware of the weather, for she wasn't even wearing a coat. He sucked in his breath at the sight of her but fought to harness the urge that shot through him. He needed a clear head to weigh his options.

He rarely ever took a chance on a spur of the moment opportunity such as this, and he did not like to hunt in unfamiliar territory. It was only the late hour and the isolated road that eased his concerns. As he debated, his hunger continued to mount as did his anxiety because his hapless victim was moving further away from him, albeit at a slow pace. Part of his hesitation was due to the woman's hair. It wasn't as long as he preferred, and yet, he still fantasized how it would feel – the silky texture of it, the feather lightness of it in his hands.

Finally, he made his decision and slipped silently out of his car, following her on foot for some distance, staying carefully out of sight although she seemed oblivious to her surroundings anyway. Despite his excitement, he vowed that if she did not move off the road, he would abandon the chase, for it was too risky to overtake her out in the open, no matter how isolated the area. It also concerned him to be moving away from his car.

If it was one thing he prided himself on, it was his discipline – in being able to weigh the risks, on indulging himself *only* when the conditions were exactly right. If the risk was ever too great, he was more than capable of pulling out, of setting aside his hunger, even after the stress of the last several months.

The woman suddenly stopped, and he feared for a moment she had sensed something. He needn't have worried though, for it was obvious she was simply undecided about continuing along the road or taking a shortcut through an adjacent meadow. She kept looking first one way and then the other.

His breath hitched in his throat as he awaited her decision...

Mercifully, she was oblivious to the evil that stalked her as she entered the field. And, of course, she could never have known her own actions had just sealed her fate. The sound of her soft laughter echoed his own delight as his shadow soundlessly closed the distance between them...

He arrived in Sudbury late at night and pulled into an economy motel off the beaten track, the kind of place where one paid up front in cash by the month, week, day, or even in some cases, by the hour. He figured he would chance a room rather than spend any more nights in his car, for he was stiff and sore, and besides, this was hardly the type of place where anyone minded anyone else's business. The desk clerk, a large hulk of a man with a shaved head and tattooed forearms, barely batted an eye when checking him in, asking no questions and going through the motions with as few words as possible. He was obviously the kind of man who did not 'trouble trouble unless it troubled him'.

Entering the room assigned to him, he noted sourly it was just as dingy as the rest of the motel – its only furnishings were a lumpy bed covered with a faded floral spread; a small desk and chair squeezed into one corner of the room; and a cheap older model TV. The first thing he did was take a long shower to wash away the grime of his travel days, and as he did so, he ruminated on the parable of the prodigal son. The only difference with his situation was his mother was in no shape to give him her blessing, and even if she had been, he doubted she would bestow it upon him anyway.

He hated the nursing home the minute he walked into it early the next morning. If he had not come all this way, he would have turned around and walked straight out. The drab institutional green paint; the outdated, shabby furniture in the lobby; and the harsh buzzing of the fluorescent lighting, all contributed to set him ill at ease. The pungent smell of antiseptic did little to mask the stench of the place – a musky, decaying odour that permeated his nostrils and soured his stomach. He looked around with indifference at the scraps of human life seemingly abandoned in their wheelchairs, many of them drooling and incoherent. The odd one scrutinized him with sad, imploring eyes as though desperate for a kind word or gesture.

As he approached the desk, a patient lunged at him from out of nowhere – a disheveled woman with wild, unkempt hair who reeked of urine and glared at him with crazed eyes. Pawing at him with her claw-like hands, she shrieked abuse – "Oh, you're a devil, you are! A devil! They can't see that," she lamented as she gestured wildly at the staff and the other patients, "but *I* can. *I* know what you are! You're the devil's spawn!"

Disgusted by her contact, he retreated from her clutches, while a staff member from the reception desk attempted to guide her into the arms of an attendant who had been hastily summoned.

She would have none of it, however, and shook off all attempts to calm her. "I *know* what you are," she pointed at him. "You're a murdering devil! An evil, black devil!" she screeched.

The attendant, who by now had his arm wrapped tightly around the hysterical woman, patted her reassuringly and whispered soothing words in an attempt to distract her. "Now, now, Edna. Let's get you back to your room for a little rest, shall we?" he suggested as he tried to guide her down the hall. When this didn't work, he struggled to subdue her and finally had to resort to manhandling in order to get her back to her room.

Although thin and frail looking, she seemed to have strength far beyond her size, fiercely resisting all efforts to interrupt her tirade. As she was hauled away, she wailed a warning, "You've let the devil in and now we'll *all* pay the price, you fools!" When she realized her warning was falling on deaf ears, she swore up a blue streak, leaving the more cognisant patients shaking their heads at her antics.

He shook off the episode and approached the clerk at the front desk who gave him a sheepish look. "Sorry about that. Edna is having one of her bad days."

"No harm done. I'm here to see Debra Miller," he smiled tightly. "I'm her son."

"Oh, Mr. Miller. We've been expecting you. I'm afraid we have bad news. Your mother passed away this morning, but we had no way of reaching you. We knew you were expected though, so we thought we'd wait a little bit before calling the funeral home. I can take you to see her. She's still in her room."

"I see. Well, yes, I've been on the road. I had hoped to be here in time. I would like to see her, please."

As the clerk turned to step out from behind the desk, he held up a hand. "That's alright. I'm sure I can find my way if you just tell me the room number."

"Are you sure? I can take you there."

"No, it's fine. I'll need a minute to...collect myself."

"Of course. She's in room 109. Straight down the hall, last door on your left."

"Thank you."

He headed down the corridor, thankful it was in the opposite direction from the crazy woman who could still be heard cursing and hollering even though she was now safely locked in her room. On the way past an entertainment lounge, he noted a plump, middle-aged woman playing enthusiastically on the piano, trying to engage the disinterested patients in her care in a sing-along. Her voice grated on his nerves, and in response, he hastened his step.

Upon glancing into the room on his way past; however, he couldn't help but break into a genuine smile. A black Labrador lay on the floor beside an elderly patient who sat slumped and sleeping in his wheelchair. At the prospect of some attention, the dog rose to its feet and trotted over to nuzzle and lick his hand.

"I see you've made another friend, Chester," a young lady chuckled as she approached.

Lifting his gaze from the dog, he was immediately struck by the sight of the young woman who stood before him. She was not pretty by any stretch of the imagination, but her one glorious attribute was a mane of fiercely bright red hair that cascaded down her shoulders in tight, corkscrew spirals. Realizing he was staring, he cleared his throat self-consciously. "Hello." Nodding to the dog, he asked, "I take it this is Chester?"

"Yes," she replied, smiling warmly. "He's keeping Bill company this morning." With a nod of her head, she indicated the patient in the wheelchair who was snoring softly. "I'm Clarissa. Chester comes in with me every Friday morning to see the patients. He's kind of a regular," she added, giving the dog an affectionate pat.

"He's yours?" he asked with interest.

"Yes, I've had him since he was a puppy. He'll be four next month."

Kneeling down to pet the dog, he remarked, "He's beautiful. You're very lucky. I move around too much to keep a dog, but if I could, I'd love one just like him."

"Yes, he's pretty special. *All* the patients adore him." At this comment, she leaned closer and whispered, "But he gets terribly spoiled here, you know."

He would have preferred to spend more time with the dog, but resigning himself to the task at hand, he stood up, albeit with reluctance. "I'd best get going. I'm here to see my mother."

"Maybe she'd like a visit from Chester later?" Clarissa offered.

"I don't think so. She passed away this morning."

"Oh, I'm so sorry." The young woman instinctively reached out to touch his arm.

He looked down at her hand as if greatly puzzled to see it in contact with his arm. Catching wind of his reaction, the girl quickly retracted it, suddenly embarrassed by the intimacy of her impulsive gesture towards a perfect stranger. In response, he gave her a tight, controlled smile. Anxious to break the tension, he nodded curtly and left the room.

As he made his way down the corridor, he battled against the urge her contact had stirred in him. It was too soon for one thing. It had been less than a week since his last kill. And he did not need the complication of a kill in the very vicinity he was staying in. He could ditch her body elsewhere, but surely in the course of investigating her disappearance, the police would check out the nursing home where she volunteered. No, he could not risk it. He could not risk any connection whatsoever with her. As much as his desires were aroused, he could not give in to them.

To distract himself, he focused his thoughts on his mother. She had been distant and emotionally unavailable to him for most of his childhood, ever since... Well, no matter. He had simply kept to himself, carefully concealing the devastation he'd felt at her rejection. He had fended for himself until he'd been old enough to run away. At the age of sixteen, he had simply packed a backpack, stole what money he could find in the house, and walked out. He knew they would not miss him or even bother to look for him – his mother undoubtedly relieved he had left, his step-father likely only indifferent.

He was very sure she had never confided her suspicions to his step-father, but nonetheless, his relationship with the man had never been more than one of mutual tolerance anyway. Granted, at first his step-father had made a token effort to gain the trust and affection of his young stepson, but in finding no response time and again, he had simply given up. Over the years, he'd spent more and more time at the office – it became his only means of escape from an unbearable marriage. Gradually, the bottle became his sole source of solace whenever he was at home.

Over the years, his mother had often taken to her bed for days at a time or listless and disheveled, she would wander aimlessly through the house. As a boy, he would sometimes stand at her closed door and lean his ear carefully against it through which he could hear her crying softly.

Entering her room tonight, he looked dispassionately at the woman who had been his whole world for the early part of his childhood. She was only in her early sixties, and yet she looked much older. Her disease had taken its toll, not only on her mind, but on her body as well. He had never even heard of her condition – Lewy Body Dementia. The nurses had explained to him that it involved not only physical symptoms (often misdiagnosed as Parkinson's), but dementia and vivid hallucinations as well. His mother required round-the-clock care because her disease had taken her mind completely, leaving her child-like and unable to look after herself.

Not having had any contact with his mother for years, he only found out about her condition when he happened to run into an old neighbour while passing through Sudbury the previous year. He learned from this encounter that his stepfather had been dead for several years, having drunk himself into an early grave. His mother had been placed in a subsidized nursing home as there had been no one else to care for her. Upon learning this news, he'd begun his weekly phone calls to the nursing home, never talking to his mother because she would not have known him anyway, but always asking the nurses for an update on her condition. He could not say what drove him to do that after all the years of their estrangement.

Taking a seat on the chair beside her bed, he reached out to touch her hand, not out of any desire to hold it one last time, but more out of morbid curiosity. He had seen dead bodies before, of course, but those had always been the result of his own actions. It felt strange to sit beside someone who had not died at his own hands. Oh, to be sure, he had fantasized over the years about taking his mother's life. Her rejection had instilled that in him. But there was still some part of him, some *small* part tucked away in the back of his mind that found the idea abhorrent. Perhaps it was the one remaining shred of decency left in him. Ah, he shook his head – now he was being sentimental.

He remembered the countless times when it would have been so easy to wrap his hands around her slender neck; to take in the soft shock that would register in her eyes in that moment; to note the exact millisecond when she would actually comprehend her fate; to watch her eyes roll back in her head; and to hear her last breath as it eased out of her limp body like the gentle sigh of the wind through tall grass. He had been sorely tempted to do so whenever he caught her studying him when she thought he was unaware of her doing so. It was as if she was puzzled how something like him could have possibly come from someone like her.

As he grasped her hand tentatively in his own, he noted the faint warmth he found there. He marveled how the skin moved so easily over muscle and bone, almost as if it had detached itself somehow in the dying process. He couldn't remember the last time he'd held her hand. No doubt it had been when he was a little boy. How he had longed for some gesture from her – some touch, some sign of affection, some affirmation of her love for him, that she still loved him despite…

And then it simply hadn't mattered anymore. He remembered precisely when he first became aware of his *lack* of feelings. He'd come home from school early one day when he was twelve years old, feigning illness to find his mother wondering the house with a bloodied nose and a black eye. She was searching for her car keys in order to drive herself to the hospital. He'd understood intuitively the real reason for her injuries – his stepfather had taken his frustrations out on her even though his mother insisted she had fallen down the stairs. It had puzzled him at first – his lack of emotion that day. He'd felt nothing for his mother – not pity, not sympathy, not even anger towards his step-father. Nothing. That realization had been quite …liberating. He'd finally felt free from an overwhelming need for her approval, her attention, her love. So why had he come back now after all these years? What did it matter now?

His recollections were interrupted by a gentle knock at the door after which a nurse quietly entered the room. "Good morning, Mr. Miller. I'm Angela, one of your mother's nurses. Your mother passed away in her sleep earlier." She approached the bedside with a sympathetic smile. "It was painless and peaceful," she assured him.

"Thank you. I'm glad. Of course, I *wish* I had been here with her," he lied. His attention was riveted when the nurse took out a brush from the bedside table and slowly began to stroke his mother's long grey locks, fanning them out across her pillow.

"She has such *lovely* hair," the nurse exclaimed.

He stared transfixed. When she replaced the brush and turned to leave the room, she told him, "Take your time with your goodbyes, Mr. Miller. There's no rush. We'll call the funeral home when you're done."

He found his voice just as she reached the door. "This may be an old-fashioned request," he said as he turned to address her, "but I was hoping I might have a lock of my mother's hair." He phrased the question with as much sincerity as he could muster without over doing it. "You know, something to remember her by…"

Tess' cell phone was ringing and she couldn't find the damn thing. She was forever setting it down and forgetting where she'd left it. Finally spying it on her bed, she pounced to answer it before her voicemail kicked in. The screen indicated the caller – Detective McLean. Her pulse raced whenever she saw his name, prompting her to pause momentarily in order to collect her scattered wits. She was more infatuated than ever with the young detective, especially now when she knew of his interest in her.

They had spoken often on the phone in recent weeks, their conversations initially focusing on the case and then gradually becoming more personal. She learned he was from a family of policemen – his father, grandfather and an uncle had all served on the local police force. Unlike her, McLean was from a large, close-knit family – in addition to two brothers and three sisters, he had several nieces, nephews, and cousins. He had only been promoted to detective three years ago after working for five years as a patrol officer. Before that, he had obtained a degree in criminal justice.

"Hi, McLean." Tess made a deliberate attempt to sound casual.

"Hi, Tess. How are you?"

"I'm fine, thanks. Knee deep in research as usual. What's up?" She desperately wanted to know if he daydreamed about her as often as she did about him, but she was far too shy to ask. Her thoughts were racing a mile a minute when she suddenly realized she hadn't been paying attention to what he'd just said.

"Tess, are you there?"

"Yeah, I'm sorry. What did you say?" She was mortified he might mistake her wandering thoughts for lack of interest.

"Is this a bad time? Should I call back?"

"No, it's fine. I'm fine," she groaned inwardly.

"I said there's been a development. I was hoping you could drop by the station today so I could give you an update."

"Good news or bad news?" she asked tentatively.

"Both. Come in and we can go over things."

Had there been another killing she wondered? As awful as this thought was, at least she had not been witness to it. Couldn't he just tell her over the phone? Did he *want* her to come into the station so he could see her? Her heart leapt at the thought.

"OK. I have a class this afternoon, but I could be there by 4:00."

"Sounds good. See you then, Tess."

Later in the afternoon, Tess paused at the entrance to the police station, taking a deep, steading breath before she entered the building. As she headed for McLean's office, her thoughts turned to the possibility of another murder. If there *had* been another one, why hadn't she heard anything about it on the news? And who was the victim? In any case, she was undoubtedly someone's daughter, sister, or possibly even mother. Tess' spirits plummeted with this knowledge, for it meant there would be another grieving family out there. She suddenly felt ashamed at her earlier sense of relief at *not* having experienced a sighting. How could she be so selfish to put her own peace of mind above someone else's life? Was it just a fluke she had been able to channel Katie Bishop's murder? Had that been a 'perfect storm' of sorts? Were those conditions unlikely to occur again? Unfortunately, she didn't have any answers. Despite years with her gift, she still had yet to truly understand it.

Her thoughts were cut short when she reached McLean's office. She stood awkwardly in the doorway unsure of entering, for the young detective was engaged in an animated conversation on the phone. He had his back to her, so she was able to study him unabashedly which she innocently proceeded to do. Although his individual features were rather sharp and angular, put together, they lent him a uniqueness she found attractive. His lanky frame made him look younger than his years as did his haircut. In addition, he had a habit of running his hands through his cropped hair, which only made it stand wildly on end, giving him a boyish look. He was the type of detective who dressed professionally, always in a suit and tie, although on this day, he had already shed the jacket and loosened the tie.

He definitely intrigued her. Despite his job, he did not appear to be jaded, and in his profession, he undoubtedly saw some pretty awful things. But maybe that was because he was still young; maybe years of cases like this eventually took their toll. It was hard to tell but she admired his outlook nevertheless. Even more than this though, she sensed a kindness in him which drew her to him. Her musings were interrupted when he sensed her presence and turned around, catching her eye. He smiled a warm greeting and motioned for her to take a seat.

"Sounds good, John. I've got to go. I've got someone in my office. OK, will do. Bye." He hung up the phone with an exasperated sigh. "Why is it when *you* need something, nobody's got time for you, but when *they* need it...?" He rolled his eyes in mock frustration and her stomach flip flopped. "Thanks for coming in, Tess," his voice softened. He moved around to the front of the desk in order to close the distance between them which only made her blush furiously. Noting her reaction, he deliberately kept things casual. "How are you? How's school?" he asked with genuine interest.

"Good, thanks," she replied. "I'm trying to finish a paper. Well, my supervisor is trying to finish a paper, but I have a lead role in it," she added proudly.

"Ah, so you'll be a published author then?" He sounded impressed.

"Well, nothing most people would read," she admitted with a laugh.

"I always thought Astronomy was just looking through telescopes, but I suppose it's a lot more than that, huh?" he asked.

"Yeah, that's the glamorous side of things. Most of the work isn't so exciting, I'm afraid. You have to have a real passion for its ultimate goal," she explained.

"Which is?"

"Understanding our universe." She gestured broadly with her hands and rolled her eyes.

"Ah, pretty lofty goal," he chuckled, nodding his head. "Right now, I'm trying to understand this case." He sighed and resumed his seat behind his desk. Pulling out a file folder from the mess in front of him, he opened it. "Our surveillance hasn't picked up on anything which tells me he doesn't know who you are or where you live. That's the good news."

Just then, Baxter stuck his head in the doorway. "You tell her yet?" he asked impatiently.

"No, not yet. I was just about to." A deep blush crept up McLean's face, and he pretended to busy himself with the contents of the file folder.

"Hi to you too, Baxter," Tess grinned at the senior detective. "Or should I say *Grampa* Baxter?" she teased. McLean had been the one to tell Tess about Baxter's twin grandsons delivered by C-section a month earlier. She couldn't help but feel vindicated with that news.

The burly detective simply grunted an acknowledgement and settled his bulk into the seat next to her. Tess took the hint and grew suddenly thoughtful. "There's been another murder, hasn't there?" she asked, knowing the answer but not really wanting to have it actually confirmed.

"How do you know? You *saw* it?" Baxter quipped, as sarcastic as ever.

"No, just a guess." Tess felt rather sheepish she had only a hunch to go on.

"As a matter of fact, there has been another murder. The victim was discovered yesterday." McLean confirmed her suspicions.

"Where? Here?"

"No. In a small town in southern Manitoba," McLean replied.

"*Manitoba?* But how do you know it's him? That's a long way from here." Tess looked between the two detectives, her eyes narrowing. "Come on; spill it. What makes you think it's related?"

"Let's just say the MO is the same," Baxter replied dryly.

"You mean manual strangulation, no sexual assault, no robbery…" Tess rattled off what they all knew to be true. "And the victim was young, anywhere from mid-teens to mid-twenties," she added.

McLean chuckled and shook his head. "She'd have made one helluva detective, Ed."

Tess beamed, inordinately pleased she had impressed them, particularly McLean.

"We've been working closely with the RCMP," McLean explained, "to see if there are any unsolved cases in Canada with this guy's MO. When this victim was found, they contacted us."

Tess' face grew serious as something dawned on her. "You know it's him because she's missing her hair, isn't she? *That's* how you know it's him!" She felt a sudden, intense rush of relief for this all but confirmed the fact their killer was indeed halfway across the country.

"We can't comment, Tess." Baxter was ever the professional, always by the book. "But we're sure it's him," he added, his voice softening, knowing the relief such news would undoubtedly impart.

"Wow, what a relief!" she blurted out. As soon as the words were out of her mouth, she winced and attempted to backtrack. "I mean that's *awful* for that poor girl, of course, but it is *so* good to have him gone, you know?" she attempted to explain.

"Yes, I'm sure it is, Tess. And we hope he'll be caught. We're assisting the RCMP in any way we can," McLean assured her.

"I wonder if that's why I never picked up on anything. Why I never had a sighting this time, I mean." Tess seemed to be talking to herself. "Maybe I only picked up on the Katie Bishop murder because it was local? Maybe our connection is related to proximity?" She looked up, her brows knitted in concentration.

"Could be, Tess. Could be." McLean nodded thoughtfully.

"In light of this development, we're going to scale back your surveillance." Baxter was all business.

Tess nodded. "I understand. I know that costs money. Do you...do you think he'll come *back*?" she asked hesitantly as if she didn't really want to know the likelihood of such a possibility.

"Hard to say," Baxter shrugged. "Could be things were getting a little too hot for him here, so he's moved on," he speculated. "My bet is he's heading east, maybe Toronto. Easy to get lost in a city that size."

Tess turned to McLean, hoping he would agree so her nightmare would indeed be at an end.

"I agree. Don't worry, Tess. I'm sure he's gone."

McLean sounded so rational, so convincing, Tess *almost* believed him. If it wasn't for a niggling doubt at the back of her mind, she would have been convinced.

"Something's not right, Ed," McLean voiced his concern when the two men were alone in his office after Tess had departed.

Baxter sighed in exasperation and was quick to brush off his partner's apprehension. "He *took* the hair trophy, Jay. How many guys have that MO? He's our guy alright."

"Hey, I'm the first one to *want* him to be our guy because then he's thousands of kilometers away from here, from Tess."

Baxter shot him a cautionary look.

Realizing he was blushing furiously, McLean continued, "It means he's likely headed east, I know, but it's all a bit too easy, don't you think? It's like it's contrived. It's like he's popped up there and is making a point of saying, 'Hey guys – Look! I'm over here!' It's like he *wants* us to know that. His victim was left out in plain view in a field, Ed. Granted, it was on a back road, but she wasn't concealed in any way. Katie Bishop was hidden deep in the woods. It was pure luck she was found at all. If those hikers hadn't been lost and hadn't had their dog with them..."

Baxter headed for the door. "You're overthinking this, Jay. Who cares why he's down east or why he wants everyone to know it. He's out of *our* hair. Let the RCMP have a crack at him. If he's getting cocky, he'll likely trip up at some point." He turned around and studied his partner, pointing a finger at him. "Off the record, Jay – don't let your feelings for Tess cloud your judgement." His tone was fatherly but stern, and he put up a hand to stave off any protest. "Don't deny it."

McLean raked a hand through his hair, embarrassed but also relieved that his feelings were finally out in the open. "I wasn't. I just hope you're right, Ed. I hope this gut feeling I have is wrong. *Believe* me; I really hope it's wrong."

Changing the subject, Baxter asked, "Have we heard anything from our inquiries in Washington or Oregon? This guy *has* to have come from somewhere. I can't believe he's lived here his whole life without ever killing before, and yet, we have nothing to tie him to – no murders, no missing persons. He must have come from *somewhere*. My hunch is he's come up from the States, maybe up the west coast," he speculated, scratching the stubble on his chin.

"I know our guys are on it," McLean assured him, "but you know, there are probably hundreds of unsolved murders and disappearances of young women up and down the west coast over the last decade or so, and if the bodies weren't found at all, no one would be the wiser about the missing hair. Or if the bodies weren't found right away, the absence of hair could simply be chalked up to scavenging by animals."

Baxter raised an eyebrow in mild annoyance.

McLean rose from behind his desk and held his hands up in a defensive gesture. "All I'm saying is, although his MO is distinctive, it may have easily been overlooked in many of his previous victims, making it hard to establish a link to our case, that's all. But we'll make inquiries. I know the guys are on it."

JUNE

"Hey, Tess, are you coming for drinks tonight?" One of Tess' fellow graduate students stood at the door to the Astronomy lab as undergraduate students filed past her.

"No, I don't think so. I'm going to head up to the dome. I've got a school tour first thing tomorrow to prep for, and I also want to get these lab books marked," she answered rather dejectedly.

"Ah, come on. Andy is flying out to Germany tomorrow for his post doc, and we're going to celebrate."

"I've already said goodbye to Andy," Tess replied distractedly. "I saw him this afternoon."

"Well, if you change your mind, we'll be over in the grad lounge."

"Hmm? OK, maybe later."

It was several hours later when Tess finally put down her pen and attempted to massage life back into her stiff, cramped hand. She was pleased to have finished all of her marking instead of leaving it to the last minute as she usually did. Sitting up in the telescope dome assembly room on the top floor of her building, she had been free of distractions. It was her favourite place to work after hours, affording her the privacy and solitude she craved when she needed to concentrate. It was the size of a small classroom, and it served as a gathering point for tours of the main telescope inside the dome itself as well as a number of smaller telescopes located on an outside viewing platform. Neat rows of chairs were stacked against one wall and a large instructor's desk sat at the front of the room. Posters of galaxies, stars, and planets adorned every square inch of the wall space and even the ceiling, giving the impression of gazing out at the heavens. Checking her watch, Tess noted it was almost 11:00 p.m. She had warned Leah she would be marking late, but if she stayed much longer, it would no doubt cause worry. Time to go.

As she stood to pack up, she experienced a sudden rush of dizziness so powerful it caused her to stumble back into her seat, momentarily stunned. Her heart sank as she felt nausea wash over her stronger than ever before followed quickly by the usual humming in the back of her head. Instinctively lowering her head and closing her eyes, she waited with trepidation as to what her sighting would herald. As she did so, icy fingers of dread crept stealthily up her spine and wrapped themselves tightly around her chest, squeezing the breath from her. And then she saw him. The night janitor. He lay sprawled on his back in an ever widening pool of blood, a shocked, puzzled expression frozen on his lifeless face.

She knew what that meant – *he* was in the building! This realization left her incapacitated with a terror so overwhelming she feared she would pass out. Panting heavily from the shock, she struggled in vain to think clearly. One thing she knew for certain – she was essentially trapped. The only way to access the fifth floor on which the dome facility was located was via the elevator or the main stairwell, either of which he could be using at this very minute. *And* there was no fire escape ladder from the roof.

Shaking her head to clear it, Tess made a grab for her cell phone but realized with dismay it wasn't where she thought she'd put it. After frantically groping around on the desktop in a feeble attempt to locate it, it suddenly dawned on her she must have left it in the lab downstairs. That knowledge was a crushing blow. Would her notorious forgetfulness cost her her life? She tried to calm down, knowing she had to think fast because it was very likely she had only minutes at most.

Thankful she always wore her keys on a lanyard around her neck while at school, Tess quickly ducked her head to remove them and managed to unlock the roof exit door despite her trembling hands. Leaving it slightly ajar, she spun around and searched wildly for a hiding place. On one side of the assembly room, a ramp led up to the dome itself, but Tess knew that was a dead end. There was only one door in and out of the dome. Hiding in there was not an option. A custom series of shelving, cubbies, and storage cupboards lined the opposite wall, and a crawlspace of sorts ran underneath the dome. That was it. Those were her choices. She could hide in one of those or she could hide out on the roof. Even if he had the building keys, there was still a possibility he may not have the one for the crawlspace, but she wasn't willing to bet her life on it. In a split second, she made her decision, but first, she crossed back over to the assembly room door. Out of sheer desperation she locked it, knowing full well the futility of doing so if he had a master key, but somehow, one more locked door between them provided her with some small measure of comfort. As she turned, she heard the distinct sound of the elevator engaging…

Through the glass assembly room door, which looked out onto the small foyer, she could see the elevator light indicating the second floor. Suddenly realizing she could make a break for the stairwell since it was obvious he was in the elevator, she fumbled with her keys in a desperate attempt to unlock the door again, but in her panic, her hands simply couldn't move fast enough. They shook so violently, the keys slipped through her fingers and fell to the ground. Fighting back tears, she lunged after them. As she snatched them off the floor, she looked up in time to see the elevator passing the third floor…

Abandoning all hope of fleeing at this point, she spun around, shut off the lights, and dashed across the room to slip inside one of the cupboards. As she turned to close the cupboard door, her eye fell on her book bag sitting beside the desk, its bulk illuminated by the red emergency lighting. In a flash, she jumped out of her hiding place to kick it underneath the desk and then dove back inside the relative safety of her enclosure. Once inside its dark interior, she battled not only her panic, but claustrophobia as well.

Waiting in breathless silence, she suddenly remembered the phone in the dome – *there was a phone inside the dome!* It had only recently been installed when the telephone system had been upgraded in the building a few weeks ago. Her heart sank. It was too late! She had already played her cards.

Tess felt the scream well up from deep within her and roll through her body straining for release, but she knew she must not make a sound. Instead, she listened in tortured silence at his attempts to unlock the assembly room door. It took several tries before he located the correct key, and with every passing second, she agonized whether she should have attempted to hide out on the roof. There was a mechanical shed out there. Maybe she could have eluded him and slipped back inside undetected. But she knew there was no turning back now. And then she heard a 'whoosh' as the assembly room door opened...

She could not hear him after that, but she hoped he would believe she had fled out onto the roof. Seconds passed as she braced herself for discovery. If he opened the cupboard, she was prepared to launch herself at him. Perhaps with an element of surprise, she could overpower him. Agonizing seconds passed and then she heard the roof exit door swing open. It was practically beside her hiding place, so she felt it as well as heard it. The crunch of gravel alerted her to the fact he had stepped out onto the roof. Another second or two, and she heard the door close. She counted all the way to ten before she allowed herself to act, figuring if he stayed out there that long, he would explore the roof before coming back in. As she eased the cupboard door open an inch, she prayed it wouldn't squeak. When it didn't, she opened it wider. From her vantage point, she could see the roof exit door, and it was indeed closed.

Wasting no time, she slipped out of the cupboard and headed immediately for the assembly room door. As she did so, a shape emerged soundlessly from the shadows to block her path. In her haste, she almost ran headlong into it. As it stepped into view of the red emergency lighting,

Tess' eyes widened, a look of recognition flaring in their depths. Recoiling in terror, she backed away, shaking her head slowly in disbelief.

"Now, now. *That's* not nice." He nodded towards the roof exit door. "Why, I'm getting the *distinct* impression you're trying to avoid me, my dear." He made a point of pouting at her. Taking a step closer, he seemed to revel in her terror. "Do you smell that, Tessa?" He leaned even closer and sniffed the air melodramatically, sucking in a deep, exaggerated breath. When she didn't reply, he answered his own question. "It's fear, Tessa, and it is my *aph-ro-di-siac.*" He pronounced the word slowly, emphasizing each syllable in order to draw out the sick thrill he was experiencing. It reminded her of someone licking their fingers after an especially decadent dessert.

Catching the look of revulsion on her face, he seemed momentarily offended but quickly recovered and continued, "I *knew* you would provide me with good sport, Tessa, and you haven't disappointed me." Seeing the abject fear on her face, he let out an exaggerated sigh. "Ah, but when it comes right down to it, I can see you're like all the rest. You'll simper and cower...and beg."

With his taunt, she slowly backed away from him and desperately scanned the room for anything within reach she could use as a weapon, quickly coming to the conclusion there was nothing at hand. Spotting the fire alarm on the wall to her right, perhaps a meter away, she tried to gauge the time it would take to lunge and pull it. Even if she could manage it, surely he would be upon her.

He caught her gaze and broke out into a huge grin, seemingly thrilled at the prospect of such an attempt. "Ah, clever girl. Clever girl!" he exclaimed, rubbing his hands together vigorously. "But you'd spoil all our fun, now wouldn't you?" he admonished, wagging a finger back and forth.

What he did next completely threw her. Rather than rushing her as she'd expected, he gestured instead for her to pull the alarm. His bushy eyebrows rose in mock challenge as he did so. She frowned from sheer frustration at the fact he was so cruelly toying with her. Well, she'd be damned if she was going to go cowering and begging! Hanging her head as if to signal defeat, she suddenly made an unexpected, desperate lunge at the alarm. She missed it by less than an inch as he was on her in that same instant, crashing into her so hard it knocked the wind right out of her. Both of them landed in a heap against the wall. To make matters worse, she smacked the back of her head, momentarily stunning herself.

He hauled her away from the alarm and quickly flipped her onto her stomach on the hard concrete floor, pinning both her arms behind her back with the full force of his weight on one knee. She was amazed at his strength. In a pathetic attempt to scream, she found herself moaning. And then she felt a sting on her arm after which he released his hold.

Rolling onto her back in a feeble attempt to right herself, she found her limbs simply would not obey what her mind commanded them to do. Instead, she lay helpless, floundering and flopping like some kind of beached fish that instinctively continues to fight for survival. Despite her disorientation, she knew she was at his mercy. All she could do was pray the end would be quick.

He stood over her, immensely pleased with himself, gloating and cackling. The effects of the drug distorted his features, stretching his broad smile into an ugly slash that seemed to split his entire face in half. This, combined with the deranged look in his dark, fathomless eyes, gave her the impression of some unearthly creature, something that had left its humanity behind long ago.

And then the blackness took her.

"What do you mean, she's missing?" The fear in McLean's voice was palatable as he grabbed his keys and wallet from his nightstand.

"Her roommate Leah just called dispatch. Tess didn't come home tonight, and she isn't answering her cell. I've sent a unit over to her house. She was last seen on campus this afternoon, so I've also alerted campus security at the university. We need to get up there and check it out. I'll pick you up in ten." As a seasoned pro, Baxter concealed his apprehension well, but not well enough to escape his partner's notice.

It was a quiet ride up to the university as both detectives were lost deep in thought. Finally, McLean broke the silence. "We should have kept a unit with her," he chided himself forlornly, shaking his head.

"Don't beat yourself up about it, Jay. We had a credible lead our suspect was halfway across the country." Baxter stole a glance at his partner and winced inwardly at the agony he witnessed on the young detective's face. There were no further reassurances he could give, so he didn't make any attempt to. Being a cop at times had its drawbacks – sometimes knowledge was a dangerous thing.

Baxter was thankful when the campus came into view as he could focus on getting over to the correct building. Luckily, the Science building was easily identifiable by the large astronomical dome on its roof. The senior detective quickly swung into the adjacent parking lot and pulled his car up to the main entrance where several campus security officers were gathered.

The security supervisor stepped forward and introduced himself after which he was quick to give a report. "Miss Walker would have had very limited access in this building after hours – only the two Astronomy labs on the main floor and the dome structure on the roof. There are several high level research labs in this building, so essentially, the second, third, and fourth floors would have all been off limits to her."

All of a sudden, a distraught security officer came tearing out of the building. He plowed into the group of fellow officers, crumpling into a heap in their midst. Out of breath and wheezing noisily, he tried desperately to collect himself while everyone looked on impatiently.

"What is it, Don? What's the matter? Did you find her?" His supervisor was concerned for his young charge.

All the security officer could do for the moment was shake his head in response. As a result, McLean felt the coil in his gut relax ever so slightly. At least she hadn't been found, but *somebody* had been; by the officer's reaction, that was obvious. Finally, the officer managed to blurt out, "No, it's not her. It's the janitor. In...in the basement. In the mechanical room." He clutched at his stomach as if he was going to be physically sick, prompting the two detectives to exchange knowing glances. How often in their careers do security officers see something like that? It had to be rough. And the guy was just a kid, probably no more than twenty-five. He would undoubtedly be haunted by *that* sight for some time to come.

As the two detectives headed towards the building, the poor man managed to collect himself enough to shout after them, "I didn't touch anything. I remembered not to." He hung his head and began to sob, muttering incoherently.

McLean turned and held up his arm in acknowledgement. "Good job, Don. Thanks."

As they entered the building, they encountered several other security officers in a huddle; apparently, news spread fast. "I don't want anyone else down there, do you hear me?"

Baxter barked at the group. "Just send me down the next couple of police officers and the crime lab crew when they get here; got it?" Their heads bobbed in unison. "Where is this mechanical room?"

"First door to your left as you enter the basement, sir," the security supervisor informed them as he joined the group, "but the door will be locked. I can take you," he volunteered. "OK, then. Come with us." On the way, Baxter called for backup and the crime lab team.

As they entered the basement, both detectives donned gloves. Baxter handed a pair to the supervisor and eyed him impatiently as the man struggled self-consciously to fit his rather large hands into the standard size issue. Once at the door to the mechanical room, the supervisor quickly keyed it open and stepped aside as if he did not want to be party to the scene within.

"I want all your men gloved and I want that *now*," ordered Baxter. "They don't touch *anything* if they don't have to and certainly not without gloves; got it?"

The supervisor swallowed hard and nodded his understanding after which he quickly left to brief his men.

An odour hit McLean squarely in the face upon entering the room, a tangy, almost metallic smell. He recognized it immediately. Once you've smelled it, you never forgot it. Sure enough, a few feet into the room lay the janitor, his throat opened up by a neat slice from ear to ear. It was clear he had quickly bled out as evidenced by the large pool of blood underneath his body.

"Poor bastard," Baxter exclaimed, shaking his head as he flipped out a small notepad. He proceeded to conduct an initial investigation of the scene, making notes as he went, careful not to disturb anything. "Do you see that, Jay?" He pointed with his pencil towards the body.

McLean tried to focus on the scene before him. "See what?" he replied distractedly.

"The empty key ring on his belt."

Both men looked up at the same instant, their expressions grim.

"Ah, Geez. That means he would have had access anywhere in the building…" McLean felt a chill run up his spine.

A thorough search of the room failed to produce a murder weapon or any other clues for that matter, and because several other police officers had arrived along with a member of the crime scene lab, the two detectives left in search of the security supervisor who had initially briefed them. They found him in the main lobby of the building taking reports from his men.

"You said Miss Walker would have had limited access in this building after hours. I want to see everywhere she would have been able to go," Baxter commanded.

"Well, here on the main floor, she would have had keys for the two Astronomy labs located in the A-wing corridor," the supervisor explained. "I can show you those."

"Fine. Let's go." Baxter nodded briskly.

Once into the A-wing, the supervisor stopped mid-way down the hallway. "These are the two Astronomy labs," he indicated, pointing out the two adjacent rooms. "As you can see," he explained as he moved to stand beside the door on the right, "the schedule on this door indicates Miss Walker taught a lab section this afternoon from 3:30 – 6:30."

"Alright. Let's take a look." Baxter gave the man a curt nod.

A quick inspection of the first lab room revealed a cell phone left in plain view on the instructor's desk.

"Anyone touch it?" Baxter raised an eyebrow.

"No, sir," the supervisor assured him.

Picking it up carefully in his gloved hand, McLean activated the screen. There was no need to speculate whose phone it was because it was not locked and the background photo that lit up was one of Tess and Leah. His stomach dropped. Had the killer confronted Tess in this room? A closer inspection yielded no clues – there was no apparent sign of a struggle, and there were no other personal items like a jacket or a purse. A similar search of the other Astronomy lab came up empty as well, so it was decided the dome facility on the roof warranted a look.

As the three men stepped into the elevator, the supervisor waved a pass card to engage it.

"Would Tess, I mean, would Miss Walker have had one of those?" McLean asked.

"Yes. The elevator is locked down at 5:00 p.m. after which time you need a pass card to engage it. Miss Walker would have had one, as well as keys for anything in the dome structure on the roof," the supervisor explained.

"And I take it the janitor would have had one of those pass cards as well?' Baxter asked.

"Yes, of course."

The three men rode up the elevator in silence. Upon reaching the fifth floor, the supervisor crossed the small foyer to slip his key into the lock on the assembly room door. "That's strange," he mumbled.

"What is?" Baxter asked coming up behind him.

"The door. It's unlocked," the supervisor frowned. "It shouldn't be."

The senior detective gave his partner a quick look of support and then cautiously pushed the door open. The room was eerily lit by red emergency lighting, giving the scene before them an unearthly glow. Baxter quickly flipped on the overhead lights to dispel the mood and stepped inside followed closely by his partner.

At first glance, nothing seemed amiss. Chairs were neatly stacked against one wall, leaving the center of the room open. The only thing of note was a cupboard door that stood open, but upon closer inspection, it revealed nothing out of the ordinary. At the front of the room, the sole desk was stacked with lab notebooks, but nothing else. Baxter made note of the course and lab section number as a reminder to check if Tess was listed as the instructor.

McLean, who by this point had spotted something stashed under the desk, bent down to retrieve it, hauling out a distinctive green book bag in the process. He did not need to open it, for he knew immediately who it belonged to. How many times had he seen Tess carrying it? Going through the motions with a heavy heart anyway, he quickly confirmed his worst fears – her wallet was inside. He buckled with this knowledge, collapsing into the chair in front of the desk and hanging his head in his hands.

Baxter laid a hand on his young partner's shoulder and held it there. "Take a minute, Jay," he advised. Wanting to give his partner time to collect himself, Baxter walked over to the roof exit door. When the handle turned and the door opened, he gave the supervisor a quizzical look.

"That shouldn't be unlocked either," the supervisor confirmed.

"Would the janitor have had a key?" Baxter knew the answer but asked the question anyway.

The supervisor nodded his head solemnly.

"Would Miss Walker have had the key?"

"Yes. There are a number of smaller telescopes out on the roof viewing platform for students to use," the supervisor explained.

"Have you got a flashlight?" Baxter asked, his face grim.

"There must be some up here somewhere. Let me take a look." The supervisor seemed relieved to be able to do something and began to root through the drawers and cabinets in earnest. He soon came across a whole drawer of them.

In the meantime, McLean had joined the two men. "What about the dome? Do you think she would have gone in there?"

"If she did, it would have been a dead end..." The supervisor stopped himself mid-sentence.

"We'll check it out after we have a look out here, Jay." Baxter's tone was firm, but gentle, and he motioned his partner toward the roof exit door, passing him a flashlight as he did so.

All three men headed out on to the roof, the crunch of gravel announcing their every step, the beams from their flashlights sending pale shafts of light into the dark night. Baxter had a lump in the pit of his stomach at the thought of Tess out on the roof with that psycho. For the first time in his life, he prayed they *wouldn't* find anything.

Upon closer inspection, it was evident there weren't many places to hide. The individual telescope mounts were too small to crouch behind, and the venting stacks were located on the other side of the dome itself, so there was no way to get over to them. The only other structure of any size was a mechanical shed at the far end of the roof. A quick circle around it, however, turned up nothing. And then an awful thought struck Baxter.

"The janitor would be able to access this shed with a master key, right?" He turned to the supervisor for confirmation.

"Well, it's not somewhere a janitor would need access to, but if he had the building master, then yes, he could have accessed it."

"But Tess couldn't, right?"

"Right."

At first, the supervisor didn't appear to grasp the detective's line of reasoning, but you could clearly see when he put two and two together.

"You don't think he'd stick her in there?" he asked warily.

"Open it."

The supervisor moved forward to unlock the door to the shed, but his hands were shaking so badly, it took several tries before he could even get the key in the lock. Feeling foolish, he quickly stepped out of the way once his job was done. Baxter took the lead in opening the door but turned around at the threshold and put out an arm to block his partner's entry.

"Let me do it, Jay," he said gently.

His partner nodded with relief and turned around. Walking a few paces away, he sucked in a lungful of the brisk night air and turned up the collar of his coat.

The shed was a small structure used to house equipment and tools. It was neatly kept, so a quick flip of the light switch revealed there was…no body. Baxter released the breath he had been holding and quickly called out to his partner to relieve the young man's anguish. "Nothing, Jay."

The supervisor, who had been expecting another gory scene, poked his head into the shed for good measure just to be sure. Shrugging his shoulders, he muttered to himself, "Don't know why he'd go to all the trouble of hiding her in here when he could have just pushed her off…"

Both detectives' heads snapped up.

Realizing he'd put his foot in his mouth for a second time, the supervisor backed away, retreating as inconspicuously as possible towards the roof exit door.

McLean immediately ran to the roof parapet and peered over the side of the building, straining his eyes, willing them to see through the darkness. Despite the lack of lighting, he ran along the perimeter of the roof, half expecting to see Tess' vacant expression staring back up at him.

"Get your men to check the perimeter grounds of the building!" Baxter barked at the supervisor who jumped at the order and ducked back into the building like a truant schoolboy. "And leave me your keys!" Baxter roared after him. "Come on, Jay. Let's check out the dome." The tone of his voice made it clear he expected professionalism from his colleague, so McLean meekly followed his lead. A quick check of the dome itself, however, revealed nothing amiss, and the two detectives were back to square one.

"She was pretty well trapped up here, so what did he *do* with her?" Baxter began to brainstorm while pacing the small room, scowling in frustration. "If he killed her..." he started to say before wincing at his choice of words and throwing his partner an apologetic look, "...why wouldn't he just leave her here? Why bother to take her?"

"Maybe he wanted to dump the body. Ah, Jesus, I can't believe I just said that." McLean backed up against the nearest wall and leaned against it for support, his hands buried deep in the pockets of his overcoat.

"*Or* maybe he simply knocked her out or chocked her into submission," Baxter hypothesized. "Maybe killing her wasn't in his plan. Think about it, Jay. He *knows* she's psychic, just like him. That's *got* to be a draw. Hell, maybe this is an abduction case, not a murder." Offering up this scenario in an attempt to bolster his partner's flagging spirits, Baxter tried to sound upbeat. "Come on. Let's do our job." Without waiting for a reply, he turned to leave but stopped short at the door when he realized his partner was not following his lead.

Instead, McLean was taking one last look at the open cupboard, attempting to fold his lanky frame so he could step inside. His height prevented him from doing so, but that did not deter his train of thought. Turning to his partner, his face full of hope, he exclaimed, "*She* would have fit, Ed." He proceeded to examine every square inch of the cupboard in a desperate attempt to find something, anything.

Dropping down on all fours, he reached with his pen underneath the lip of the cupboard and moved it along the length of the wall unit and out the far end. His excitement mounted as he could hear he'd swept something along. The first thing to come into view was a thumbtack and his heart sank. However, along with a dust ball, he next caught sight of something else – something plastic. Carefully picking it up, he held it triumphantly in front of his face. It was a syringe cap.

Baxter stepped closer to better view the object, and a look of comprehension dawned on his face. "Unless we've got some addicts using this room to shoot up, I'd say he drugged her."

"Then she *is* alive, Ed!" McLean's smile was tentative at first and then spread to encompass his whole face.

Once the two detectives returned to the main lobby of the building, McLean voiced the question they had both been pondering. "How do you think he got her out of the building once he sedated her? Carrying her out would be taking quite a risk."

"I'm thinking I want to know where the janitor's cart is," Baxter speculated as he made a bee-line for the security supervisor who cringed upon seeing the burly detective bearing down upon him. "Have your men located a janitor's cart anywhere in the building?" Baxter demanded.

"If...if you come with me sir, we found it d...down on the loading bay," the supervisor stammered as he led the two men down the staircase into the basement. Passing through double doors onto the loading dock, they immediately spied the janitor's cart abandoned at the foot of the ramp.

"Please tell me your men haven't touched it," Baxter turned and glared at the poor man.

"No, sir. All they did was report it." The supervisor shook his head vehemently and stepped back.

"Good. We'll get the lab guys on it." Baxter proceeded to circle the cart, leaning over to peer into the large garbage bin it contained. "What do you think, Jay? Large enough to hide someone in, eh? And all he does is leave it here while he brings his car down the ramp."

"Sounds plausible," McLean agreed as he stood with his head tilted back, scanning the walls of the loading dock. "I don't suppose we'd be lucky enough to have a surveillance camera out here," he asked the supervisor forlornly.

"Sorry, sir," the supervisor replied sheepishly. "We've never had a need for one," he was quick to add.

Knowing Tess had been stashed and then loaded on this very spot made McLean's gut roll over. What did that maniac want with her? Would they find her in time? And even if they did, what would he have done with her in the meantime?

Tess woke sluggishly to a dull, persistent throbbing at the back of her head. She tried to roll over in a feeble attempt to sit up but only succeeded in making herself nauseous. At first, she couldn't recall the reason for her headache or for the grogginess she was experiencing, so she forced herself to take slow, deep breaths in an attempt to clear her mind. She wanted to call out to Leah for assistance but was afraid of what that would do to the pain in her head.

Gradually, she became aware of an offensive odour – a damp, musty smell – but in her confused state, she had trouble placing it. She wrinkled her nose and wracked her muddled brain for a comparable memory. This was something stale and moldy like a damp cardboard box. In order to get away from the pungent smell, she tried to lift her head but only succeeded in making herself nauseous again.

While fighting for control over her disorientation, a nagging unease began to worm its way into her consciousness. She slowly opened her eyes, and as she did so, her heart sank. The room she was in was lit by a single window – one that was obviously in a basement. She squinted at it for several seconds before her brain could comprehend the fact it was barred. Groaning, she closed her eyes, and it all came rushing back to her in a moment of clarity. Wishing she could find herself back in her own bedroom with something as trivial as a hangover when she re-opened her eyes, she knew that would not be the case.

As she lay there shocked and defeated, Tess listened intently for any noise, any sound to indicate *he* was nearby. Despite straining her ears for several agonizing minutes, she heard…nothing.

Gradually, she came to the conclusion she was alone, at least for the moment, so she tried to focus on her predicament. She was alive, that much was evident by the headache that plagued her. At least he hadn't killed her outright, and he'd had ample opportunity to do so. So why hadn't he?

When she shifted her weight, she became aware of the fact she was lying on an old, stained mattress in one corner of the room. That would account for the damp, musty smell. When she realized there was no bedding, she hugged herself, suddenly aware of being chilled. Taking care not to lift her head, she scanned the room as best she could. It was a typical undeveloped basement – concrete floors, unfinished drywall, and a single light bulb hanging from the ceiling. From her vantage point on the mattress, she had a direct view of the door which she naturally assumed was locked. The only other furniture besides the lumpy mattress upon which she lay was a single chair placed in the center of the room. She feebly groped around on the mattress for her book bag before realizing, of course, it wouldn't be there.

In the opposite corner of the room, she spied a laundry sink and a toilet, the sight of which gave her immeasurable relief, for almost as strong as her panic was her mortification at the simple fact she had to pee…urgently. The only trouble was she couldn't raise her head without feeling like she was going to pass out, so that would have to wait for now. To distract herself, she went over the sequence of events leading up to her abduction. Realizing he hadn't taken her watch, she was able to check the time. One o'clock. Counting backward, she came to the conclusion she'd been unconscious for at least fourteen hours. Not knowing what he'd drugged her with or the dosage, she had no way of knowing if she had already slept away a full day or possibly even more.

She remembered with dismay that the blow to the back of her head had *not* caused her blackout – she'd been drugged. She remembered all too well the sting on her arm and the distorting effects of the drug before the blackness had taken her. In examining her arm, she noted tenderness at the injection site. What had he drugged her with? As her mind began to clear, she reached up to feel the back of her head and found a dandy of a goose egg back there.

As she lay there, Tess wrestled with the fear of what he would do with her. She was quite certain his motive was not rape; she hadn't sensed any kind of sexual perversion with him. So if sexual torture was not his thing, just what *was* his motive for keeping her alive? He obviously knew of her ability. Did he want to 'compare notes', so to speak? How long would he keep her? And what would happen when he tired of her? She *had* to keep him interested. She *had* to pose no threat to him. She *had* to outwit him. But how?

Less than an hour later, footsteps above her head alerted her to the fact he was home. Her stomach clenched, and she began to tremble so violently, her teeth chattered. Slapping a hand over her mouth in an attempt to stifle the scream she so desperately wanted to utter, she was forced to give in to her panic silently lest he hear her. She knew she had to get herself up and ambulatory or she was a sitting duck, so she hauled herself carefully onto her knees. Pausing only long enough to catch her breath, she used the wall for support and cautiously rose to a standing position, taking special care not to move her head unnecessarily. Edging her way along the wall, she made it over to the toilet and mercifully managed to relieve herself. She did not flush, fearful he would hear. She reasoned that every minute she was able to move about and regain her stability could make a difference when he came for her.

Continuing to inch along the wall, she made her way over to the door and quietly tried to open it. The door knob turned easily enough, but when she applied pressure against the door itself, it wouldn't budge. Something on the other side was barring it. Stranger still, there was a keyable lock on *her* side of the door. It was as if someone wanted to be able to lock themself *inside* the room. It took a few seconds for the implications of that to sink in, the very thought of which left her weak in the knees.

Sick with worry, she forced herself to concentrate on walking around the perimeter of the room using the wall for support. The waiting was awful knowing he was just feet above her head doing God knows what. At one point, forgetting about no sudden head movements, she glanced down at her watch to check the time again. Instantly, dizziness washed over her, leaving her sweating profusely. Leaning against the wall, holding her face against its cool surface, she waited for the wave of nausea to subside. When it didn't, she realized what was really going on. No! No! She slid down to the floor with a groan while the humming in her head grew louder. She was helpless to stop it.

McLean paced the conference room, his hand massaging his temples in a vain attempt to relieve a tension headache. He had only been able to grab a few hours of fitful sleep the previous night on the couch in the staff lounge, and he had eaten nothing so far this morning. The very thought of food made him physically sick. At most, he could only stomach a strong cup of coffee. It had been less than eight hours since Tess' disappearance, and in that time, a search for her had been mobilized, and a command post had been set up.

A unit clerk stuck her head in the open doorway and advised McLean about a woman asking to see him. His adrenaline kicked into high gear with this news, and he rushed headlong into lobby. Upon spying Leah, his face fell, after which he made a concerted effort to appear collected.

"I want to help," she told him resolutely as he walked up to her. "Please give me *something* to do." The look she gave him was full of determination, and yet, her anguish was plain to see. Although he tried hard not to show it, it matched his own.

"We've set up a command post downstairs where we're organizing volunteers," he told her. "You're welcome to help out there." He tried to sound positive for her sake. Despite her obvious beauty, she looked haggard. Her hair was pulled back in a severe pony tail, and her otherwise striking face was devoid of any makeup, revealing just how truly exhausted she was. No doubt she'd had a sleepless night as well.

"Absolutely. Our phone has been ringing off the hook at home with people from Tess' department who want to help out, so I can bring some of them with me," she said smiling tentatively, relieved at the prospect of having something to occupy her time.

"We need to blanket the university with flyers," McLean told her. "It's not a large campus; maybe *someone* saw *something*. They may not even realize what they saw is significant, but we need them to come forward. In cases like this, tips from the public can provide invaluable leads. In the meantime, has anything else come to mind you haven't already told us? Anything at all?"

Leah shook her head forlornly. "Oh, God. I wish I'd called her earlier and told her to come home. I got watching a movie."

"Hey, don't blame yourself," he was quick to advise her. "There's no way you could have known. There's no way any of us could have known."

She looked up at him. "Do you think he came back specifically for her?" she asked in a voice full of dread.

"I don't know. She's a loose end..." McLean seemed to forget who he was talking to. "Sorry." He was quick to apologize, shifting uncomfortably on his feet. "We're re-releasing his sketch in the hope it triggers something." He stopped short of telling her about the syringe cap, even though he would have liked to bring her up to speed, if for no other reason than to give her hope.

Almost as if she read his mind, Leah asked him, "Do you have any leads? Any *at all?*" She looked at him with such utter despair; McLean was forced to look away.

"Not much, I'm afraid." At least that wasn't a lie. He wanted to confess to her the lack of clues pointed to a very sophisticated killer, one who would undoubtedly be hard to track, but he didn't want to upset her any more than she already was. It was always such a delicate balance dealing with relatives and friends of the victim. You didn't want to scare them, but neither did you want to give them false hope. In this case, Tess' own wits could be the key factor in keeping her alive long enough for them to find her. Of course, the question no one could answer was – how long did they have? He shook off such thoughts and returned his attention to Tess' friend.

"We have a team of guys working on this, Leah. It's our number one priority. I can assure you we'll do everything we can," he promised her, but his words, although full of conviction, did little to bolster his own sagging doubts.

"I know you will, and I appreciate that. If you don't mind me saying so, you look awful. Let me at least get you guys something to eat," she offered.

McLean held up a hand in protest. "No, I'm fine. Really. We're fine."

"I insist. If I go and get you something then you'll have more time to spend on the case," she reasoned. As she turned to leave, she paused, "There's something you should know, Detective." She looked at him as if reluctant to spill a secret. "She talks about you *all* the time. It's really getting nauseating."

The look he gave her was one of appreciation tinged with regret.

"So you'd better ask her out at the end of all this," she admonished. Her jest was light hearted, but both of them knew the worry behind her words.

He came to her basement room later that afternoon, by which point an exhausted Tess sat huddled on her mattress, praying she didn't look as unsteady as she felt. His entrance was preceded by the scraping sound of bolts being slid back on the door, a sound that threw her into a complete panic. His presence as he entered the room seemed to suck out all of the air, leaving her floundering and breathless.

He took no notice of her at first but proceeded to key the interior lock, effectively locking them both in. Witnessing his actions, an intense fear gripped Tess' gut, prompting her to slide farther back on her mattress to put more distance between them. It was only when she had backed into the very corner of the wall, did she realize she could go no farther.

Noting her reaction, her captor simply grinned, after which he placed a dinner tray on the single chair in the room. Turning around, he addressed her properly, his manner and tone a complete surprise. "I've brought you a tray, my dear. You *must* be famished!"

She sat in speechless terror. Despite that, her stomach began to growl in earnest, testament to the fact she was indeed starving. She did not want to accept *anything* from him, however, so she was frustrated beyond measure by what she saw as a betrayal by her own body.

"Ah, of *course* you are, you poor thing. I've made you some supper." He grinned again, obviously amused at her apparent discomfort. "Don't worry; I'm not going to stay to watch you eat. I must run." As he started to turn, he suddenly remembered the items he had tucked in his arm. "Oh, I've also brought you some shampoo, a towel and a hair brush." He held up the items and flashed her a brilliant smile as he proceeded to place them at the laundry sink. "I must insist on one thing, Tessa – please be sure to wash your hair daily.

After all, we wouldn't want it to get all limp and... *lifeless*, now would we?" When she didn't reply, he answered his own question, "No, no. That wouldn't do at all."

As he turned to leave, he cautioned her, "I know you won't try anything foolish, my dear. After all, I wouldn't want to have to do anything before we've even had a chance to get to know one another, now would I?" Quickly keying the lock open, he tossed her a wave as he sailed over the threshold and out of sight. Seconds later, she heard the definite sounds of first one and then a second bolt being slid back into place.

Only once his footsteps had receded was she able to release the breath she hadn't even realized she'd been holding. In his presence, she had felt like she was drowning – drowning in her own fear. Taking several deep, cleansing breaths, she attempted to calm her erratic pulse. Despite her fear, she could not ignore for long the delicious aroma of the meal on the tray before her. Still guarded, she gingerly crawled off the mattress to examine it – a pasta dish on a paper plate and some juice in a foam cup. No cutlery of any kind. It figured. After only a moment's hesitation, she tore into the food with a desperation she could barely control, at first self-conscious about using her fingers, but soon losing all sense of propriety. Despite her revulsion of him, she knew she had to eat. Logic told her she would need every ounce of strength, every faculty she possessed in order to plan her escape.

After wolfing down her dinner and feeling much stronger for it, Tess cautiously eyed the sole window in her room. Although it was barred, she knew she could at least get *some* perspective as to her whereabouts, and she knew she needed to do that before it got dark. At first, she was doubtful she could get up on the chair in her condition, but she soon came to the conclusion she could accomplish it if she was exceedingly careful.

Setting her dinner tray on the floor, she slowly slid the chair underneath the window, careful not to make any noise as she did so. Once it was properly situated, she used the wall for support and climbed onto the chair's seat with painstaking care, keeping her head level so as not to trigger any dizziness. The *last* thing she needed was to take a fall.

Standing on her tiptoes and using the bars for balance, she found she could look through the bottom half of the window, enabling her to take note of her immediate surroundings. It was as she had suspected – a rural setting. The window looked out onto a thickly forested yard, and there were no other buildings or houses in sight.

Sighing heavily, she carefully stepped down off the chair and took a seat on it, spending the next anxious hour contemplating her confinement. A sense of purpose settled over her borne out of the necessity for single-minded focus on the predicament she found herself in. Knowing that the first 24 to 48 hours were critical in any abduction case, she knew she had to think fast.

Her mind raced, trying to conjure up a plausible escape scenario with the things she had at hand. Taking stock of her room, she made a mental list of the things at her disposal: a twin-sized mattress; a plastic chair; one light bulb; a thin towel; a bottle of shampoo; a small hairbrush; and finally, her watch, clothing and shoes. She discounted the plastic dinner tray, paper plate and foam cup as he would undoubtedly collect those items daily. For a brief instant, she speculated about a strangulation attempt using the towel, but she quickly ruled out such a notion. Manual strangulation required strength a woman her size simply did not possess.

And so she sat for a long time, worrying her lower lip as she often did when deep in thought. Finally, she came to a conclusion – her only chance, she believed, was to incapacitate her captor long enough to get his keys. She estimated she would need perhaps ten to fifteen seconds to get the keys, unlock the door to her room, and make a break for it. The speed with which she could accomplish such a thing would all depend on how many keys were on his keychain. Unfortunately, she was still feeling the effects of the drug he had injected her with. She knew she would have to wait for her dizziness to subside before she made any move. For now, she was still too unsteady on her feet to confront him. Annoyed, she wondered how long it would take for the drug to wear off.

Rising from the chair, ever careful of her precarious balance, her eye fell on the hairbrush sitting atop the towel at the sink. She stared at it intensely for several seconds before carefully making her way over to it. Picking it up, she examined it closely, her pulse quickening when she realized it was made from a light-coloured wood.

Like a thief with something inordinately precious, she made her way back along the wall to her mattress, feeling like she could literally dance along. Carefully lowering herself to her knees and holding the brush by the end with the bristles, she rubbed the side of the handle along the rough concrete floor for a moment or two and then examined the result. The clear finish had been scraped away! Her heart soared.

Easing herself off the mattress, she proceeded to tug it away from the wall. Several nasty looking spiders exposed from their hiding place scurried away towards another dark corner of the room, but she paid them no heed. Instead, she began in earnest to scrape one side of the elongated oval brush handle against the concrete floor, a difficult endeavour with her dizziness that would not allow her to bend over her work. Instead, she had to hold her head level and work the brush by feel. After several minutes of exertion, she held the brush up in front of her once again and examined her handiwork, elated to see a *slightly* noticeable difference in the shape of the handle. It would require a great deal of effort to sharpen it, but she knew she could do it.

Realizing her captor might have heard the scraping upstairs, she paused and listened intently. After several minutes, she was finally satisfied she hadn't attracted his notice, but she chastised herself anyway for her stupidity. Surely at *some* point, he had to go out, she reasoned. Vowing to wait for such an opportunity, she pushed the mattress back in place and waited...

After what seemed like ages, but in reality was actually less than an hour later, she distinctly heard the sound of a door opening and closing followed soon after by a car engine. She came to the conclusion there was an exterior basement door close to her room because she not only heard the door, but felt it as well in the subtle vibration of the adjacent wall. Hearing the car engine so soon after the door led her to believe the car was probably parked close to the house. That was a relief. At least she should be able to hear him come and go.

Not wasting any time after her captor's departure, Tess yanked her mattress out from the wall once again and immediately set to work. Holding her watch in front of her face, she noted the time – 4:30 p.m. With a goal now firmly in mind, she attacked her work with a feverish intensity, rubbing the brush handle repeatedly along the rough concrete floor. She felt like some kind of medieval master craftsman honing a fine blade against a sharpening stone, knowing that the hours of labour would be well worth the effort. As she suspected, colour from the wood stained the concrete, but she would hide any such evidence underneath the mattress.

Less than ten minutes into her work, she realized with dismay she had a problem; the bristles were digging into the palm of her hand. Continuing as she was would likely lead to an abrasion. Cursing under her breath, she brainstormed for a solution, finally striping off one of her socks to use as a glove. Relief soon gave way to delight as she discovered an added benefit of her makeshift glove – it actually gave her a better grip.

She had to pause often during the course of the evening, for she had no idea how long her captor would be gone. Closing her eyes and stilling her breathing, she strained her ears for any sign of his impending return. While she listened, she flexed her cramped hands, rubbing and stretching out her fingers, gently coaxing life back into them. Her breaks also allowed the brush handle to cool off as it grew quite warm while she worked. The *last* thing she needed was the smell of burning wood. That would be sure to give her away.

Holding the brush up in front of her at one point, she noted with pride how the once oval-shaped handle was now trimmed slightly on both sides into a more tapered shape. Several more hours should fashion it into something she could use.

While busy sharpening the brush, Tess used the time to strategize on the best course of action for her escape plan. Clearly, her best chance at injuring her captor was while he was carrying her food tray. With both his hands occupied, he would have little opportunity to defend himself. That meant moving toward him as soon as he entered the room, before he had a chance to set the tray down. Would he be suspicious of her actions when she had cowered before in his presence?

As the hour neared 11:00 p.m., Tess couldn't believe her good fortune in being able to work for so long, but she grew increasingly anxious as to her captor's whereabouts. Where would he have gone? Only minutes later, her nerves sprang into high gear with the sound of an approaching car crunching in a gravel driveway, forcing her to put an immediate stop to her work. Although exhausted and sore, she scrambled to stand up, her back muscles screaming out in protest. Ever careful of her wobbly balance, she made her way stiffly over to the sink. To anyone watching, she must have appeared comical, like an intoxicated old woman in a hurry. Quickly, she washed her hands and rinsed off the brush, leaving it bristle end in plain sight at the sink, it's newly fashioned handle hidden underneath the towel.

Making her way back over to her mattress, she was shoving it back into place along the wall when she heard the door to the house open and close. As she sat down, her eye fell on her discarded sock which she promptly snatched up. Turning it inside out, she clumsily put it back on, a difficult task given her panic and her aching hands.

Taking a deep breath, she sat cross-legged on her mattress and prepared herself for his entrance into her room, thankful she at least had the light on. She had never been one to be afraid of the dark, but if he came at her, she'd much rather see him coming than not.

To her consternation, he never came to her room, and as the anxious minutes ticked by, she began to wonder about the reason for that. Suddenly, a thought dawned on her – could it be because he had some sort of camera set up? Why hadn't she thought of that earlier? How could she have been so *stupid?* Eyes darting to and fro, she rose from her mattress and methodically began to check every square inch of her room. So busy was she with her efforts, she was badly startled by a knock on the door some minutes later.

"Tess?" he called her name. "Just checking in. I shall do so any time I return. Is that clear?"

She stood dumbfounded and breathless.

"Tess?"

Not wanting to give him any reason to enter her room, she stuttered a hasty reply, "Y...Yes, I understand."

"Good then. Sleep tight, my dear. We shall visit more in the morning."

Her heart dropped at his words.

By the end of that first exhausting day, an extensive and fruitless search had been conducted of the two local hospitals and dozens of medical clinics in the city for an employee who matched the killer's sketch. At one point, a surgical orderly caused a flurry of excitement. Not only did he resemble the sketch, but he had not shown up for his shift that afternoon. Upon further investigation, however, it was discovered he had been in a car accident up island and was in the hospital in Nanaimo. Such dead-end leads were hard on everyone. They looked promising at first, allowing hopes to be raised, and then when they didn't pan out, those hopes were dashed. Such roller coaster ups and downs took a toll, particularly when everyone was working on minimal sleep. It wasn't long before the smallest thing could cause tension as everyone's nerves began to fray.

It was late in the day when the two detectives regrouped with their team and conceded the fact they were stymied. "OK. *Think!*" McLean tried to brainstorm. "Where else would someone have access to syringes and sedatives?"

Before anyone else could answer, Baxter took the lead and began barking orders, "I want a list of every pharmacy, every nursing home, hell, even every dental clinic in town, and I want that NOW!"

Having been given their marching orders, everyone scattered like rats off a sinking ship. You did *not* want to be around Detective Baxter when he was in a foul mood.

Sighing heavily as if exhausted at the prospect of the task ahead, Baxter turned to his partner. "It's going to take us a while to canvass those, Jay."

At first, McLean didn't seem to hear his partner's comment as he appeared deep in thought. "Wait! Wait a minute," he suddenly announced. Grabbing a seat in front of a computer terminal, he quickly keyed in a search. "Veterinarians would have syringes and sedatives, right?" he asked, his voice barely able to contain the emotions he was struggling with.

"I didn't think of that, but you're right," Baxter nodded thoughtfully. "We'll add them to the list."

McLean turned from the screen. "Check those out first, Ed. Tess told me she sensed this guy had some kind of connection with animals." Ignoring his partner's skeptical frown, he continued, "Just humour me, Ed. I have a feeling about this." The look he gave his partner was a tortured one.

"Come on you pansies," the senior detective bellowed when he caught his men staring. "You heard him. Let's get a move on!" Some of the officers mumbled amongst themselves, prompting him to add, "What? You got somethin' more *important* to do tonight, boys?"

No one dared answer.

Tess woke with a start. Her heart was racing and she was shivering from a cold sweat. Rolling over on the mattress, she curled into a fetal position, wrapping her arms around her knees in an attempt to warm herself. She must have been dreaming, but thankfully, she couldn't remember about what. It was still dark save for a pale shaft of moonlight shining through the sole window in her room, allowing her to check her watch – 5:00 a.m. She listened intently for any sign to indicate her captor was up, but the only thing to disturb the stillness of the early morning hour was a soft but incessant chorus from what she could only surmise were frogs. This all but confirmed her belief she was in a rural setting because she knew you didn't hear *that* in the city. And yet, she had no way of knowing how far he'd taken her. For all she knew, she may no longer even be on the island on which she lived.

As she lay restless and cold, she wondered if Leah was asleep or if she was lying troubled and fearful as well. Were Detectives Baxter and McLean looking for her? She smiled wistfully when she thought of McLean and her infatuation with him. Their relationship had barely begun, and now she doubted she would ever get the chance to explore it further. She vowed if she ever got out of this, she would ask *him* out. Her thoughts drifted to her beloved guardian, and she was thankful Emmy had never lived to endure her abduction. Sighing heavily, she whispered, "If you're up there, Emmy, I could really use some help."

Tess knew when her captor stirred from his bed later in the morning because she could hear his shower. It simply floored her that people like him had any normalcy to their lives. How could a person be such a monster on the inside, so insidiously evil, and yet for all intents and purposes, lead a seemingly ordinary life – working, shopping, cooking, and even sometimes maintaining what appeared to be a perfectly normal marriage or family life?

As she struggled to rise and get her stiff limbs warmed up, she was relieved to find the effects of the drug had finally worn off. She was still a bit unsteady on her feet, undoubtedly because of the blow she'd taken to the back of her head. As she began to pace the room, her thoughts turned to her captor. She knew he fed off fear, so it was crucial she reasoned, not to show him any. That would be no easy task. She was quite literally terrified of him. How the hell was she going to hide that fact? 'Get angry, Tess! Get bloody angry!' she reproached herself. If he expected her to cower and beg, he bloody well had another thing coming.

By the time he entered her room carrying a breakfast tray some time later, he encountered a very different young woman. After locking the door behind him, he narrowed his eyes at her, immediately suspicious of the change in her demeanour, for Tess sat cross legged on her mattress with her arms folded defiantly in front of her chest, glaring at him. Before he could say a word, she demanded, "What are you going to do with me?"

He smiled broadly at her, obviously impressed with her spunk. "Why, kill you of course!" he replied matter-of-factly as he set the tray down on the corner of the mattress, prompting a skittish response from her. When he saw the horrified look on her face, he stepped back and chuckled, "Come now, Tessa. What did you *think* I was going to do with you?" He smiled wickedly at her but then checked himself. "Oh, I don't mean right this *minute*. Now tell me, Tess. You don't mind me calling you that, do you? After all, I feel like we already know one other. Now tell me, how long have you had your ability?" He settled himself on the lone chair in the room, crossed his legs, and eagerly awaited her response much like a little boy who had settled himself down to hear a good story.

Well, she would have none of it. She would not give him the satisfaction of picking her brain apart in order to satisfy his idle curiosity and then disposing of her afterwards. She was admittedly terrified of him, but her voice when she found it was strong and calm.

"How long have you been killing women?"

The directness of her question didn't faze him at all.

"Ah, so you're curious too. Let's see. Well, I made my first kill when I was all of eighteen. But it was a messy business, I must confess." He rolled his eyes and wrinkled his nose in mock disgust. "I was *such* an amateur back then."

"No, I mean your very *first* kill," she replied undaunted.

That threw him. He cocked his head and squinted at her, almost as if he was trying to read her mind. He reminded her of an insect sizing up its prey before it struck.

She steeled herself before continuing, "You know...your sister."

His eyebrows shot up.

When he did not respond, she pressed further, "In the bathtub." She could not help the slow smile that crept upon her face at having bested him.

His shocked expression quickly gave way to one of grudging admiration, and he seemed to study her then, smirking knowingly. "So you can see into the past, can you? Tell me, do you all of a sudden just *know* things or do you actually *see* them?" He stood up as if agitated and began to pace the room. "Did you see, for instance, how *easily* she slipped under the water, Tess?" He gestured broadly with his hands in a dramatic fashion much like an actor on a stage. "No protest." He shook his head with deliberate care as though to better convince her. "No protest at all."

His excitement mounting, he continued, "And did you see how her little blonde curls fanned out around her face? Those curls my mother loved to comb *every single* night." He seemed on the verge of working himself up into a frenzy, but in a matter of seconds, he reigned in his emotions. "And did you see how she just *lay* there staring up at me, mouth gaping like a beached fish. So trusting. So innocent. Her little hand reaching out..." He extended his arm as though to grasp something elusive in the air above him. "It was so... *touching*."

Tess hated to sink to his level, but she just couldn't help herself. "Everyone believed it was an accident, didn't they?" she asked him. "After all, how could a little boy do something like that? On purpose? But your mother knew, didn't she?"

A fleeting, pained expression crossed his face.

Tess felt a stab of perverse pleasure at having wounded him with that truth, and she didn't stop there. "And she changed afterwards toward you, didn't she? She withdrew. Sort of like her love for you just kind of...died."

The look he threw her literally took her breath away. It was filled with such pure and utter venom, Tess felt the hairs on the back of her neck stand on end, and she feared she had gone too far. His response surprised her, however, for he merely brought both hands together in front of his face and closed his eyes as if deep in meditation. Opening them seconds later, he levelled his gaze at her, giving her a forced, tight smile. "Touché, Tess, touché." His voice was low and deadly serious. "But remember, two can play that game. We're alike you and I. We're kindred souls." Without another word, he rose and headed for the door. As he keyed the lock open, he caught her comment.

"We're not alike at all," she said softly. "I have no skel-etons in my closet."

As the dozens of local vet clinics and animal hospitals were being checked out, McLean stood in his office pouring over a map on the wall. As each location was cleared and radioed in, he ticked it off on the map. His frustration was mounting as he still trusted a gut feeling, and yet, it hadn't produced any leads. What if he was wrong? What if he was steering them in the wrong direction? Would they waste precious time when they should be looking elsewhere?

Other than the syringe cap, they had no other leads. Tess' bank and credit cards had not been used since her disappearance, and the records for her home, cell and office phones had not produced any suspicious numbers. She had taken the bus up to the university on the day of her disappearance, so there was no need to track her car. It still sat in her driveway. The graduate student who had stopped by the lab at 6:30 p.m. that night confirmed Tess had been planning to head up to the dome to set up for a tour and do some marking. This grad student had no recollection of seeing a janitor in the building despite the fact the janitorial shift had started an hour earlier. She also confirmed it was not unusual for Tess to work late. Leah hadn't reported Tess missing until 11:45 p.m. This timeframe had given the killer plenty of time to make his move.

McLean's head ached from hours of endless speculation. He wondered what Tess must have been thinking when she actually saw the killer face-to-face. Squeezing his eyes shut, he winced as if in physical pain. She must have been *so* terrified. And he had not been there to protect her. That ate away at him. All the months of searching for this guy, and all the months of assuring her they would find him, had all been for naught. In the end, they had failed her. *He* had failed her. It was that simple.

Sighing wearily, he moved to stand in front of the window from which he looked out over the city, his mind awash with worry and guilt. Was Tess already dead? Was she lying at this very minute in some wooded area where she would never be found? Or would her weathered bones be discovered months or maybe even years from now? He shook his head to clear it. He *had* to stop thinking such thoughts. It wasn't helping anything. If anyone had a chance of surviving, it was Tess. He marvelled not only at her presence of mind, but also at her courage, in attempting to save herself by hiding in that cupboard. She must have had only minutes if not seconds to make such a choice, and yet, she had acted. '*Stay strong,* Tess', he willed her. '*Stay strong*'.

Just then, Baxter entered the conference room in search of his partner. Never one for physical displays of affection, he couldn't help but place a hand on his partner's shoulder. They stood in awkward silence for several seconds, each of them well aware of the dwindling odds of locating Tess alive. In an attempt to offer some consolation, Baxter advised his young charge, "Don't give up, Jay. We may hit something yet. We're not only checking every vet clinic in town, but also those from Sooke all the way out to Sidney." As he spoke the words, he knew how hollow they sounded. Both of them knew only too well that the clock was ticking and a killer had the upper hand.

To her utter dismay, Tess had no opportunity to work on the hairbrush during the second day of her captivity because although she heard the basement door to the house open and close several times, she did not hear a car. To err on the side of caution, she had to assume her captor was working outside but had not left the property, making it too risky to work on the brush. If he happened to pass by her window and look in...

Thinking back on their conversation that morning, she chided herself roundly for her stupidity. True, she mustn't show fear, but to deliberately provoke him was madness. It was as though some sick need within her had been awakened, some primal desire to wound him, to strike out at him *first* before he could hurt her. Never in her life had she ever used her ability that way, and it sickened her to have stooped to such a low level. She *had* to be more careful. She could not risk angering him again. She knew the key to her survival was playing to his ego. Suddenly, her thoughts were interrupted by the sound of a bolt sliding...

Tess stood sick with fear at the touch of his fingers lacing idly through her hair, struggling against an overwhelming urge to throw up. She hated the mounting sense of helplessness she was experiencing, and it was all she could do not to cringe. Closing her eyes, she waited in tortured silence for his hands to settle around her neck. If they did, she knew what she would do – *fight!* She was certain her struggles would only excite him further, and she already knew how strong he was, but she had no choice. She would *not* go like a lamb to the slaughter.

A soft puff of breath on the side of her neck startled her, bringing her back to reality, sending shivers of apprehension down her spine.

"Now, Tess. That wasn't so bad, was it?" he drawled lazily in her ear.

As she turned to face him, she deliberately took a step back to create some distance between them. "I...I know you have a...a thing for hair," she stammered, trying to disguise her disgust.

"Do you now?" he grinned, clearly amused.

"Yes, an...and if you want my hair, you can have it. Just... cut it off." She knew he would see that for what it was – a plea for her life.

"Now, Tess. Let's not be rash," he drawled. "Besides, I usually collect...*afterwards.*" Stepping closer to her, he closed the gap between them once again. "It's a little ritual I have, quite private, you know," he whispered in her ear. With the back of his hand, he reached up to gently stroke the full length of her hair. Her horrified reaction seemed to delight him, and for full effect, he held up a lock of her hair and inhaled deeply and dramatically.

Some wild part of her wished she could rip out her hair by the roots and strike a match to it right in front of him just to wipe that smug grin off his face.

"Sit down, Tess. *Relax*," his voice was soothing as he gestured to the sole chair in the room. As he watched her cautiously lower herself onto the chair and sit uneasily on the edge of its seat, he began to stroll around the room, hands laced behind his back.

Nervously, she glanced in the direction of the sink.

"I actually have a request of you this afternoon. Well, not really a *request* per se, but I *will* need your cooperation." He smiled broadly at her.

She eyed him warily, afraid of where this was leading.

"You see, Tess. I am a collector of sorts, but I have never indulged in a fantasy of mine."

Her breath hitched in her throat.

"If you will permit me this one indulgence..." He stood before her in all sincerity. "I've never seen a finer head of hair than yours. So thick, so glossy." He reached out to touch her hair again, but she instinctively pulled away, forcing him to drop his arm to his side. He scowled at her before his mask of civility slid back into place.

Tess' mind raced. What could he want of her? As if his possible intentions weren't hard enough to bear, she stood rooted to the spot in tortured silence, rendered speechless when he moved over to the sink and picked up the shampoo bottle, holding it up to his nose, grinning almost shyly at her. She couldn't help it – her eyes darted to the hairbrush whose altered handle was concealed by the towel only inches from where he was standing. If he picked up either, the brush or the towel, she would be caught. Luckily, he appeared engrossed in the heady fragrance of his shampoo. Although her insides felt like they were tied in knots, Tess struggled to keep her composure and desperately tried to think of some way to distract him.

Gesturing for her to join him, he began to roll up his sleeves.

"You...you want t...to *wash* my hair?" she stuttered, flabbergasted.

"Please, *do* indulge me," he cajoled her, raising his eyebrows in mock sincerity.

Quickly sizing up her options, she knew she basically had no choice. A refusal would only anger him, in which case, he might force her. And then he was sure to be doubly angry upon discovering the brush. Her mind in turmoil, Tess reluctantly picked up the chair and carried it over to the sink. As she did so, wild thoughts raced through her mind. Should she throw the chair at him or try to pin him against the wall with it? Even as she schemed, she knew it was no use. The chair was a cheap plastic thing, unlikely to inflict much pain or be very useful. In an attempt to stall for time, she made a show of placing the chair just so in front of the sink, but his impatient sigh forced her to finally take a seat. It wasn't until after she straightened that she realized she would essentially be sitting with her back to him, her throat exposed. This thought nearly undid her.

He caught whiff of her fear and used all of his charm to persuade her, holding his hands up to convince her he had nothing up his sleeves. "I give you my word, Tess. I only want to wash your hair; that's all. It's such a simple request, no?"

Worried he would restrain her if she balked, she sighed deeply in resignation. Steeling herself, she slid back in the chair to lean her head against the edge of the sink.

Thrilled at her capitulation, he rubbed his hands together. "*Good* girl! *Good* girl! Now, you must tell me if the water is too hot," he advised as he turned on the taps.

The touch of his hands through her hair sickened her, raising bile in the back of her throat, causing her to grimace.

Undaunted by her reaction, he proceeded to lather shampoo through her long locks, his hands massaging sensuously from scalp to tip *over* and *over* again for what seemed like an eternity. The sickly sweet fragrance of his shampoo clung in Tess' nostrils, turning her stomach. True to his word, he was gentle, but in spite of his promise, Tess sat in breathless apprehension. She never took her eyes off his face, watching it intently for any indication that the momentary thrill he was experiencing would be replaced by a frenzied need to kill. She needn't have worried, for he was lost to his bliss, eyes rolled back in his head, a depraved grin splitting his face.

⚜ ⚜ ⚜

When it was finally over, he squeezed the water from her long locks and reached for the towel. In her desperation, Tess contemplated biting his arm as it reached past her face, but if truth be told, she was paralyzed with fear. Closing her eyes in anticipation of his fury, she sat trembling and breathless. God knows what he would do to her. Grabbing the end of the towel, he jerked it toward him causing the hairbrush to slip off the lip of the sink and clatter to the floor. He made no comment, nor did he attempt to retrieve it, but instead, wrapped up her mass of wet hair and patted her shoulder.

Confused, she opened her eyes and sat up. Frowning, she craned her neck to look back at him, fearful of the rage she would find there. Instead, she was astonished to simply discover a satiated look on his face. Stupidly, she looked around for the brush but couldn't spot it. Had it fallen underneath the sink?

"Leave it," he waved at her.

She sat dumbfounded before him, her eyes darting to and fro, hardly able to believe her luck.

Sighing contentedly, he grinned like a Cheshire cat and acted like they were now the best of friends after having shared such an intimate experience. "Now, tell me, Tess," he asked her in all seriousness as he moved to stand in front of her. "Have you had your ability all of your life?" His interest appeared genuine, and he waited patiently for her answer.

Tess faced a dilemma – she could refuse to answer his questions, which she desperately wanted to do, or she could play along, the mere thought of which galled her. By keeping him interested and engaged though, he might forget about the brush. And maybe after some conversation, he would simply leave her to dry and comb out her hair by herself. On the one hand, she felt like she was being forced to sell her very soul, but on the other, it was better than losing her life. She was not naïve – she knew the futility in attempting to form any kind of relationship with him in the hope he would spare her. Sociopaths like him didn't feel *anything* for *anyone*. She just needed to keep him distracted for now, and so reluctantly, she answered his question. "No."

Undeterred by her curt response, he continued, "How old were you when you realized you had it?"

"Ten."

"And what was that circumstance?"

"A car accident."

"Ah," he sounded intrigued. "So you never had the ability before the accident, but you had it afterwards?" He stroked his chin absently.

"Yes."

"How extraordinary! Is this the same car accident in which your parents were killed?" he raised his eyebrows at her in mock innocence.

Tess' head jerked up.

The look of dismay on her face pleased him immensely. "Such a *tragedy* to be orphaned at such a young age. Ah, well. What do they say? If something doesn't kill you, it makes you stronger, no?"

She closed her eyes and turned her head away with a pained, defeated expression. A crushing sense of helplessness flooded over her with the understanding he had free reign to her private life. She was left feeling incredibly violated, like he had taken away some precious part of her. When she could bear to look up at him again, she found he was grinning at her with a smug, self-satisfied expression as if to say... *Touché.*

Well, she deserved it. How could she have thought to spar with this man? This... *thing*? She was *not* on his level, nor did she want to be. Her revelation yesterday about his sister was foolhardy. She had unwittingly poked a hornet's nest, and now she had been stung. What other weakness of hers would he find to exploit? Aside from her very real fear of losing her life at this man's hands, her more immediate concern was losing herself in all of this. Would he strip her of that first before he finished her off? Would she lose her very soul to him as well as her life?

Her agonized thoughts were interrupted by a clearing of his throat. Believing his control over her was now well established, he continued with his line of questioning as he paced the room. "So tell me, Tess, how do your visions come on? Do you have any warning at all?"

After a moment's hesitation, she answered dully, "Yes."

When it was apparent she was not about to provide details, he prompted her, "A headache? Blurred vision? Lights?" He flashed her a look that compelled her to answer.

"A buzzing here," she indicated the back of her head. "And nausea."

"Ah, that's unfortunate. I myself suffer no real ill effects. Just a little dizziness. How often do you channel?" He stopped directly in front of her, forcing her to look up at him.

With only a few feet between them, Tess fought the urge to launch herself at him. She had no desire to share such intimate knowledge of her ability with him. It outraged her to have to do so. With a sigh of resignation, she replied wearily, "I…I don't know. It usually comes on of its own accord. I don't have much control over it."

"Oh, I think you have more control than you realize, Tess. I've grown quite good at controlling mine in certain circumstances." He did not elaborate but smiled mischievously at her.

Under his piercing stare, she dropped her eyes.

"And, of course, I want to hear *all* about your first time..."

Her head snapped back up.

"*Channeling*, my dear," he laughed. "Your first time channeling. But I must be gracious. I'm not being a very good host, am I? You may ask *me* a question." He folded his arms across his chest and rocked back on his heels. "After all, we have no more secrets between us, now do we?" he grinned.

Caught off guard, Tess was at a loss for words. Struggling to regain her composure, she blurted out the first thing to pop into her head. "How many women have you killed?" She was mortified the minute the words tumbled out of her mouth, but rather than anger him, her question actually seemed to amuse him.

"Good question, Tess. But if I told you..." He paused and leaned toward her for dramatic effect. "I'd have to kill you, now wouldn't I?"

The blood drained from her face.

He waved good-naturedly at her. "You mustn't mind me," he chuckled. "I'm afraid I have a rather morbid sense of humour."

How ludicrous for a serial killer to joke about something like that! And why had she even asked such a question in the first place? A big part of her didn't *want* to know the answer. But if he had been killing for years, how many women had there been?

"Let's see. I have a strict rule of thumb – no more than two in any one location." He seemed to be doing a mental calculation, but then simply threw his hands up in a dismissive gesture. "Let's just say over the years, I've moved around *a lot*."

"But *why*?" Tess blurted out.

He sighed wearily and turned away from her, walking to the far side of the room by her mattress where he lounged against the wall. "I suppose this is the point where I confess I hear voices telling me to do it, or I was abused as a child, or I have anger management problems, but it's really none of those, Tess." He levelled his gaze at her. "I just...*want* to," he stated plainly as he shrugged nonchalantly.

When she made no comment, he asked her, "Haven't you ever given in to an urge, Tess, only to find it becomes stronger?"

His words made her skin crawl, and she flinched in disgust.

"Ah, I've offended you." He straightened his shoulders as if to shrug off her disapproval.

"Don't you feel *any* guilt? Any remorse at all?"

"I'm sorry to disappoint you, Tess, but no. What I do feel is release, but sadly, it never lasts." He gave her a playful pout and then suddenly grew serious. "It's not the bloodlust you see in the movies, Tess. Quite the contrary. I personally find gore extremely distasteful." He wrinkled his nose. "It's a messy, messy business for which I have no appetite. I *only* resort to it if circumstances dictate it, but I certainly do not enjoy it." He shook his head vigorously. "And I'm no sadist, Tess. I take no pleasure in inflicting pain on anyone." He caught her incredulous look. "Ah, no. You're wrong if you think that."

He approached her slowly and knelt down on his haunches in front of her, his hands pressed together in front of his mouth.

For a brief instant, she feared he would spy the hairbrush from his vantage point, but he was lost in his speech.

"You see, it's the power, Tess. The power to hold another person's life within your hands." With this statement, he lowered his arms and extended them in front of her, unfurling his fingers with deliberate care so she was staring into the palms of his hands. "To feel the pulse of their life force; to take in the last breath to leave their body; to look into their eyes knowing yours are the very last thing they will see in this world." His own eyes bored into hers, leaving her no escape from his madness.

Lowering his hands, he rested them briefly on her knees, prompting Tess to suck in her breath and bite her lower lip. Every fibre of her being screamed out in protest at the vileness of his touch. Straightening suddenly and rising in front of her so she was forced to lift her head in order to maintain eye contact, he continued, "Do you know what I see there, Tess? *Time and time again?*" He smiled lazily, drawing out the suspense, taking obvious pleasure from her distress. "I see wonder. It's a marvelous thing, death is. I see their wonder as they greet it."

She couldn't help herself – she gagged.

Chuckling at her reaction, he clapped his hands together. "Now. Let's brush out that lovely hair of yours," he drawled as he reached to remove the towel from her hair.

Her stomach dropped at his words, and she hung her head and closed her eyes, trying to prepare herself for discovery.

Mistaking her despair for unwillingness, he coaxed her, "Come now, Tess." His voice was low and persuasive. "Don't deny me such a simple pleasure."

She felt the towel fall away and then his hands were upon her hair as he extended it to its full length. Even with her eyes closed, she could sense his wonder. What she did not see was his hand reaching inside his jacket…

And then…slowly…gently, she felt the soft bristles of a brush working through her hair; rhythmic strokes that under any other circumstance would have been pleasurable.

As comprehension dawned, Tess was at once horrified and baffled. Her eyes snapped open. Turning warily to face her captor, she had to blink twice before she could actually process what she was seeing. When he caught her incredulous look, which he mistook for admiration, he held the brush aloft for her to see.

"It's lovely, isn't it?" he exclaimed proudly as he turned the antique silver hairbrush this way and that. "It's a family heirloom."

McLean and Baxter sat in Mrs. Peterson's sunny kitchen and politely declined her offer of tea and cookies. Both of them were impatient to get to the task at hand although neither wanted to appear rude. When Leah had informed McLean that her neighbour, Mrs. Peterson, wanted to speak with the police, it had taken him a minute to recognize the name. Tess had mentioned a Mrs. Peterson once – the nosy neighbour. With this recollection, he had grabbed his partner, and together, they'd rushed over to speak with the woman. Nosy neighbours were a godsend in cases like this.

"Now, Mrs. Peterson," McLean began. "We understand you want to speak with us in relation to a suspicious man in your neighbourhood." He smiled kindly to set her at ease.

Although in her early nineties, Mrs. Peterson was far from frail. She looked like someone who had spent a good portion of her life outdoors. Her tanned face was heavily lined, and she moved with an easy grace for someone her age. It was obvious she still possessed most of her faculties as she managed in her own home, having outlived her husband by some dozen years. As she bustled around in her kitchen, she exuded a nervous energy McLean found endearing. When she finally took a seat at the table with them, she turned her keen eye to the flyer in her hand.

"Well, when Leah brought over Tess' flyer, I took a good look at the police sketch. It didn't really resemble a fellow I chatted with a few weeks ago, but because I've never seen him before in the neighborhood...and now with Tess missing and all... Well, I just thought I should report him all the same."

"And where was this, Mrs. Peterson?" Baxter asked.

"Across the street in the park," she indicated, pointing out the front window. The row of houses in which both Tess and Mrs. Peterson lived faced a large open green space complete with playground, soccer pitch, baseball diamond, and tennis courts. "Oh, it can be a nuisance living across from that at times with all the noise from teenagers on the weekends. I've phoned the police more than once about their shenanigans," she chuckled, shaking her head. "But I do so love to watch the young children. There's nothing like a child at play to keep one young at heart." She winked at them.

"Yes, yes. I'm sure you're right. Now, this man. He was in the park, you say?" Baxter tried to steer the old lady back on track.

"Yes, right over there." She directed their attention to a park bench almost directly in front of her house. "The bench by the big oak tree. I sit there sometimes for a rest after my walk. He was sitting there too that day. He wasn't with any of the children in the playground," she advised them with a knowing nod of her head.

"How do you know?"

"Because I asked him. Ever since all that surveillance with Tess, I've been very wary of strangers. But he was such a *nice* young man."

"Young? How young?" McLean interjected.

"Oh dear, when you're my age, 'young' is a relative term, I'm afraid," she laughed. "If I was to hazard a guess, and you understand it's just a guess, mind you, I would say he was in his forties. Yes," she said, nodding her head as though to convince herself, "somewhere in his forties." She looked at them then, trying to gauge if her information was at all helpful, but both detectives merely nodded.

"Did he give you his name?" McLean asked. Of course, they knew their killer would never use his real name, but knowing a name could nevertheless prove useful in eliminating this person.

"Let me see, now. Yes, he did give me his name. It was David, I believe."

"Any surname?" McLean probed, hoping she would not pick up on the anxious edge to his voice he found hard to mask once his emotions were in play.

After a moment's hesitation, the elderly woman admitted, "Well, if he did, I'm afraid it escapes me." Witnessing the disappointment on the young detective's face, she was quick to add, "But I do remember he said our neighbourhood would be perfect for him and his wife."

"Can you remember what else you talked about?" Baxter asked.

"Well, let me see." Mrs. Peterson puckered her lips and frowned as if deep in concentration. "I seem to recall he asked me a few questions about our neighbourhood. Was it safe? What were our taxes like? That sort of thing." Looking up, she clapped her hands together as if to congratulate herself for remembering so much of their conversation.

"Did you leave first or did he?"

"Why, he did," she replied.

"When he left, did he get in a car?" With this question, both detectives leaned in.

Mrs. Peterson took a moment to answer as though she had to think about it. "Well, no. He just walked off across the park. Yes, yes. I remember thinking how tall he was," she mused.

"Did anything about this guy strike you as odd, Mrs. Peterson? Anything about his demeanour, an accent, a tattoo?" McLean was grasping at straws and he knew it. And more importantly, he had to tread carefully so as not to lead the witness.

"Now that you mention it..." Her brows knitted together in concentration. "There was a large scar on his cheek, the right one, I believe. Poor fellow. He had concealer on it so it wasn't very noticeable until you were right up close." Noticing the puzzled looks on the detectives' faces, she continued, "Oh, I used to be a nurse in my day, so I know all the tricks of the trade for concealing scars. He hid it pretty well, just not well enough for *my* keen eye," she explained as she winked at them.

Both detectives sighed heavily and put their notebooks away. This didn't match their sketch. And without any other information to go on, they decided this lead was not worth chasing. Although Mrs. Peterson invited them to stay for tea, they took their leave, graciously accepting the cookies she insisted on pressing into their hands.

Tess knew she'd been incredibly lucky. Using his antique hairbrush, her captor had stroked her hair for ages, fussing and fawning over its weight, texture and colour. Engrossed in his fantasy, he had forgotten all about the hairbrush on the floor under the sink. He'd stood perhaps feet from it the entire time. Tess retrieved it the moment he left, carefully setting it back on the lip of the sink, its handle concealed once again underneath the now damp towel. Afterwards, she had waited, hoping against hope he would leave the house again like he had the day before, so she would have the opportunity to fashion the brush into something sharper.

Later in the day, after he had delivered her dinner tray, she heard the basement door open and close, and her heart almost skipped a beat when a car engine started. Glancing down at her watch, she noted the time – 4:30 p.m. Same as yesterday. Would he be gone until late again, she wondered? Of course, she had no way of knowing, but she was determined to make the most of whatever time she *did* have. It crossed her mind he might have some kind of evening job like a night clerk at a motel or a janitor, but whatever the reason for his absence, she was elated.

It took only a few minutes to devour the simple meal he had prepared for her after which Tess turned her attention to the task at hand. Quickly retrieving the hairbrush from the sink and sliding out the mattress from the wall, she put on her sock 'glove' once again and set to work, fueled by the horror of his frank intention to kill her at some point. This was day two of her captivity. How many more days would he keep her? She decided then and there she *had* to finish her weapon tonight. To wait even one more day could cost her her life. As the reality of that settled over her – the grim, stark fact she was going to attack a man with nothing more than a crudely sharpened brush handle – her resolution faltered. Who was she kidding? He was not a large man by any means, but a woman her size had virtually *no* chance against someone who outweighed her by a good forty pounds. Not to mention this man was incredibly agile and inordinately strong for his size.

Sitting back on her haunches, she closed her eyes and briefly gave in to her despair before the face of her beloved guardian came to her. Breathing deeply, it was as if she could *feel* Emmy's presence, and for a brief instant, she was certain she caught a hint of lavender, Emmy's favourite perfume. Opening her eyes, Tess took comfort from the steadfast belief her guardian was with her, even now. She remembered fondly how Emmy had always told her she could do whatever she set her mind to, so she vowed to live up to the faith her guardian had always placed in her. And so, she resolved to see her plan through.

With any luck, she would have the element of surprise on her side. *He* had always benefited from that in the past. With the tables now turned, she was hoping he would be thoroughly unprepared for a planned attack. All she needed was seconds, mere seconds to wound him, get the keys, and make her escape.

Suddenly, something dawned on her – she had been so focused on a plan of escape from her room, she hadn't given any thought as to what she would do if it was actually successful! She knew he had a keychain with multiple keys; she had heard the keys jingling when he locked and unlocked her door. Surely the door to the house wouldn't be locked from the inside, would it? If so, would she have time to figure out which key to use? She knew the basement door was near her room. She decided she would try for it first. If it was indeed locked from the inside, she wouldn't waste any time trying his different keys. Instead, she would simply bolt upstairs and make her escape through a door or a window on that level. Surely, they couldn't all be locked or barred, could they?

If she was *very* lucky, his keychain would also include a key to his car. If it didn't, what would she do then? What if his house was out in the middle of nowhere? True panic descended on her in that instant and in her desperation, Tess wasted precious time struggling to regain her composure.

"*Think! Think!*" she finally scolded herself. Realizing it would be foolish to run down the road if he indeed had the car keys on another keychain, she decided she would try for a neighbor's, and if there weren't any, she would strike out cross country. She knew he could probably track her easily enough, but she really had no other alternative. Admittedly, he had moved around a lot, so hopefully, he hadn't lived on his property very long. Maybe he didn't know the surrounding area very well; at least that would level the playing field. Thankfully, it was late in June, which meant the nights would be cool but not unbearable if she had to spend a few days hiking her way out.

Feeling somewhat better after her strategizing session, Tess set to work once again with the hairbrush, carefully pausing time and again to listen for the sound of a car that would signal her captor's return. As the hours ticked by, the brush in her hand began to take shape, the once oval handle gradually crafted into a crude dagger.

Rationalizing his likely return at the same time as the previous evening, Tess rose gingerly from her mattress just after 10:30 p.m. in order to clean up. She didn't think it possible to be stiffer than last night, but her legs felt like jelly as she struggled to stand, and her arm ached and throbbed from hours of concentrated effort. She hoped she hadn't overdone it. In addition to the element of surprise, she also needed strength and agility, no matter how sore she was.

After washing and drying both her hands and the brush, she spent some time planning the actual attack. Holding the brush in front of her, she admired her handiwork. Although small, the dagger would definitely do some damage if she could plunge it into her captor. She debated where to land her blow and decided his chest would present the largest target. All she had to do was avoid his breastbone. A blow to either side would suffice.

Testing out the feel of the dagger in her hand, Tess turned it this way and that, trying to gauge the easiest to way to hold it in order to get the best grip. She practiced whipping it out of her back pocket and lunging forward with a quick stabbing motion. Hopefully, she would be able to wound him before he even knew what had happened.

Preoccupied as she was, Tess never even heard the car's approach; it was only the muffled sound of a car door that alerted her to the fact her captor had returned. Glancing quickly at her watch, she noted the time – 11:05 p.m. He was back! Quickly replacing the brush handle under the towel at the sink, she scurried back over to her mattress, shoving it against the wall before she hurriedly put her sock back on. Lying down on her mattress facing the door, she waited. She was not prepared to launch her plan of attack until he brought her breakfast tray in the morning, so it was crucial if he entered her room tonight that he didn't notice anything amiss. She needn't have worried, for as with the previous night, he simply knocked on her door to check on her.

Before sleep had a chance to overtake her, she crept soundlessly to the sink and retrieved her make-shift dagger, taking it to bed with her. As she lay still and silent, she prayed that the one thing she was counting on – her captor's overconfidence – would be his downfall.

The sound of a bolt being slid back on the door woke Tess the next morning, prompting her eyes to fly open. "*Shit! Shit! Shit!*" she cursed as she flailed around on the mattress for the hairbrush. She'd been so exhausted from her exertions the previous night, she'd slept late. Instead of waking in the pre-dawn hours as she had on the previous two mornings, she hadn't stirred even when the sun rose. And now she *had* to act or risk exposure with her weapon – she had nowhere to hide it. Thankfully, she immediately spied the brush on the floor beside her mattress where she must have kicked it during the night. Snatching it up and stuffing it into her back pocket, she rose hastily and swatted at her wrinkled clothes to straighten them. Her captor entered the room and turned to key the lock, giving her time to catch her breath.

Feigning interest in the food he carried, Tess licked her lips and moved forward with her arms outstretched as if to take the tray from him, all the while praying he would not sense her intentions. Surely, her outstretched arms posed no threat as he could clearly see her upraised, empty palms. He appeared momentarily taken aback by her eagerness, but then simply smirked at her, clearly amused by it. As he continued into the room; however, his smile slowly faded...

Tess followed his gaze and realized with horror he was staring at the condition of her right hand. Even though she had used her 'sock' glove yesterday, her concentrated efforts had produced a large, angry-looking blister. Her heart sank. Knowing her element of surprise had now been compromised but desperate to launch her plan of attack anyway, she reached behind her back and pulled out the brush, rushing him as she did so.

In life or death situations where one must choose to act in a matter of a split second, it is said adrenalin kicks in and instinct simply takes over, often making one's actions a blur, but if truth be told, Tess was hyper-aware of the movement of every single muscle in her body. It was like she was part of a movie that was playing out in excruciatingly slow motion.

The moment he saw Tess come at him with her hand-made dagger, her captor recoiled in alarm and dropped the breakfast tray he was carrying. As it fell, the tray glanced off Tess' knee, upsetting its contents, causing her to falter. As she began to fall, Tess lunged forward and made a vain attempt to plunge her weapon into her captor's chest. Instead, it glanced off his left arm, slicing open his sleeve in the process. As Tess sprawled onto her side, the hairbrush flew from her hand and clattered along the concrete floor coming to rest against the wall underneath the window. She landed heavily on her right hip, the jarring pain momentarily stunning her. Catching her breath, she turned to face her captor and was elated to discover that the blow *had* felled him, for he was crouched against the opposite wall of the room, one hand covering his injured arm.

When he looked up at her, it was with a mixture of shock and disbelief as though he couldn't quite fathom what had just happened. Recovering swiftly, he broke into a lopsided grin. "*Brilliant* plan, my dear!" he exclaimed, spittle escaping from his mouth at the force of his words. "Simply *brilliant!*" The look he gave her was one of fiendish delight behind which lurked a hint of grudging admiration. His mood changed instantaneously, however, when he noted the degree of injury to his arm. Narrowing his gaze and motioning with a quick toss of his head, his voice suddenly flat and deadly serious, he challenged her – "Now come and get the key…"

❧ ❧ ❧

Tess swallowed hard. Biting her lip, she looked longingly at the hairbrush resting against the far wall much closer to him than to her. She was plagued with indecision. True, he was probably in shock, but she did not underestimate, not even for a minute, his agility even while wounded. And even if she managed to get to the brush first, she would realistically have only seconds before he'd be upon her, at which point, he could very well use it on *her*! She *had* to face facts – the element of surprise that had been to her advantage was now gone, and with it, perhaps her best chance at freedom. It was a harsh reality to face.

She had to fight against the urge to scream out her frustration, but knowing such a display would only amuse him, she restrained herself. She knew he would savour every morsel of her despair. Well, she would bloody well rob him of that. It was the least she could do. "You're bleeding quite a bit there." She pointed to his arm in an attempt to distract him.

The hand covering his wound was bright red, and blood had already seeped down the sleeve of his shirt to his elbow.

Carefully pushing herself into a sitting position facing him, wincing at the stabbing pain in her hip as she did so, she motioned with her head. "You're in no shape to make it to the door." Tess knew her attempt at bravado must look unconvincing, but she continued anyway, "Let's just talk about this, OK?"

He did not respond but simply cocked his head at her as if sizing her up.

Tess swallowed past the lump in her throat and attempted to reason with him. "You let me go and I *swear* I won't go to the police for at least 24 hours. You'll have plenty of time to get away. I...I...don't even know your name."

"Ah, you're a clever girl, Tess," he finally spoke, shaking his head slowly back and forth. "Such a *clever* girl. Trying to stall while I bleed. Weaken your opponent to the point where you have the upper hand, no? I am *duly* impressed," he clucked, "but I can assure you, this is only a flesh wound. A few stitches, and I'll be as good as new," he boasted.

Tess' face fell.

"But most definitely," he advised her as he wagged a bloody finger at her without letting go of his arm, "I will not underestimate you again, my dear. You can be certain of that!" He spoke as though he was admonishing a naughty child. Gritting his teeth, he made an attempt to stand.

"How do you know I won't try again before you get to the door?" Tess glared at him, rising to her knees despite her sore hip, her body language making it clear she was prepared to make a break for the hairbrush. Hoping to intimidate him, but knowing the futility of such a gesture, she began to look wildly about her for any other way to stop him, her eye dismissing the spilt breakfast on the floor between them.

"Why, I don't," he shrugged nonchalantly as he straightened, albeit shakily. "That's what I love about you, Tess – your *un-predict-ability*." He pronounced the word slowly with relish. Wincing, he leaned against the wall for support. "But you and I both know you're no match for me. Granted, you've had your little fun, but to think you can outwit *me?*" When he caught her defeated look, he grew conciliatory. "Ah, come now, my dear. Notwithstanding my superior intellect, I've had *so* much more practice at this than you." His stare was mesmerizing, incapacitating her will to fight. Before she knew it, he had moved along the wall to the hairbrush and had begun to gently kick it along in front of him towards the door.

Not knowing what else to do, Tess snatched up the small plastic dinner tray and moved to block the door, holding the tray in front of her like some kind of shield.

He raised his eyebrows as if to say, '*Really?*' and for a moment, both of them simply stared at one another.

"Get out of the way, Tess," he finally spoke. Although it was a command, his voice was strangely quiet. It had a patient quality to it much like a parent talking to a small child who was being petulant.

"No."

"No?" he cocked his head. "Do you know what I will do to you if you do *not?*" he asked her.

Her mouth fell open and a gasp tumbled from it.

"Ah, yes. I can see you know what I'm capable of," he nodded wickedly.

"Give me the key." Tess held out one hand shakily. She couldn't quite believe she had demanded that of him, and by his reaction, neither could he.

"*What?*"

"You heard me. Give me the key," she repeated herself, this time with more authority.

"Ah, Tess. You *are* marvelous." He lowered his head slightly as if to signal capitulation and then a bloody hand shot out at her, trapping her against the door, his fingers digging cruelly into the soft flesh on either side of her neck. As his sweaty face leaned into hers, his sour breath assaulting her senses, he tightened his grip, causing Tess to squirm and thrash. Releasing her hold on the dinner tray, she raised her hands to clutch wildly at her throat, clawing and digging at his fingers in a vain attempt to loosen his hold. Horrid, strangled little sounds emanated from her mouth as her lips moved wordlessly. Had his hand not been slick with blood, he would no doubt have been capable of lifting her completely off her feet. As it was, he had her pinned against the door in a vice-like grip. Within seconds, her colour began to change from red to a bluish purple. Just as her vision was beginning to fade, he flicked his wrist and tossed her aside with no more effort than one would toss away a cigarette butt.

Landing in a heap on the floor, painfully jolting her hip once again, Tess ravenously sucked air into her starved lungs, her hands feverishly massaging her throat as she did so. Incapacitated by a spasm of choking and gagging, eyes watering profusely, she was only vaguely aware he had keyed open the door.

"You have seriously tried my patience today, Tess," he admonished her before breaking out into a huge grin. "But *what* a day it's been!" he exclaimed as he kicked the hairbrush out into the hallway and slammed the door behind him. A second later, the grating sound of bolts being slid back into place echoed deafeningly in her ears.

Tess sat for a long time afterwards huddled against the wall on the cold concrete floor with her knees drawn up, her arms wrapped around them, head bowed. Deep in shock, she was too stunned to even cry. The minutes ticked by, marked only by her ragged breathing. The ache of her bruised throat was nothing compared to the anguish she felt at her failed escape attempt. Without question, he would be doubly careful with her from now on. *If* he kept her around at all, that is.

Gradually, her head cleared, and as it did, she listened acutely for the sound of the exterior door and the car, figuring he would *have* to seek medical attention for the wound on his arm. After all, surely it would require stitches. Occasionally, she could detect faint footsteps on the floor above her in another part of the house. As the minutes stretched into an hour, she grew perplexed, finally admitting to herself the possibility that perhaps he wasn't hurt as badly as she had assumed. Or was he simply refusing to go to a hospital or a medical clinic for fear of being identified? She had no way of knowing, but the mere prospect of his wound only being superficial left her sorely dejected. She had to fight back the flood of despair threatening to overwhelm her.

Finally, she stirred, driven by an overwhelming thirst. The throbbing in her neck had worsened and her throat felt parched and raw almost as though tiny glass shards were dislodged every time she swallowed. Spying the foam cup on the floor in front of her, she crawled stiffly over to it and then stood and made her way unsteadily to the sink. Filling the cup, she drank greedily, the first gulp feeling like a firebrand down her throat, causing her to wince and squeeze her eyes shut. The next few gulps were easier, and afterwards, she tenderly massaged her neck with her free hand in an attempt to ease her discomfort.

Despondent and defeated, she sought the refuge of her mattress where she lay curled up, numb with fear. It was hours later before hunger finally drove her from her bed. She rose stiffly, wincing at her sore hip, and stood to examine her breakfast that was strewn across the floor. Gingerly kneeling down, she forlornly picked up a ripe strawberry, dusted it off and made a face before taking a hesitant bite. She tried to chew and swallow carefully so as not to aggravate her bruised throat. At first, she worried about any permanent damage, but being able to breathe and pass food down her throat eased her fears somewhat. Despite her disgust, she scooped up the cold scrambled eggs from the floor with her fingers and ate them along with the rest of her fruit. She forced herself to eat because she was under no illusion whatsoever that he would bring her a dinner tray later in the day.

It was the end of day three, almost 72 hours since Tess had been reported missing, and they were no closer to finding her. This fact was weighing heavily on all the police officers involved although they tried their best not to show it in front of the dozens of volunteers who had gathered at the search command post at the police station that evening. Many of them were Tess' colleagues from the university – faculty, staff, and fellow graduate students who had taken time out of their professional and personal lives to aid in the search. Leah had been instrumental in organizing them into various groups to put up posters and hand out leaflets at the university, to comb the nearby woods and campus buildings for any evidence, and to spread the word to neighboring residents in case anyone may have noticed anything amiss that night.

The university's astronomical dome was housed on the top of the Science building situated on the southeast side of the campus bordering a large wood known to locals as *Mystic Vale*. This area encompassed several hectares of heavily wooded trails and deep ravines, making it difficult terrain to search. Although the police were certain the suspect had removed Tess from her building by car, they did not rule out the possibility he had then taken a secondary road on campus from which he could have accessed Mystic Vale. And so, it had taken dozens of volunteers hours to tramp inch by inch through the dense brush and trees, prodding and checking every possible hiding place where evidence could have been stashed. Despite their best efforts, they were unsuccessful in turning up anything other than a few discarded beer bottles and joint stubs from young party goers who often used the woods to pass away a few idle hours.

One promising lead from the day's efforts came from a fellow graduate student who remembered a rather odd character at one of the weekly Astronomy Open Houses several weeks prior. An excited Leah steered this student through the crowd of volunteers who were taking a few minutes to grab a quick coffee and muffin before heading home for the night.

"Detective McLean!" Leah called out. "Hey, McLean!" she waved.

Hearing his name, McLean turned around to face her, his face unable to conceal the strain of the last three days. "Hey, Leah," he greeted her in a voice that revealed his exhaustion.

Guiding the graduate student to a stop in front of the young detective, Leah couldn't contain her excitement. "You've *got* to listen to this!"

McLean perked up at the sense of urgency in her voice.

"Ryan here says he remembers a weirdo at one of the Astro Open Houses a few weeks back," Leah informed him. "Right, Ryan?"

The graduate student held out his hand in greeting. "Hi. I'm Ryan Withers."

McLean straightened, clearly intrigued and shook the young man's hand. "Hi. Detective McLean. Jay McLean. Nice to meet you. Come on. We can talk easier in here." He indicated a door to a small side office, signalling to his partner as he did so.

Ryan and Leah followed his lead and both of them took a seat at the table in the centre of the room. McLean remained standing as his partner entered and curtly introduced himself.

"Name's Detective Baxter," he spoke directly to Ryan while simply nodding at Leah.

"Hi, I'm Ryan."

"Anything I can get you guys? A coffee?" McLean asked them.

"I'm fine. I've got to get going soon. I have a lab to teach first thing tomorrow morning," Ryan explained.

"Tell them what you told me, Ryan." Leah, who could barely contain her excitement, nudged him.

"I'm one of the grad students who run the Astronomy Open Houses on Wednesday evenings," he began to explain. "That's where we invite the public to tour the astronomical dome on our building. We talk about the main telescope and we let them look through the smaller ones mounted out on the roof. It's an outreach program," he added. When he witnessed the impatient looks directed at him, Ryan moved along with his story. "Anyway, when Leah came to speak with us today about anything unusual in the last few weeks, it got me thinking about this guy who came to one of the open houses back in May. Leah showed us a sketch of your suspect, and it kind of looked like this guy."

"Did you get his name?" Baxter crossed his beefy arms and frowned.

"Nope, he never gave it." Ryan shrugged his shoulders.

"What was it about this guy that made you remember him?" McLean asked.

"Well, quite frankly, he was not your 'run of the mill' member of the public," Ryan admitted. "I've done a lot of these open houses over the years and we get the same type of people coming out – amateur astronomers, retirees, families with little kids, or students who have a career inter-est in Astronomy, and he just didn't fit into any of those categories."

"How so?" Baxter prompted him.

"Well, for one thing. He asked a lot of questions."

"That's unusual?" Baxter threw Ryan a skeptical look.

"No, not at all," Ryan attempted to explain. "It was more the *type* of questions he was asking. Instead of asking how the telescopes work and what you can see with them, he seemed more interested in the dome facility."

"An engineering background?" McLean speculated.

"No, I don't think so. It was more like – Was there access off the roof from the viewing platform? Did the dome only have one door? Things like that. It just struck me as odd. He didn't spend any time looking through the telescopes, just kind of snooped around."

McLean began to pace the room. "Did he stay long? The entire session, I mean."

"Yup," Ryan nodded.

"You're sure?" Baxter narrowed his eyes.

"Yes, I'm sure," Ryan answered resolutely, "because it ticked me off when he hung around," he added.

"How come you didn't call campus security?" Although Baxter's question was blunt, it didn't seem to offend the young man.

In response, Ryan simply shrugged his shoulders. "Hey, the guy was creepy but he wasn't doing anything disruptive. It crossed my mind he was casing the place for something to steal, but there's really nothing a person can take from up there, you know. It's not like he could remove the smaller telescopes. They're bolted down. So I just shrugged it off until today when Leah came to talk to us."

"Did you see him anywhere in the building after the session?" Baxter asked.

"We always escort the group out of the building," Ryan assured them.

"How big was this group? You sure he left with it?" McLean seemed anxious for confirmation of that fact.

"Any group I've had is usually too big to go down the elevator together, so I always make everyone walk down the stairs," Ryan chuckled. "Some of them complain, but it keeps them all together. Believe me; I checked to make sure this guy was with us."

"Do you remember what evening this was? You said it was back in May?" Baxter flipped out his notepad and pen.

"I know exactly what night it was," Ryan assured him. "Open Houses are every Wednesday night, weather permitting, and I only did one session in May. It was the night of the 25th."

"And have you seen this guy since?" Baxter asked.

"Nope. Just the once." Ryan shook his head.

McLean stood feet apart, hands braced on the tabletop. "And this guy, you say he *sort of* resembled the sketch? How would you describe him?"

"Let's see. He had long hair pulled back in a ponytail." Ryan gestured with his own hair. "And he wore a baseball cap. Can't remember any insignia on it or anything. He was tall, probably six foot and thin, maybe 140 or 150. Kinda reminded me of one of those carny guys."

"Carny guys?" McLean cocked his head and looked over at his partner to see if he understood the reference, but Baxter simply gave him a blank stare.

Ryan looked between the two detectives before attempting to explain. "You know – the kind of lean, wiry guys who run the rides at those traveling carnies." he chuckled. "Sorry," he held up a hand, "I don't mean to be rude or anything."

"Anything else? Any birthmarks, tattoos, missing teeth? Anything like that?" McLean asked as they wrapped up the interview.

"He had a beard." Ryan ran his fingers over his own clean-shaven face. "Well, I guess you'd call it a beard. It was pretty scruffy. And it didn't cover his scar very well."

"Scar?" Both detectives' exclaimed in unison as they looked over at one another in disbelief.

"Yeah," Ryan raised his hand to his own cheek. "Right here. A big one."

His arm was throbbing as he drove home from work later that evening. The painkiller he'd taken had yet to kick in. The ugly gash made by her makeshift dagger had required several stitches to close, and he had stayed late after his shift to sew it up. As luck would have it, the wound was on his non-dominant arm, so he was able to stitch it up himself by standing in front of a mirror. It had been an awkward and slow procedure, but when it was done, he was more than pleased with the result. He did not doubt his arm would be sore for some time, but at least it was nothing more than a flesh wound. No artery had been involved. Plus, he still had full use of his arm.

How clever she had been – to have devised such a resourceful plan so quickly and with so little at her disposal. He *had* to admire her ingenuity. Examining the modified hairbrush, he'd come to the conclusion she had been able to sharpen it on the rough concrete floor, any evidence undoubtedly washed off or covered up by her mattress.

Facing such a shrewd opponent was indeed invigorating, but being caught off guard needled his ego more than he cared to admit. Of course, he *had* come out the winner, but if truth be told, he'd been caught with his pants down. That *never* happened. *Ever.* Thinking back on it, he *had* picked up on a peculiar smell in her room. It had been hard to place so he'd naturally assumed it was a *female* smell. Having no experience as an adult living with a woman, he was totally unfamiliar with their…body odour. How was he supposed to know what they smelled like? With hindsight, he now realized the smell in her room was from her efforts to sharpen the brush. How strange his senses had not alerted him.

Despite breaking his cardinal rule about not bringing a victim to his home, despite this morning's close call, and even despite the dull ache in his arm, he still had no regrets.

None whatsoever. She was a fascinating creature. He simply couldn't remember a time when he'd felt more exhilarated. Realistically though, he knew he had to be very careful around her from now on. Her unpredictability was entertaining, but it was also risky.

With his wound, he had not taken her a dinner tray before he left for work, but once back home after his shift, he quickly put together something for her to eat. It was only a sandwich and a glass of milk, but as it was close to midnight, he figured she would devour it. No sense in starving the poor girl he thought to himself with a chuckle.

As he descended the stairs to deliver her meal, he pondered what her frame of mind would be; after all, she'd had all day to think about her actions. Was she remorseful? Resigned? Scared? Oh, he hoped she was scared. He hoped to see that reflected plainly on her face.

As he slid the first bolt back, he paused when he detected shuffling on the other side of the door. Leaning his ear against it, he listened intently, trying to gauge her whereabouts in the room. He did not want to be ambushed as he entered. He had never worried about such a possibility before with her, but now, he was not taking any chances. Quietly setting the tray on the floor bedside him, he knelt down soundlessly on his knees and lowered his head to look under the door. A sliver of light emanated from inside the room. It amused him to know she slept with the light on. Frightened of the dark, was she? Squinting to see under the door, he could not detect any shadow or any indication she was there. Rising to his full height, he decided to be diligent.

"Tess. I've brought you something to eat."

No response.

"I'm going to open the door, Tess, but when I do, I want to see you on your mattress, is that clear? I'm afraid I'm going to insist on such measures from now on, my dear, as you've proven yourself entirely untrustworthy." He raised a hand to stifle the smirk tugging at the corners of his mouth. No response.

Slowly lowering his hand, he frowned. Pursing his lips, he debated what to do. Well, he was *not* going to plead with her to cooperate. If she chose not to, *she* would suffer the consequences. It was that simple. Making a show of sliding the second bolt noisily, he slowly opened the door...

From his vantage point, his eye immediately fell on the mattress. He had strategically placed it in the left-hand corner of the room so it was the first thing he saw when he opened the door. He needn't have worried, for she lay curled up in a fetal position on the mattress, her eyes huge, her expression one of dread. Realizing he was hunched over as though prepared for a possible attack, he straightened and made a show of entering the room. Unsure if this was some new ploy to throw him off his guard, he swiftly set the tray down on the chair by the door and backed away to stand directly in the doorframe.

"Come now, my dear. You *must* be famished. I've brought you something to eat. Nothing fancy at this hour of course. Just a sandwich and a glass of milk." When he noted her wary reaction, he added – "A token."

She stared blankly at him.

"Why, to show there are no hard feelings, my dear." Bowing his head curtly to demonstrate his sincerity, he turned abruptly and closed and re-bolted the door.

Tess was dumbfounded. Heart still slamming against her chest, she rose and tore into the sandwich.

Tess woke on the fourth morning of her captivity suffering from lethargy and a dull headache. Something wasn't right. She struggled to lift her head, but even this simple act seemed to take a colossal effort. Sinking back down on her mattress, she let out a guttural moan. The last time she'd felt like this...Her eyes flew open. Oh, God, No! The last time she'd felt like this...

He had drugged her *again*! But how? *Why?* She forced her sluggish mind to concentrate, to go over the sequence of events from the previous evening, but it was hard to focus on any single train of thought. Had he injected her again? With effort, she distinctly remembered his departure from her room the night before. Drugs injected directly into one's system took affect quickly, didn't they? If he *had* injected her, she reasoned, she would not have remembered his leave taking. This conclusion calmed her, but only momentarily.

Had he injected her as she slept? That possibility made her sick to her stomach. It was bad enough she was on eggshells every waking minute, frightened out of her wits, but now even her sleep was to be invaded? Sleep was her *only* refuge. She tried to calm herself and reason logically. She was a light sleeper. Surely she would have heard the bolts on the door. Surely she would have felt the needle.

That left only one scenario – he had drugged her food. The *son-of a-bitch*! She had been frightened by such a possibility from the very start, but her back had been against a wall. If she hadn't eaten, she would be too weak to fight for her life when the time came. But why drug her *now*? He obviously hadn't done so in order to kill her. And that wasn't his style anyway. He fed off his victim's fear.

Had he drugged her in order to move her? Tess peered around at her surroundings, squinting in an attempt to bring things into focus. It was not quite dawn, but what precious little moonlight filtered through the window made it possible to discern the now familiar confines of her room – the lone chair, the barred window, the door. No, she had not been moved. She was truly stumped.

She realized the dosage this time must have been less, for she didn't feel as groggy. The sluggishness and headache were there, but they weren't nearly as bad as last time. Did he only need her unconscious for a short period of time?

As she lay there confused and frightened, a dread crept stealthily over her. Had he violated her? She hadn't sensed any sexual perversion with him, but maybe she'd been wrong. Maybe he wasn't capable of normal sexual relations. Maybe the only way he felt able to engage in them was when his partner/victim was unconscious. After all, there would be no need for pretence or foreplay or cooperation of any kind. He could simply take what he wanted. And of course, there would be no performance anxiety, so to speak. That would seem to fit with his narcissistic personality.

With immense relief, she realized she was still fully clothed. This fact, however, brought with it only a fleeting reprieve, for he would have had plenty of time to put her clothes back on. Overwhelmed by uncertainty, she began to sob quietly, hugging herself in a futile attempt to protect her battered state of mind. She was devastated to think her first time (and possibly her last) would be with someone, some...*thing* like him.

Gradually, she became aware of something amiss. She couldn't quite put her finger on it at first. It was only the vaguest of sensations, just a subtle awareness of something...different. Finally, a realization broke over her – she could feel cool air on the back of her neck. This in itself was strange, but even stranger still was the sensation she experienced when she lifted her head. She could not feel the weight of her...hair.

Tess sat bolt upright with this insight despite her lethargy and wooziness, and her hands flew automatically to examine her head. It was gone! Her hair was gone! The bastard had left her with mere inches! Opening her mouth, she let out a blood curdling scream that pierced the calm stillness of the morning.

On the floor above her, he smiled.

When he entered her room later in the morning with her breakfast tray, he was met with a defiant glare. Tess sat in her usual cross-legged fashion on the mattress, her arms folded tightly against her chest, her posture rigid and tense. If he thought his latest move would leave her defeated, he was in for a rude awakening. She was positively fuming.

As he finished keying the interior lock, he was met with a blistering tongue lashing.

"*Why?*" she demanded. "*Why* don't you just get it over with?"

"Oh, but my dear, we're having so much *fun!*" He smirked as he held up his hands in a defensive gesture. "I know. I know," he chuckled. "You're angry with me. You must excuse my indulgence last night. I usually have more self-control than that."

"You sick son-of-a- bitch!" she spat the curse word at him.

"My, my. You are direct, aren't you?" He grinned as he straightened after setting her tray down on the chair. "No matter; I like that. One knows where they stand that way, don't they? You don't mind if I stay a few minutes, do you?" he asked. "I take it you haven't had time to fashion anything else, hmm?" Without waiting for her to answer, he moved to lounge against the wall only feet from her mattress with an effort that was both languid and fluid like a cat.

His proximity spooked her, prompting her to rise quickly off the mattress which only caused her to stumble, forcing her to grab onto the chair for support. As she breathed in the aroma of the delicious-looking meal, her stomach let out a fierce growl. Humiliated at her continual dependence on him and still fuming, she reached her breaking point. Picking up the tray, she hurled it at him with as much force as she could muster in her weakened condition. It was a futile effort, for he easily ducked out of the way, and as a result, the tray hit the wall behind him, splattering her breakfast in a sticky mess that ran down to the floor.

The look on his face was priceless. If he was to take her life this very minute, she would not regret her outburst. It was *worth* it.

"Why feed me if you're just going to kill me?" she screeched at him.

Moving effortlessly to stand directly in front of her, careful to keep a safe distance, he took his time in answering. "You've asked an honest question, Tess," he said, measuring his words, "and I shall endeavour to give you an honest answer."

She thought he would toy with her once again, but his mood suddenly shifted as he readily confessed, "Let's just say, in my *line of work*, I don't get the chance to make many 'connections'. I've always been much more comfortable with animals than with people, you see." With this admission, he seemed to get distracted. "You must remind me to bring Winnifred down to meet you. She's my tabby cat. We get along just fine, her and me. But you..." His voice took on a vague quality as though he was talking more to himself. "You *know* what it's like to be different, Tess. I know you do. And you know what it's like to keep a secret." At this he gently touched his chest. "Here, inside." He levelled his gaze at her, daring her to deny his words.

Tess stood dumbfounded in morbid fascination of the serial killer who stood before her baring his soul to her.

Shaking off his melancholy, he admitted, "It's – how shall I say? – refreshing not to have to pretend. With you there is no pretense."

Despite the consequences of possibly angering him, she wearily replied, "I don't condone what you do. Surely, you must know that."

He gave a quick, matter-of-fact nod. "Yes, yes. Of course. But there's a part of you, Tess, I know there is, a part that understands the importance of being true to one's nature. I sense that in you." He caught the look she gave him, to which he was quick to add, "There's a beast in all of us, Tess. I've just unfettered mine; that's all."

"We've got a hit, Jay," Baxter grinned like a schoolboy as he stuck his head in his partner's office. It was early in the afternoon of the fourth day, and both detectives had spent another sleepless night bunked down on the couches in the staff lounge in order to grab a few fitful hours of sleep. The strain was beginning to show on everyone from the unit clerk all the way up to the chief of police who had requested a briefing the night before.

McLean, who had been on the phone, immediately hung up and looked up with such obvious relief that Baxter winced.

"Come on. I'll fill you in."

The young detective wasted no time sprinting down the hall to catch up with his partner.

"Name's Roy Lange. A co-worker in a vet clinic out in Sidney ID'ed him. Your hunch was right, Jay." Baxter clapped his partner on the back before moving around behind his desk to sit down, stretching both of his feet out on the desktop in a gesture of triumph. "He's our guy alright!" With his hands laced behind his head, he leaned back and basked in the moment.

"Is he in custody?" McLean asked cautiously.

"His address is a PO box in Sidney. He gave it when he first moved here and has never provided a street address." Baxter caught his partner's skeptical look and brushed it off. "Don't worry, Jay. We'll nab him at work. He's scheduled for a shift tonight at 6:00."

"Has he been in to work since Tess was taken?"

"Come on, Jay. We both know this guy's smart enough not to alter his normal routine," Baxter advised.

Although McLean knew that to be true, he still seemed unconvinced and an awkward silence hung in the air prompting Baxter to throw his partner an annoyed look.

"*What?*" Baxter finally demanded, dropping his feet to the floor and sitting forward in his chair.

"I don't know, Ed," McLean sighed as though he had the weight of the world on his shoulders. "He's been one step ahead of us for months now. How come this co-worker hasn't come forward before this?"

"How the hell am I supposed to know? And who cares, Jay. She's ID'ed him now. The guy probably lies pretty low. For Christ's sake, he works night shift cleaning cages after the vet clinic closes."

"You're probably right," McLean conceded. "It's just this guy is no dummy, Ed. I don't think we should underestimate him."

Baxter sighed and spoke in a fatherly tone to his young partner, "The guys are running a background check on him as we speak. Hell, maybe you're right. Maybe he's some *Harvard* graduate!" He slapped his desk and guffawed loudly at his jest.

Just then the phone rang.

"Baxter here. Talk to me." As the senior detective proceeded to listen to the call, his confident swagger slowly dissipated like a flagging sail in a dying wind, and as it did so, he deliberately turned his back on his partner. "Uh huh… yup…uh huh. Alright, thanks." Hanging up the phone, he turned around and cleared his throat several times. He then took his time pouring himself a glass of water. When he finally made eye contact with his partner, his look was sheepish. He simply shrugged his shoulders as if to minimize the news. "Fake identity. Roy Lange died in a house fire twelve years ago."

McLean shook his head and dropped into a chair as though he no longer had the strength to support himself. For a long moment, neither detective said anything.

"You can bet it's all under a fake ID or a stolen one – SIN number, driver's license, car registration." McLean seemed to be talking to himself. "This guy is fucking meticulous," he muttered miserably.

"But not infallible, Jay. The syringe cap proves that. We'll nab him when he shows up for his shift tonight," Baxter replied resolutely. "In the meantime, the guys have brought in the co-worker. Let's see if we can get anything from her."

The two detectives entered the interrogation room moments later with grim determination, their faces haggard from lack of sleep and stress. The woman waiting patiently for them was seated primly at the table, her hands folded neatly together on the table top. She was a large, fleshy woman who, despite her size, still seemed at ease in the confines of her small chair. She took obvious pride in her attire, for she was neatly dressed in a floral print top and matching skirt. The overwhelming aroma of perfume filled the tiny room making McLean wince at the thought of spending any length of time in there. Despite that, he smiled warmly at the woman in an attempt to put her at ease. He needn't have worried, for Nora Evans wasn't the least bit intimidated. Quite the contrary – she was in her element.

Baxter spoke up first after both men had settled themselves in the opposite two seats. "Good afternoon, Ms. Evans. I'm Detective Baxter and this is my partner, Detective McLean."

The woman gave each of them a curt nod, after which she announced, "It's *Miss* Evans. Thank you, Detective."

Whereas that dressing down would have made McLean blush, Baxter simply cleared his throat and made an exaggerated point of addressing the woman correctly. "Of course, *Miss* Evans. Thank you for coming down to the station today. We'd like to ask you a few questions."

"Yes, so your officers told me," she replied with an air of self-importance.

"We understand you work evenings at the vet clinic doing the books, is that correct?"

She seemed indignant at his question. "Yes, but I do a lot of other duties as well – typing, filing, supply orders…"

Baxter cut her off before she could launch into a full-blown job description. "Yes, of course. Thank you for the clarification." He made a show of bringing out the sketch from the folder in his hand after which he set it down on the table in front of her. Sliding it towards her, he asked, "Are you able to identify this person?"

"Well, when the officers showed me this sketch," she said as she pointed to the flyer, "I thought to myself – Nora, that sort of looks like Roy. Same thin face, same large ears."

"Roy *who*, Miss Evans?" Baxter asked, an edge of strain barely discernible in his voice.

"Why, Roy Lange. The man who works at the vet clinic in the evenings with me," she explained. All of a sudden, she leaned against the table, her ample chest spilling onto its surface. "Now, don't you dare tell me he's wanted for some kind of sexual attack!" Without even waiting for an answer, she prattled on as though she'd been given one. "I just *knew* it. He gave me the eebbie-geebbies from the get go. Pretending to be some loner, playing hard to get when he's really out satisfying his carnal lust under the cover of darkness. How many women has he attacked?"

"Slow down, Miss Evans. He's simply a person of interest in a case we're working on," Baxter attempted to explain.

"Person of interest?" she cocked her head. "What's that mean?"

"It means we want to speak with him," McLean answered with infinite patience. "Now, can you tell us anything about him? Anything at all?"

Nora appeared deep in thought for a moment before answering. "He's terribly unsociable, you know. Hardly utters a word. Comes in to do his shift and disappears into the back without so much as a 'howdy-do'. Why, sometimes I think he likes animals better than he likes people! I hear him talking to them back there friendly as all get out, but whenever *I* ask him a question, he clams right up. I find it most *disrespectful.*" She turned her head to the side as if she suddenly found the sketch in front of her distasteful.

"I see. So he never told you much about himself then," McLean stated dully.

"I should say not! I haven't been able to pull two words out of that man's mouth. You'd need pliers to get him to say *anything,*" she muttered.

"We'd like to ask you a few things about his habits then." Baxter took a different tactic. "Do you know if he's punctual for his shifts?"

"Like clockwork. If it's one thing I'll say for the man, he takes pride in getting to work on time. I remember working with this fella once…"

Baxter cut her off before she could get sidetracked. "Do you know *how* he gets to work?"

"Not a clue. I don't hear him until he's at the back door. I always check to make sure it's him, you know. The doors are locked, of course, but a woman can never be too careful these days." Her head bobbed up and down, and she narrowed her eyes knowingly at the two detectives. "He has his own key, and I'm never there when he finishes his shift. I only work until around eight while he stays until he's done, which is always after I leave."

"You're expecting him to be on shift tonight with you, correct?"

"You can check with Dr. Anderson, but yes, tonight is his regular shift," she answered. "I won't be there though. Dr. Anderson said I can take the day off."

It was clear she would add little else to the investigation and that their time would be better spent at the clinic in preparation for their suspect's shift, so the two detectives rose simultaneously from the table.

"Well, thank you for coming in today, Ms…I mean *Miss* Evans. You've been very helpful, but we don't want to take up any more of your time. If we think of anything else, we'll give you a call. You gave our officers your contact information, correct?" Baxter was at his most charming.

"Why, yes, but I don't take calls late at night, you know." She seemed vexed at being dismissed so soon, especially when she had learned nothing about the enigma of a man she worked with. "I don't mind telling you that now I'm spooked!" she balked. "I think I'm going to take a few days and go up island to see my sister until all of this is settled. I can give you her contact information."

"Very good. Good plan," Baxter smiled tightly, one eyebrow raised.

As both men turned to leave, McLean paused in the doorway. "Oh, one other thing, Miss Evans. Does Roy happen to have a scar, here on his cheek?" He indicated a large scar running from his cheekbone down the right side of his face.

"Why, yes. Yes, he does. Guess I don't think much about it anymore, but how did *you* know?"

"I just don't get it." Baxter made no effort to conceal his frustration as he wove in and out of heavy traffic on the highway out to the vet clinic. "I've pulled every warm body I can spare to canvass every gas station, every bank, and every grocery store in Sidney, and no one's ever *seen* this guy. It's like he parachutes into work every day!"

"It's because we're looking in the wrong place," McLean stated dully, staring blankly out his window at the passing scenery. "He doesn't live anywhere near Sidney, Ed. He may work there, but he sure as hell doesn't live there."

McLean's logic made sense and Baxter ran with it. "Where then?"

"My guess is somewhere rural. Somewhere isolated. Somewhere with few neighbors to get in the way. Maybe up in the Highlands or out in Sooke."

"Alright. I'll get our guys to canvass out there. Somebody has *got* to know this guy." Baxter shook his head, irritation bristling in his voice.

"Do you think she's even still alive, Ed?" McLean finally asked the question they had both been pondering all day. "It's been four days," he stated flatly.

"I'm not even going to go there, Jay." Baxter shook his head but failed to bolster even his own sagging doubts.

They rode in silence for several minutes before Baxter could no longer stand the tension. Attempting to distract his partner's train of thought, he asked, "Hey, Jay, you wanna know *why* I think he took her?" When his partner didn't respond, he continued anyway, "I think this guy's probably lived his whole life as an outsider. I'd lay odds he was the kid in school everyone kicked around. And I'd bet he took it too, took the abuse. And now he's found someone out there who's *just* like him. Someone who knows what it's like to be different." When he noted the lack of response from his young partner, Baxter continued, "Don't you see, Jay? That could buy us some time…"

The vet clinic was located on the outskirts of Sidney, a quaint, picturesque municipality some twenty minutes north of Victoria. Often referred to as a seniors' community, it attracted retirees from all over Canada who were drawn there by its small-town feel and mild climate. It offered a quiet, unhurried lifestyle where you could get to know your neighbors, and you weren't afraid to walk the streets at night.

As the two detectives approached the clinic, they were careful to park their unmarked car well down the block as an added precaution. They had arranged to meet with the owner at 4:00 p.m., two hours before their suspect was due for his shift. Despite knowing his alias, they knew virtually nothing else for their efforts other than where he worked. This sting *had* to net him.

As the detectives entered the clinic, an uneasiness settled over McLean, leaving him feeling queasy as though he'd eaten something that hadn't agreed with him. He tried to shake off the feeling and chalked it up to nerves, but it persisted. He prayed his misgivings were wrong, but from his experience, he knew that when everything rode on only one thing, it invariably went wrong.

A bell attached to the front door chimed announcing their entry. The clinic although small was bright and cheery. Posters of dogs, cats, birds, hamsters, and every other kind of pet imaginable adorned the walls in the sitting area. From the back room, a rather young, bald man appeared and smiled at them, extending his hand in greeting as he approached.

"Good afternoon, gentlemen. Detectives Baxter and McLean, I presume."

Both detectives shook the man's hand. "*You're* Dr. Anderson?" Baxter asked with surprise.

"Yes, I am." At this, the vet nodded towards the back. "I've let my staff leave early today as you requested except for Alex who will leave by 5:30. I would prefer to stay on the premises if that's permitted. We have several sick animals in house, and I don't want to leave them."

"Sorry, Doc, not possible, but let's coordinate how we're going to handle this." Baxter sounded much like a school teacher addressing a student.

The vet frowned slightly as he escorted them to the rear of the clinic into his office. On the way, he called to an employee who appeared in gown and gloves and directed the man to monitor the front desk. "I don't want to be interrupted for the next hour, Alex, unless it's an emergency." The vet's tone was warm but authoritative.

"No problem, Dr. Anderson," the employee replied, giving the two detectives a curious perusal as he disappeared down the hall. If he was suspicious of the two men in suits or wondered why the clinic was seriously understaffed on this particular afternoon, he did not ask any questions.

As the vet closed his office door, he caught Baxter's offhand remark. "Either I'm gettin older or they're crankin these guys out of med school younger and younger!"

Dr. Anderson conspicuously cleared his throat and sat down at his desk with a tight smile. "I'm 38 this year Detective, but I'll take that as a compliment," he commented dryly. "Now, may I ask what your interest is in Roy? I wasn't here this afternoon when your officers came to the clinic, but I understand they went to Nora's house to speak with her." The vet looked back and forth between the two detectives.

"He's a person of interest in a disappearance we're investigating," Baxter's tone was brusque, not rude per se, but curt enough to squelch any further inquiries. The vet took the hint and sat back in his chair in apparent acceptance but commented all the same, "You know, I've never had any trouble with Roy. None whatsoever. He's reliable and he does his job well with no complaints. He's reserved, yes, and he minds his own business, but that's not a crime. I just want to say that up front."

"Duly noted, Doc. Now, you told us this Roy has worked for you for, what was it? Less than a year?" Baxter's tone was sarcastic, and he made a show of fumbling through his notepad and readying his pen.

"Yes, I hired him last summer. I know that's not a lot of time to really know a person, but I do know Roy is genuinely good with animals and that often translates to a caring personality." He raised his eyebrow as if to invite any further comment.

"OK, so the guy's a peach, but we still need to speak with him," Baxter retorted. "Now, does this look like him?" He produced a copy of the sketch from the folder in his hand and passed it to the vet.

"Oh, for heaven's sake!" Dr. Anderson exclaimed. "*This* is what you have to go on? This could match any number of thin, middle-aged men." After examining the sketch further, he added, "And besides, Roy has a prominent scar on his face, here." He traced his finger along the right cheekbone. "Even with his beard, it's hard to miss," he advised them. Holding the sketch closer, he frowned. "I've *seen* this sketch recently. It's in relation to some missing woman, isn't it?" he asked, comprehension dawning. "Is *that* what all these measures are for?"

Baxter simply shrugged matter-of-factly.

The vet shook his head and frowned again as he handed the sketch back. "I'm sorry detectives; I just *can't* believe

Roy is mixed up in anything like that. He's a gentle, quiet person."

"Still waters run deep, Doc." Baxter fired back. "Now look, we're obligated to follow every lead, so let's just check this out. If he's not our man, then you've got nothing to worry about."

"But if he is..." The vet looked aghast at the thought. "Then Nora..." he gasped, his voice full of concern.

"We've spoken with Nora. If he *is* our guy, she's probably done the smart thing not to engage him. She's given us some information. We understand, for instance, he's punctual for his shifts."

"Yes," the vet massaged his temple and attempted to focus on the detective's comment. "I'm not usually here during his shift, but on the occasions when I am, he actually arrives a few minutes *before* his shift."

Baxter continued with his line of questioning. "Do you know *how* he gets to work?"

"I'm quite sure he takes the bus. I've offered to give him a ride home now and then when I've had to work late, but he always politely declined, saying the walk to the bus did him good."

As the vet explained all this, McLean's thoughts raced. If this was their guy, there was no way he would take the bus and risk establishing a routine from which he could be identified by the driver or by other passengers. And they already knew he had used a car to abduct Tess. A quick check of vehicle registrations, however, had not produced anything under the name, Roy Lange. Undoubtedly, that was only one of many aliases he used.

McLean was jolted out of his reverie by Baxter clearing his throat. "Now, when he comes on shift, does he enter through the front door or the back entrance?" Baxter asked.

"Back."

"Always?"

"Always. There is no need for him to come in the front. As you saw, that is the reception area," the vet replied, a slight annoyance audible in his voice by this point.

"Good. Once he arrives on shift, what does he do? Does he punch in? Does he get changed? Does he scrub up?" Baxter fired off questions in rapid succession.

"He knows the routine, but he always greets the animals first. He's always eager to see them."

McLean interrupted with a different line of questioning. "How easy are your records to check? Do you have everything stored electronically?"

"Why, yes. Nowadays, we enter everything on the computer." The vet was wary where this was leading.

"How are they filed?"

"By the pet owner's name. Why?"

"If I gave you a person's surname, could you look up on your computer and tell me if anyone by that surname ever brought their pet in here?" McLean knew he was grasping at straws, but he also knew most leads in an investigation were where you least expected them to be.

"Our electronic records on this computer date back to 2000. If it's been since then, then yes, I could tell you."

"Have you ever had a customer by the name of Bishop?" McLean asked.

The vet regarded him for a moment with a vague uneasiness.

"I could get a search warrant, but that would take time we don't have," McLean said in a voice tight with strain.

The vet decided his cooperation would undoubtedly speed things along, so he turned to the computer on his desk, and in a matter of minutes produced a result. "I have two Bishops in the system."

"Any by the given name George or Sandra or even Katie?"

"No, none of those names," the vet looked up at both detectives, his face registering shock. "Surely you aren't referring to that murdered teenager?" he asked. "I was out of town when that happened last year, but I've heard about her case. You *can't* be serious you suspect Roy had anything to do with *a murder* in addition to this missing woman?"

"We can't comment, Doc," Baxter flatly informed the vet.

McLean wasn't at all surprised by the findings. He doubted this killer would risk any connection to his victim, however remote, but it had been worth a shot. Quickly switching gears, he focused on another line of questioning. "How likely would it be for Mr. Lange to get his hands on a sedative?"

Dr. Anderson frowned and shook his head. "Not very likely. We have strict inventory control procedures and a pass-coded med room." Having said that, he looked between the two detectives and was forced to admit, "But I suppose anything is possible if a person is clever enough."

"Going over inventory records will take time we don't have, Jay," Baxter pointed out, turning his attention back to the vet. "So here's what we're gonna do, Doc. My partner and I will be on the premises when the suspect…ah, when Mr. Lange enters. The front entrance is going to be locked so we don't lose him out of that access point. And we'll have the building surrounded."

"The minute he enters the building, he's ours," McLean assured the now worried man sitting across from them.

"You don't understand. I'm still unconvinced about Roy, but if what you suspect is true, then I am concerned for my animals." The vet's gaze drifted toward his office door. "I don't think he'd harm them, of course, just that any altercation could frighten them. I'd like to check their cages to be sure they're secure."

"Fill your boots, Doc," Baxter quipped.

As the worried vet proceeded to inspect the cages and tend to some of the sicker animals, the two detectives checked in with their back-up officers. There were no sightings of the suspect, but they still had another hour to go. A team of police officers were out of sight in neighboring buildings, and plain-clothes officers were stationed at the closest bus stops, just in case. No matter which direction the suspect came from, he would be spotted well before entering the clinic.

It was an agonizing wait. For the first time in his career, McLean wasn't sure he could control himself when he came face to face with this guy. And even if they did nab him, the creep was unlikely to admit to anything, least of all Tess' whereabouts. Was she even still alive?

On his drive to work that evening, he spent time reflecting on Tess' failed escape plan. He would never admit it, of course, but shearing her hair had been a simple matter of payback. Because he considered such primitive emotions as revenge to be beneath him, he was able to rationalize his actions – if he was going to keep her around, she needed to be taught a lesson. After all, he couldn't very well have her running the show, now could he? He smirked when he recalled her defiant reaction. It pleased him immensely that she was a fighter. Oh, he could still sense her fear because she couldn't hide it entirely, but her bravado amused him no end.

His thoughts were cut short as he approached his exit off the highway. He'd continued to work his shifts at the vet clinic even after the abduction for the simple reason he loved the animals he cared for. He also knew it was unwise to alter any routine because such a course of action might only serve to attract notice.

When it came to getting to work, he was exceedingly careful. The bus would have entailed several transfers, not to mention it was a routine he could not risk establishing. Instead, he took his car and always varied his route, sometimes taking the main highway, sometimes taking any number of secondary roads. The vet clinic in which he worked was located on the outskirts of Sidney, and he always parked his car far enough away that he doubted anyone would make a connection to the clinic. And to be doubly careful, he always varied *where* he parked his car.

As he was pressed for time this evening, he decided to take the main highway leading directly up the peninsula to Sidney. Once having taken the appropriate exit off the highway, he grew annoyed at the pace of traffic that had slowed to a crawl through a construction zone. As he sat drumming his fingers impatiently on the steering wheel, he spied a familiar face in the car approaching him through the traffic light – it was Dr. Anderson. He immediately pulled his hat lower on his head and reached over on the pretence of accessing the glove compartment, making sure he remained that way until the vet's car had passed by. He needn't have worried for Dr. Anderson was preoccupied, talking animatedly on a cell phone the whole time.

While it had only taken a few seconds for the vet's car to pass, it was as though a residue had been left in its wake, a residue he immediately picked up. And that was when he knew. He simply *knew*.

It was the doorbell! Tess was positive she had heard the doorbell. At first, she thought she was imaging it as she'd been dozing when she became aware of it, but there it was again – someone was ringing the doorbell! With this realization, she rose quickly from her mattress and stood listening intently in an effort to figure out if the caller was at the basement door. With dismay, she realized it was someone at the front door. Her heart sank.

Despite the slim chance of anyone being able to hear her, she made a rush for the door to her room, landing against it with a muffled thud, almost knocking the wind out of herself in the process. Pounding wildly, she began shouting as loudly as she could. She knew her captor was not at home. She had heard him leave at his usual hour earlier in the day, and when he'd done so on the previous three afternoons, he hadn't come home until late. Even if he *had* returned while she'd been dozing, she no longer cared. After a minute, she paused to catch her breath, willing herself to calm her laboured breathing in order to concentrate on what she could hear. Straining her ears for the slightest sound…she was met with deafening silence.

Gradually, she became aware of the thumping of her own heart as it slammed against her ribcage. Dropping her forehead against the door, she stood motionless for several seconds in the vain hope she would hear the bell again. When she did not, she became aware of her tensed muscles, and upon releasing them, it was as if they gave way causing her to slump against the door and sink slowly to the cold concrete floor. Hanging her head between her knees, she began to weep.

How cruel to be that close to a possible rescue, to be *so* close to safety and sanity, and yet be kept from it. She wished bitterly she had never even *heard* the doorbell, that she could have slept right through it. At least, she wouldn't have gotten her hopes up. To have them dashed, on top of everything else she'd had to endure, was almost more than she could bear.

Minutes passed and then she heard something. Realizing it was a dog barking, she discounted it – a dog could not have rung the doorbell. Soon after though, she was able to detect the faint but unmistakable sound of someone calling. Was it the person at the door? Had they heard her? Were they investigating? With hope beating wildly in her breast, she scrambled to her feet and moved to stand underneath the sole window in her room. Taking a deep breath, she began to scream again in earnest. She kept it up for a full half minute and then paused. She waited some more…still nothing.

Snatching the chair from the middle of the room and placing it underneath the window, she clambered onto it. Grabbing hold of the bars, she stood on tiptoe so she could scan the ground directly in front of the window. At the same time, she frantically shouted, "Help! Help me, *please*! I need help. Is anyone there?"

Frustrated, she relaxed her grip on the window bars and sank back on her heels. Just as she did so, a brief movement in her peripheral vision prompted her to turn her head, her face full of hope. A large golden retriever approached the window, its tail wagging in obvious interest. He stood assessing her full of curiosity and sniffed at the pane of glass, his wet nose leaving a dirty smudge print. Cocking his head at Tess as though he didn't know quite what to make of her, he barked a greeting.

Hoping the dog's owner would make an appearance, Tess attempted to keep the animal's attention. "Here, boy. Come here, boy," she encouraged it, holding her hand up to the window.

Despite her efforts, the dog quickly lost interest and wandered off, leaving Tess groaning in despair. It was just her luck to have a dog as her would-be-rescuer.

Just then a pair of legs, and soon after, a face came into view, startling Tess so badly she instinctively backed away, and as a consequence, almost toppled off her perch. The kindly face that peered in at her was elderly and male. Once over her initial shock, Tess reached up to press her face against the bars and pleaded for help.

"*Please*, help me. I've been kidnapped. *Please* call the police."

The old man was obviously having difficulty maintaining his balance stooped over as he was, so bending down gingerly first on one knee and then the other, he inched closer to the window, cupping his hand to his ear in an attempt to hear her.

Great. He's hard-of-hearing.

The dog began barking excitedly at that point, but his owner paid it no heed, preoccupied as he was at the window. Just as Tess opened her mouth to repeat her plea, she heard a sickening thud. The old man's expression turned from one of concern to one of surprise and pain as he slumped to the ground. When he feebly attempted to raise himself, the look in his eyes reflected the full horror of his predicament. A second equally loud thud splattered the window with blood. It was on the second blow that she saw the shovel. Shocked and sickened, she stood rooted to the spot, unable to make her limbs obey her natural flight response. And then the old man's body was dragged out of sight, disappearing from view in short, angry jerks.

Tess was vaguely aware of the dog barking furiously for several more minutes. As her body went into shock, she began to tremble violently. Instinctively, she wrapped her arms around herself to quell the tremors. And then the barking abruptly stopped. Listening intently, she was quite certain there had been no yelp. Surely, he wouldn't have killed the dog as well, would he? And what was he doing home so early anyway? She hadn't expected him for hours. All these thoughts raced through her mind as she waited in agonized silence.

With sickening clarity, she realized what this meant. An innocent man was dead, and she had been the cause. If she had just remained silent, he would have gone on his way. He would be alive this very minute if it hadn't been for her. She'd had *no* right to risk someone else's life, and yet she had. She'd thrown caution to the wind and had grabbed at the opportunity presented to her, grabbed at it with no consideration for anyone but herself. And because of her thoughtless actions, a man was dead.

Stumbling off the chair, she scurried over to her mattress where she sank against the wall in the corner of the room and began to rock herself rhythmically. She knew he would come for her. The cold, hard reality that she had perhaps minutes to live didn't even seem to register with her. She underwent an almost out-of-body experience, as though it wasn't her in this horrific predicament but someone else. It was hard to fathom *she* was the pathetic, fear-riddled woman cowering in anticipation of her captor. However much she desperately needed to use those moments to collect herself, she simply couldn't. Maybe that was a blessing, for when he finally did appear, she was past caring. She simply wanted it to be over with.

The screech of the bolts sliding back signalled his entry, and as he stepped into the room, he threw her an annoyed, exasperated look. Speaking in a carefully controlled voice, but one edged with irritation, he scolded her. "Because of you, Tess, I've had to do a most loathsome thing."

His comment immediately triggered her anger. "What? Kill a helpless old man?" she sneered at him. Her retort shocked even herself, for only moments before she had all but given up.

He simply frowned at her while he keyed the interior lock after which he set the duffel bag he had been carrying down on the chair. His actions sparked Tess to spring warily to her feet.

"So I'm next; is that it?" She was getting hysterical now as she watched him open the bag. "Bashing in the skull of an old man and killing his dog wasn't enough for one day?"

He gave her a mortified look. "I did *not* hurt his dog." He seemed distracted as he proceeded to rummage through the bag. "But it knows I hurt its owner, and I had to chase it off, poor thing."

"*That's* your definition of *loathsome*? You're insane! You are *fucking* insane!" She was screaming now, but she didn't care.

"My, my. Such colourful language. Please calm yourself, Tess." All his earlier irritation seemed to melt away in the face of her hysteria. "We have to leave. Immediately. You can cooperate or I can sedate you. The choice is yours."

He seemed so matter-of-fact about it that she burst out laughing. He was giving her a choice? He was going to kill her, but the choice was to be awake for it or to be oblivious to it? What a ludicrous choice. *Everything* about this man was ludicrous.

When he saw her disbelief, he continued, "Look, Tess. We're moving; that's all. We *have* to leave."

She backed away from him shaking her head slowly and moaning softly.

"I promise. I won't hurt you. I simply have no time to fight with you on this. Now you can make it easy on yourself and cooperate, or I will have to resort to medicating you, and I'm sure you don't want that, now do you?"

She wrapped her arms around herself to bolster her courage. "Alright. Alright. I'll go with you, but no drugs, please."

"Ah, now, good girl." He smiled broadly as he removed a length of rope from the bag. Tess gasped upon seeing it. In an attempt to win her cooperation, he assured her, "No drugs, Tess, but I *will* need to bind your wrists." When she started to protest, he raised a hand. "Merely a precaution. Merely a precaution," he insisted. "I won't bind your feet, but I do insist on your wrists. Place your hands behind your back and turn around, please."

Wordless, she shook her head. The calmness of her voice when she found it was surprising, not only to him, but to her as well. "I won't try anything. I give you my word, but I will *not* turn my back on you. Here," she held her wrists out in front of her defiantly.

For a brief moment, he scrutinized her, sizing up whether it was worth fighting with her over this one thing.

Obviously pressed for time, she hoped he would capitulate, but if she thought that, she was sorely mistaken. He made a sudden grab for her arm, twisting it cruelly and spun her around, after which he grabbed her other arm and proceeded to bind her wrists together leaving a length of rope dangling. She winced at the roughness of the rope as it bit into her flesh. Ignoring her discomfort, he turned his attention back to the duffel bag preoccupying himself with rooting through it.

Despite her rough treatment, Tess was not cowed. "Where are we going?" she demanded.

"Really, Tess. You are becoming *quite* tiresome," he scolded her. "Why, you'd try the patience of a saint." Throwing her a mischievous grin, he added, "And a saint, I'm not."

As they were about to leave the room, he produced a roll of duct tape and stripped off a piece. Tess balked and instinctively backed away, prompting him to hold up his hand. "I can't afford to have you screaming, now can I?"

Tears of frustration and helplessness rolled down her cheeks as she was forced to stand while her captor applied the tape to her mouth. He paused afterwards and awkwardly brushed aside the wetness from her cheek with his thumb. He marveled at it for a moment as if it was something foreign to him.

Moments later, he forced her to walk in front of him out of the basement tethered like a dog on a leash. He had backed the car into the carport right next to the door, and as they stepped outside, Tess took her first breath of fresh air in days. Despite her circumstances, she revelled in the luxury. True panic descended on her, however, when she spied the open trunk of the car, at which point she started straining and bucking on the rope like some wild, crazed animal. Her captor had to drop the duffel bag he was carrying and use both hands in an attempt to control her, jerking so hard on the rope, she was catapulted backwards into his arms. A searing pain shot through her shoulders. Lifting her effortlessly, he dumped her into the trunk's interior and slammed the lid shut before she even knew what had happened. Lying in the dark, coffin-like interior, numb and traumatized, she knew with agonizing clarity that her last chance at freedom may very well have just come and gone.

A s the clock struck 6:00 p.m., McLean had a sick feeling the killer would not show. By 6:01, he was certain. This realization hit him squarely in the gut. All of their careful preparations, all of the steps they had taken to nab this guy, and yet, they had nothing for their efforts. The taste of failure sat sourly in the back of the young detective's throat. Dropping heavily into a chair in the veterinarian's office, he raked a hand through his hair.

"He may still show, Jay." Baxter clapped his partner on the back even though they both knew how implausible that was given what they knew of their suspect.

McLean shook his head and grimaced. "Let's face it, Ed. He made us. I don't know how, but he did. He must have picked up on *something.*" Throwing his hands in the air, McLean continued, "And God help us now. You know what that means. If Tess is even still alive, she won't be for long."

Ed replied in a quiet, measured voice, "If you're right, and he knows we're on to him, Jay, he's going to be on the move, and she would be a huge liability."

The young detective grimaced again and nodded his understanding.

Wasting no time on further speculation, Baxter pulled out his cell phone, punched in a contact and began barking orders, "I want his sketch re-sent to all ferry points and airports on the island and contact the RCMP to alert their highway patrol. Re-send them the sketch too. And listen, for the next 24 hours, I want you guys to monitor all 911 calls from Sidney to Sooke. Call me with *anything* that doesn't sit well with you, no matter how trivial; got it?"

Satisfied his orders were being acted upon, Baxter turned his attention back to his partner who sat dejectedly with his head in his hands. "How long do you want to wait, Jay?" he asked carefully, checking his watch.

"No sense in staying. He's not coming," McLean looked up, sighing heavily.

"Alright then, let's get off our arses and get the crime lab guys in here. Maybe they can lift some prints or DNA from this guy. Call Doc Anderson and get him back here, will ya?" Baxter raised an eyebrow expectantly at his partner as though he would not tolerate self-pity, and in response, McLean duly pulled out his cell phone. He did so with a heavy heart.

Trapped in the pitch black of the trunk's interior, Tess' claustrophobia virtually consumed her, so much so, she wasn't aware of anything other than the importance of calming her breathing. It took several minutes to bring that under control, but once accomplished, she was able to think clearly. She knew a trunk couldn't possibly be airtight although she'd heard of people suffocating in them if they were trapped for any length of time. She had to wonder if it wouldn't be a blessing to simply die that way before reaching their destination. A part of her would love to be a 'fly on the wall' in that case – to see the look on his face when he opened the trunk only to be denied his sport. To cheat him out of his pleasure would be a sweet victory, even if she wasn't around to savour it.

She gently rotated her shoulders in an effort to determine if she had dislocated anything in her attempt to flee, but although sore, they seemed OK. Thank goodness. Where was he taking her? Were they really moving to another location, or was she too much of a risk to have around any longer? What should she do when he came for her? She doubted she could outrun him, and she was no match for his strength, so what did that leave?

Maybe she could fashion something out of the rope. As this idea leapt to mind, she concentrated on freeing one wrist, spending precious minutes pulling, twisting and wriggling her hands. The rope was thick and strong, but so desperate were her efforts, she eventually felt some slack, which only encouraged her to work harder. She knew she was chaffing her wrists and she figured they were probably bleeding, but that seemed trivial under the circumstances.

After what seemed like ages with no further success, her wrists numb and aching, she felt on the verge of giving up, but she knew that in doing so, she would be doomed. She *had* to free her hands and she had to do so before the trauma she was inflicting on her wrists caused them to swell. And so, she persevered with an even greater vengeance, concentrating on her dominant hand, exploring any and every conceivable position in order to free it. *Finally,* her struggles paid off – she was able to pull her right wrist loose. She had to fight the urge to bellow in triumph with her accomplishment, for although it was only one small victory, it felt like the greatest achievement of her life. Reaching up, she stripped the duct tape from her mouth, allowing her to take several deep breaths despite the stuffiness of the trunk's interior. Knowing she could not afford to waste valuable time savouring the moment, she removed the rope from her other wrist and pondered what to do with it. Could she tie the trunk lid down somehow? But what would that accomplish other than prevent him from getting at her? She would still be stuck in the trunk of a car, and he would have the luxury of waiting her out.

Surely there had to be an internal trunk release mechanism somewhere, would there not? Shifting her weight carefully so as not to make any noise, she was able to slide herself into a position whereby she faced the trunk opening. Blindly, she moved her fingers over the inner trunk hatch, searching for some type of handle or some way to access the latch mechanism. In doing so, she suddenly realized the recklessness of bailing out of the trunk of a moving car at highway speed. That in itself was foolhardy, not to mention the possibility of a dashboard light, which would indicate an open trunk lid, essentially tipping him off the minute she disengaged the latch. Granted, from her brief glance at the car as she was led from the house, it appeared to be an older model sedan, so maybe it didn't have any type of indicator, but should she take the chance? Her other choice was to wait until the car stopped. But what would popping the trunk do then other than buy her a few seconds head start? Unsure of what to do, she hesitated and wracked her brain for another idea.

Knowing there *had* to be a spare tire compartment somewhere in the trunk, she began to search frantically for a way to access it and soon came across a metal ring. In order to pull the compartment lid up; however, she had to roll to the very front of the trunk to get out of the way. Once she lifted the cover, she didn't have the necessary leverage to lift the tire itself, but she was able to feel around its contours for any tool, her fingers slipping feverishly into every nook and cranny to examine all her eyes could not see... Her heart sank. Nothing.

Gently closing the compartment cover and rolling carefully onto her back, she covered her face with her hands to stifle her anguish. '*Think*, Tess. *Think!*' she scolded herself. All of a sudden, an earlier speculation she had once contemplated made sense – that her sightings with her captor were somehow the result of proximity. The murder, the ferry and now her captivity had all produced sightings and they were all circumstances involving close physical proximity with her captor. Could she channel in his presence now? And even if she could, would it help? What if he could *tell* she was trying to channel? Such a thought turned her stomach; nevertheless, she had run out of options.

Breathing deeply in order to focus, she tried to clear her mind. It was difficult to push aside the terror coursing through her, to ignore the overwhelming feeling of dread threatening to consume her, but Tess gritted her teeth and tried to concentrate on emptying her mind. Minutes passed marked only by the soft whine of tires on pavement. As she stared into the gaping blackness of the trunk's interior, an image slashed through the darkness. Another followed in rapid succession and another. Trees. She saw trees...

⚜ ⚜ ⚜

Tess groaned and covered her eyes with her hands, curling herself into a fetal position where she lay for several minutes having all but given up. The last four days had been a nightmare. Every bone in her body ached. She was exhausted, having slept only fitfully, dozing for no more than a few hours at a time, always fearful, always on edge. In her despair, all she wanted to do was allow the gentle rocking of the car to lull her to sleep. She didn't know how long she lay in her numb, exhausted state. It could have been minutes; it could have been hours. She lost all track of time, her watch useless in the pitch dark.

Despite the fog of despair, some part of her brain refused to give up, and from out of nowhere, an idea came to her. She could attempt to kick out a tail light in order to alert another driver! She'd seen such a thing once in a movie. Kicking out the tail light would allow her to signal a driver behind them. She could use her hand, or the rope, or even a piece of her clothing. Surely, there were other motorists on the road! Her heart soared with hope. Listening carefully for several seconds in an attempt to discern the sound of other vehicles, she realized with dismay she couldn't hear any. To make matters worse, the car began to slow and turn… She held her breath…

It was a crushing blow to hear the crunch of gravel under the tires because she knew what that meant – they were heading up a logging road. She was so unnerved by this turn of events that all but confirmed her worst fears, she wet herself, the liquid warmth spreading down her legs, but she hardly took notice, her mind was so dulled and traumatized. When she finally did come to her senses, she had to wonder – How much time did she have? Would she have any chance to make a break for it, and even if she did, where would she run to?

In her moment of utter despair, Emmy's face came to her, so unexpected and so calming, she instantly felt her hopelessness melt away. She knew she *had* to fight for her life, even if it meant she died trying. She still had one chance left. She just needed to choose her moment.

Wasting no time, Tess rolled on to her stomach and began to probe methodically along the floor of the trunk, pulling back the carpet to check *every* square inch, relying solely on her sense of touch in the pitch blackness, determined to make one last, thorough search before they reached their destination. 'No stone left unturned' as Emmy would have said. After what seemed like ages, she almost cried with relief when her fingers came across a small loop of nylon fabric tucked under the far corner of the trunk. She pulled it back to reveal a small, hidden compartment behind the wheel well. Frantic now, she groped inside, searching and probing…

The 911 call came in at 7:09 p.m. An elderly woman reported her husband had taken their dog for a walk earlier in the evening, and the dog had come back alone. Not only that, it was highly agitated – it kept running down the road as if attempting to lead its mistress somewhere. Alarmed, she had called 911, fearing her husband had suffered a heart attack or had taken a fall. Because the couple lived out in East Sooke, a rural community some forty kilometers southwest of Victoria, the RCMP had responded and was on scene.

"You're sure it's the husband?" Baxter asked the RCMP constable as he knelt over the body that had been carelessly tossed in a wood shed on the remote rural acreage located down the road from the elderly couple's farm.

"Yup. Had his wallet on him and his dog led us straight here," the constable replied matter-of-factly.

"Did the wife say anything about who lives here?" Baxter stood up and flipped open his notebook.

"Some guy's been renting it for the last year. A real loner apparently. Kept to himself. They only knew him as Rick."

Baxter's pulse quickened with this news, and yet, he was careful to guard his reaction.

McLean, on the other hand, sucked in an audible breath. "Have you guys checked out the house yet?" he asked as he turned on his heel to leave.

"They're in there now," the constable replied, but the young detective was already sprinting up the driveway.

As he crossed the yard, McLean noted the old farmhouse on the property was in a dilapidated state. Its exterior was in sore need of a paint job, and the property in general looked like it had been left to fallow. The place had a sad, neglected air such that anyone passing by would naturally assume it was deserted. McLean flipped his badge at the

280

constable who stood guard at the front door and didn't even wait for Baxter to catch up before he entered the premises. He was immediately struck by how neat and tidy the interior was – an odd contrast to the exterior. Granted, there was very little furniture, but what there was, was tidily arranged. As he passed from room to room, one thing was glaringly obvious – the place was spic and span.

An RCMP constable approached McLean in the kitchen and extended his hand in greeting, introducing himself in the process. McLean distractedly shook hands as his attention was riveted elsewhere – there was a large city map tacked up on the wall beside the window. Approaching it, he could see where a number of subdivisions had been crossed off – by his calculations, about a third of the city. Quickly scanning the Oak Bay neighborhood, his worst fears were confirmed when he found Tess' street circled.

"Looks like he was pretty methodical," the constable confessed, coming up to stand behind the young detective. "And we've got something else downstairs you guys are definitely going to want take a look at." From the stricken reaction of the young detective, the constable was quick to add, "Not another body, but come on." He motioned and proceeded to lead the way down a back staircase into a dank, musty smelling basement, the type that had no doubt flooded many times over the years.

As they descended the stairs, McLean was hit by a wave of nausea at the thought of Tess having been held captive in a place like this. It rolled over him so intense, he almost doubled over. As he leaned against the wall to collect himself, he felt a reassuring hand on his shoulder. Looking up, he grimaced weakly at his partner who clapped him on the back and moved past him. Taking a deep breath, McLean followed with his heart in his throat.

At the end of a long, narrow hallway, a single door stood ajar. There the constable waited. "You'll note the door has two sliding bolts on the outside." He pointed to two thick metal bolts. "Not only that though," he explained as he swung the door open further, "it has a keyable lock on the i*nside*."

"For what?" Baxter frowned.

The constable shrugged his shoulders. "Your guess is as good as mine."

McLean had to fight the sudden surge of bile at the back of his throat as he struggled to comprehend the reason for such a thing. Just what had that maniac done with Tess in this room? It made him sick to think of what she had possibly endured at his hands. Attempting to stay focused on his job, he entered the room and immediately spied the bars on the sole window. A single, stained mattress lay in one corner of the room, and a single chair stood near the door. Walking over to the mattress, McLean knelt to examine it and realized with relief the stains were not blood, but water marks.

"Someone's definitely been down here recently." The constable pointed to the sink where a towel and a shampoo bottle sat. "The towel is still damp," he remarked.

As McLean crossed the room in order to scrutinize the items, something immediately caught his attention – several long strands of dark hair were clearly visible in the sink. His heart skipped a beat as he reached out to touch one of them. It all but confirmed Tess had been held here. Had her killer dispatched a nosy neighbour to guard that secret?

"Have you searched the property yet? This looks like a large acreage," Baxter asked the constable.

"I've got men fanning out from the house, and I've called in our canine unit. It should be here any minute," he assured them. "We found blood staining on the grass outside the window."

McLean's head snapped up.

"Judging by the blood on the old man's skull, we presume it's his, but forensics will confirm that."

McLean turned aside and winced, feeling guilty for *hoping* the blood belonged to the old man.

Baxter, who had been pacing the room, paused and stood stroking his chin. He spoke as if to himself – "It doesn't make any sense why our guy would waste valuable time disposing of Tess' body any differently than the old man's. And why would he *take* her body to dispose of it? To hide the fact she's been here? Her DNA is likely all over this room."

"But why would he take the chance of moving her, Ed?" McLean asked dully.

"Because he's done it once before, Jay. Hell, maybe he sedated her again."

McLean had to admit his partner's reasoning made sense, but a terrible thought dawned on him in that moment. Tess had told them once that this killer *enjoyed* his kills. Pressed for time, would he have moved Tess in order to kill her at his leisure? If so, where would he take her? He would have to backtrack to get to the island highway, crossing through several densely populated townships to do so. Would he take such a risk? A far simpler route would be to head up the west coast along Highway 14 – it had little traffic as it only serviced a few remote communities further up the rugged west coast of the island. And along its length, there were a number of secluded side roads and logging roads that would be ideal for their killer's needs. McLean's thoughts were interrupted by another RCMP officer who entered the room and passed something to the constable before departing.

"Well, at least we've got a description of his vehicle," the constable waived the paper in his hands. "The old man's wife was able to describe it as a green older model sedan. She thinks it may be a Honda. We'll get a bulletin out on it. Our crime lab guys and canine unit are also here, so I'll need to brief them. Excuse me." With that, he left the two detectives alone.

"I *know* what you're thinking, Jay, but there's nothing we can do until first light," Baxter warned his partner.

"She may not *have* until first light, Ed," McLean voiced the fear both men knew only too well. He then proceeded to pace the room, thinking aloud, "If I was in his shoes, I'd head up Highway 14. Can we contact the Coast Guard? They fly with night vision and infrared systems on board, don't they?"

Baxter pursed his lips but nodded his approval. "All right, Jay. I'll put in a call."

Left alone in the room, McLean struggled with the knowledge they had been *so* close. In all likelihood, they had missed Tess by less than an hour. It was a bitter pill to swallow.

As the car started to slow, Tess' breath hitched in her throat. When it finally rolled to a stop, she focused every ounce of concentration on what she could hear. It was several seconds before she heard his door open and then slam shut. She listened with a sinking feeling to his footsteps as they crunched their way along the side of the car. For a fleeting moment, she realized the irony of her situation – despite the fact she was facing death, she never felt more alive. It was as if all of her senses were on overdrive. She was never more aware of the blood coursing through her, of the kick of adrenaline, of her heart beating so wildly it felt like it would burst right out of her chest.

The key scraped in the lock after which the trunk lid was lifted in a swift movement that caught her off guard. She only had a split second to orient herself because he reached for her almost immediately. Although the light was fading now that the sun had already set, it was brighter than the dark confines of the trunk, forcing her to squint and blink in an attempt to adjust. As he hauled her out of the trunk by placing his arms underneath her armpits, she was struck by the warmth of his touch. How could something so evil possibly feel *warm*? How could the same life force beating in her breast beat in his as well? Wasting no time pondering such a thing, she scanned her surroundings and her stomach plummeted. It was as she had suspected – they were in the woods, far from anywhere no doubt.

Just then, something broke in her, and a frantic anger rose from deep within her. She discarded the pretence of being bound, shrugging off the rope, and in a swift, savage movement, she stripped off the tape from her mouth that she had replaced. "You *promised* we were just moving! You *promised* you wouldn't hurt me!" She was furious at his betrayal.

He looked thoroughly amused at her outburst. "Come now, Tess," he chuckled as he shrugged nonchalantly. "You expected *honesty*?" Diverting her attention, he motioned to her cast-off bindings. "I *knew* from the very first you would be a challenge, my dear. I just *knew* it! Why, I've so *thoroughly* enjoyed our sport, I simply have to wonder if your good friend would prove as much fun. Now what was her name?" Putting a finger to his lips, he feigned forgetfulness. "Ah, yes. Leah. Such *lovely* blonde hair."

Tess stood rooted to the spot horrified at his words.

"Ah, but I'm getting ahead of myself." At this, he consulted his watch. "I'll tell you what – I'll give you a head start." Witnessing her dumbfounded expression, he added, "I'd give you my word, but…" He shrugged his shoulders again and arched one eyebrow at her as if daring her to take up the challenge.

She backed away from him and wasted no time in making a break for the cover of the woods, formulating no plan as she ran from him other than to put distance between them. It didn't occur to her should she somehow elude him, survival in the west coast rainforest was a challenge in itself. And even if she had known this fact, it would not have changed her course of action. She would rather have taken her chances with the elements than with *him* any day of the week! Dying from exposure, although grisly in its own right, had to be less terrifying than dying at his hands.

In the distance, she could hear him calling to her, taunting her. The undergrowth was thick and tangled, and as she plowed through it, she was certain he would be able to track her. In places, it was almost impossible to make any headway. The wind storms on the west coast could be savage in the winter, resulting in a number of trees, even large ones, toppled every year. Those decaying trees, rich in nutrients, provided nurseries for a new generation of seedlings that sprouted in wild abandon. They also created obstacles as she ran, taking precious seconds to scramble over or crawl under. Huge, leafy ferns carpeted the forest floor making it difficult to discern a stable foothold causing her to trip and fall at almost every turn. It didn't help that this spring had been one of the wettest on record, creating a slick, almost slimy layer of moss on any exposed surface. Traveling a distance of only a few hundred feet had utterly drained her. Was he counting on that? But by the same token, he should be tiring as well, shouldn't he? And she should be able to hear *him* moving through the forest, shouldn't she? This logic forced her to slow her pace until she finally stopped to listen for him. She heard nothing but the odd call of a bird.

Hope welled in her breast.

Trying to think logically, she reasoned if she couldn't hear him, he couldn't hear her. And so, she started out once more. 'Stay focused, Tess. Stay focused', she coached herself. So intent was she on concentrating on her footing, she didn't even notice the trees were thinning. It was only the difference in light that finally alerted her. As the sun had already set, the fading light filtering through the tree cover was dim at best, but over the last few minutes, it was actually becoming lighter. Pushing forward, she stumbled out of the treeline, not into a clearing as she had expected, but onto the shoulder of a logging road. Undoubtedly, it was the same road they had come in on. Her heart sank, for she had no way of knowing if she had simply gone around in a circle or if she had come upon the same road at another point in the woods. It was impossible to tell. She scanned first to her right and then to her left along the length of visible road, squinting in an attempt to discern the shape of a car pulled off to the side, but she saw none.

She now faced a dilemma – either get back into the woods or follow the road. Slogging through the woods had been exhausting. She knew she would tire more quickly that way. However, the road was exposed; she'd be a sitting duck if he came along it. And she had no idea which direction to take. One way would no doubt lead her back to the car (for which she had no keys, she had to remind herself) and the other way would lead her deeper into the woods. Her thoughts were interrupted by a throat clearing…

"My, my. You are an *elusive* little thing, aren't you?" he drawled.

As she swung around, she stared in disbelief at the figure standing before her only a short distance down the road. She wanted to scream out her frustration, but she would not give him the satisfaction. Instead, she turned abruptly on her heel and made a mad dash for the trees. Within a few minutes of entering the treeline; however, she stopped short. She knew it was useless to run. She knew he would track her. This was a game to him; one he had played countless times before; one he'd surely never lost. She could tire herself out some more, or she could make a last stand now while she still had some fight left in her. The choice was hard when every fibre of her being was screaming at her to flee, but instead, she stood her ground, hunched over with her hands on her knees attempting to catch her breath, scanning the surrounding trees for some sign of him. She didn't have long to wait, for in no time at all, he emerged grinning and shaking his head.

"Ah, Tess. You never *cease* to amaze me," he chuckled.

This was it. Her moment had come…

"If you touch me," she warned, "I'll fight you with *everything* I have," she declared, her face set in a mask of grim determination.

"Ah, my dear girl. S*uch spunk!* From you, I would expect *nothing* less." His voice was like silk, and for a brief moment, she thought she caught a hint of something akin to admiration.

In the next instant, she launched herself at him. After being at his mercy for so long, the look of utter astonishment on his face as she plowed into him was one of the most satisfying moments of her life, even though it may very well be one of her last. She slammed into him so hard they both flew through the air, landing with a muffled thud on the forest floor. She landed atop him so he was at a disadvantage, having had the wind temporarily knocked out of him. Gasping for breath, he glared up at her with a look that was not only furious, but unspeakably murderous. He reminded her of some grotesque gargoyle, and she instinctively recoiled. Caught off guard, her defences down, she fell easy prey to his agility. Quickly regaining the upper hand, he flipped and straddled her.

Now that the tables were turned in his favour, he sneered in triumph as he wrapped his hands around her neck. In that instant, she felt the full horror of her situation, and all reasoning left her as she flailed and clawed at him. Her struggles only seemed to incite him further, causing him to tighten his grip. She knew she had only seconds left when a sense of calm flooded through her. Clenching her fist, she landed a blow directly on his injured arm. Although he did not release his hold on her neck, he groaned in pain and leaned to one side in an attempt to avoid another strike. Now was her chance! With a super human effort, she pushed mightily with her feet, raising her hips slightly off the ground. Reaching behind her back, under her shirt...

He never saw the blow coming. So focused was he on her desperation that seemed to fuel some sick need in him, he never saw the glint of steel as it caught a pale shaft of twilight and descended toward his temple. The blow hit its mark mightily, and he shrieked, a high-pitched wail of pain that echoed throughout the forest. One moment he was in his glory – the next, he lay motionless beside her.

She rolled away from him, choking and gasping, sucking in the crisp, cool air in ragged, rasping breaths. Her hands reached up to her throat, frantically massaging it in an effort to coax air faster into her starved lungs. Lying on her back on the forest floor, the tangy scent of rotting vegetation stung her nostrils, bringing her back to her senses.

Wasting no time, she made a feeble attempt to stand but ended up collapsing onto her knees in front of her captor, her eyes watering so badly she could barely focus. It was some time before she could speak, but when she did, she hurled her words at him – "Did I fail to mention," she panted, "that I have a tire iron, you sick *son-of-a-bitch*?" She had a death grip on the spare tire iron she had found tucked away in that hidden compartment, and so forceful was the kick of adrenaline still coursing through her system, she was prepared to use it again if he so much as fluttered an eyelid.

She desperately wanted to flee, but because she was out in the middle of nowhere, walking out of the woods was not an option. She *had* to get his car keys, but in order to do so, she would have to search his pockets. Tears of frustration welled up in her eyes because she did not want to go anywhere *near* him. Uncertain what to do, she resorted to pacing back and forth, worrying her lower lip, weighing her options.

Too afraid to prod him with the tire iron in case he made a grab for it, she slipped the weapon back into her waistband behind her back. Knowing she would feel much safer if she could somehow tie his hands, even though that meant having to touch him, she tried to brainstorm for a way to accomplish such a task. She could go back to the car to search for the rope she had discarded, but that would mean having to leave him, and she was not prepared to let him out of her sight, not even for an instant. Instead, she quickly stripped off her shirt in order to use her bra, looking around sheepishly as she did so.

'Like there's anyone else here, Tess,' she reprimanded herself.

Slipping back into her shirt, she chuckled nervously – going braless was the *least* of her worries tonight. Before she would allow herself to kneel down beside his body though, she kicked him. Nothing. She kicked him harder. Nothing. And then a terrible realization dawned on her. What if he was *dead?* 'Oh, my God! I've killed him!' she thought as she cupped her hands to her mouth, fighting the urge to throw up while backing slowly away from him.

'Calm down, Tess. For God's sake, *calm down*,' her inner voice hissed.

After taking several deep breaths, she decided she needed to know for certain. Before she could lose her nerve, she approached the body and cautiously knelt down beside it. She could not bring herself to touch his neck, but instead, placed two fingers distastefully against one of his wrists. It sickened her to do even that. Somehow, she believed he wouldn't even *feel* like a normal person. What did she expect? Scales? She shook her head in order to clear it and tried to concentrate on finding a pulse. When she did (albeit, a weak one), she dropped his wrist as though she had just touched a hot flame. She felt both relief and dread – relief at not being a murderess, and dread, that alive, he was still a threat.

Focusing on what she needed to do, she grabbed both of his hands and quickly placed them together on his stomach. As she did so, she noted a trickle of blood running down the side of his face, giving the impression he was crying blood. This image spooked her, and she scrambled backwards, kicking up debris from the forest floor as she went.

'Come on, Tess. *Focus!*' she chided herself, taking a deep, steading breath. In spite of her revulsion, she forced herself to crawl back to the body.

Using her bra, she tied his wrists as tightly as she could. All the while, she was terrified at the possibility he would regain consciousness. She knew she was likely cutting off his circulation, but too damned bad. 'So he loses his hands. That's a bad thing?' she thought to herself. Satisfied for the moment, she cautiously placed her hand against one of his front jean pockets, praying the bulge she found there was his key ring. A nervous giggle bubbled up from inside her. She was amazed she could even *think* something so crass given her predicament. Mercifully, she felt the outline of a key ring, so she steeled herself and plunged her hand into his pocket. As she did so, she feared he would somehow make a grab for her hand even though his were bound.

'Don't be stupid. You've cracked his skull,' she thought as she pulled out the car keys. Not wanting to kneel beside him for any longer than was absolutely necessary, she quickly stood up and backed away.

'OK, Go! *Go!*' a voice inside her head screamed. 'What are you *waiting* for?'

Instead of fleeing, however, she held the distinctive metallic key chain in front of her face and watched the keys dance and jingle from the tremors in her hand. Reaching to still them with her other hand and sighing heavily, she knew what she had to do. She could not leave him there. It had nothing to do with leaving him injured. After what he'd done to her, she could really care less what happened to him, but she did not want to risk the very real possibility he would regain consciousness while she was gone. What if he got away? And what if he made good on his threat? She could not live with herself if anything happened to Leah. And she did not want to live the rest of her life always looking over her shoulder. Even with her new freedom this night, she was *still* tied to him. Exhausted, she started to cry softly, standing indecisively in the middle of nowhere, desperate to leave, but torn by the possible consequences of doing so.

In the end, she accepted the fact she *had* to bring him with her, but she knew it would be no easy task. She could hardly lug his dead weight around the forest all night. Assuming she couldn't be *that* far from the car, she resigned herself to her grisly chore and hoped like hell he wouldn't regain consciousness along the way. If it came down to her life or his, she'd strike him again.

Forcing herself to slip her arms under his shoulders despite her revulsion, she proceeded to drag him inch by inch across the forest floor. Her sore shoulder muscles screamed out in protest, but in her determination, she ignored the pain. Thank God he was not a large man, or she never would have been able to manage. She was well aware branches and rocks were clawing and cutting his back and legs, but she didn't care. It seemed to take ages just to clear the treeline, but with a mighty heave, she broke out onto the shoulder of the road, at which point she paused, struggling to decide which way to go – left or right? She had a 50–50 chance of taking the right direction, but even with those odds, she agonized over the decision. She turned first one way and then the other, a scowl of indecision framing her face, making her look much younger than her years. All her instincts told her to go left, and yet, she called to mind Leah's comment any time they took a road trip: "For God's sake, Tess – you have a horrible sense of direction!"

And so she went right.

After only ten minutes, it wasn't just her shoulders that were killing her, but her back as well; however, the pain gave her something to focus on. She had to stop often and gingerly stretch out the discomfort, but even then, she was always careful never to turn her back on her captor. After another half hour of agonizingly slow progress, her anxiety level reached a feverish pitch. She just couldn't believe she hadn't spotted the car. Surely she couldn't be *that* far from it, could she? Had she gone in the wrong direction? Should she go back the other way along the road? Her throbbing muscles screamed out in protest at such a thought.

In her panic, Tess struggled to think clearly. A full moon was rising, and with it, she could just make out a curve in the road ahead. Despite the lack of much light, the blackness of the trees towering on either side of the road made it easier to discern the pale ribbon of gravel as it wound its way through the forest.

Looking back and forth between her captor and the road, Tess made up her mind. She would venture ahead to see if the car was around the next bend, but she would do so walking backwards, so at least, she would be able to keep an eye on her captor. Before doing so, she lugged him from the shoulder of the road to the very centre in order to keep him in view. It briefly crossed her mind he could easily be run over if a vehicle came along, and although such a thought was gruesome, she highly doubted the likelihood anyone would be out here at this time of night. Anyway, as far as she was concerned, he deserved far worse! And so, Tess backed away from the still form on the ground, treading carefully so as to make as little noise as possible. 'Like he can hear you, Tess,' she thought dryly to herself.

As she reached the curve in the road, she followed it as far as possible while still keeping her captor's dark form in sight. Just when she dared go no further, she spotted the outline of a car a short distance ahead. Covering her mouth with her hands, she contained the whoop of joy that welled up inside her as an intense wave of relief washed over her.

"Come on, Tess. Don't get cocky," she muttered to herself. She knew it was always at this point in a movie that something invariably went wrong...

Almost as though on cue, the stillness of the night was broken by the sound of a branch snapping. Her nerves already frayed, the noise spooked Tess, prompting her to jump and scan wildly about for its source. Peering into the shadows of the treeline with what little moonlight she had at her disposal, she couldn't make anything out. Cocking her head and listening intently for several more seconds, she heard nothing further. Wasting no time, she made her way back to her captor with her heart in her throat, her feet barely feeling like they were touching the ground. She did not run, knowing of course that it would not be wise if there was indeed something out there. Instead, she walked as soundlessly as possible, trying all the while to convince herself there were any number of nocturnal creatures in the forest, the majority of which were *not* dangerous. What she'd most likely heard, logic told her, was a deer.

It seemed to take *forever* to make her way back to her captor who lay oblivious to any danger, although in reality, it was only a matter of minutes. Upon reaching his still form, Tess paused and peered at the wall of trees to her left, straining her ears again for any hint of movement. When she still detected none, she glanced at the man who had caused her so much agony, her mind in turmoil.

'It's not worth it, Tess. Leave him!' her inner voice hissed. Shaking her head to quell her misgivings and ignoring her fear of what could be out there, she set her jaw, resolved to see her plan through. She'd gotten this far with him; she sure as hell wasn't going to quit now.

Fueled by a fierce kick of adrenalin, she hoisted her captor up once again by the shoulders. Suddenly realizing the safest course of action would be to make plenty of noise, she broke into a boisterous rendition of *99 Bottles of Beer on the Wall* – the only song she could think of. Dragging him along, she managed to round the bend in the road in less time than she anticipated. Her whole body ached by now, but at least the car was in sight, only a few dozen feet ahead. Straightening and sighing deeply with relief, she hastily dug the car keys out of her jean pocket.

When another branch snapped, this time more loudly, Tess froze. Her eyes darted to the prostrate form before her, but it lay unmoving at her feet. Groaning, she pivoted cautiously to glance behind her in time to see a shape emerge from the treeline. That was when she came to the horrible realization they were being stalked...

"You've got to be fucking joking!" The words tumbled out of her mouth of their own accord when she spied the glinting yellow eyes and heard the low, throaty growl. She had endured four days of imprisonment *and* a strangulation attempt at the hands of a deranged serial killer only to run into a *cougar*? She could *not* believe her luck.

She tried to remember what little she knew of this elusive predator from snippets of conversations with Emmy over the years and from news reports of cougar sightings and maulings on the island. There had even been several instances when an old cougar or a starving juvenile had wandered right into town, prompting public warnings to keep small pets and children indoors.

She knew they were powerful.

She knew if they ever got you by the throat, you were toast.

But what else? What else? She racked her brain.

Never break eye contact. Or was it – Never look them in the eye?

Walk away backwards *very* slowly. Or was it – Stand your ground and make yourself appear as large as possible?

Growl and bare your teeth. Or was it – don't show any aggression?

Without even thinking, Tess moved to stand behind her captor, putting the unconscious man between her and the menacing predator who was sizing them both up. Would the cougar be satisfied with an easy meal, or would its instinct be to hunt for itself? She tried to gauge how long it would take her to reach the car. If she even made it that far, she had her doubts she could actually get inside in time, but it was her only option. And so she made up her mind right then and there to abandon her captor. Why risk her life for his?

He deserved whatever he got. She had even turned around to make a break for the car only to discover her legs would not obey what her mind was commanding them to do. She quickly realized what the term 'frozen with fear' actually meant. She stood rooted to the spot, her legs refusing to move despite the urge for self-preservation that was screaming at her to flee.

Slowly, cautiously, the cougar emerged from the shadows, prompting Tess to suck in her breath. Despite her very real terror, a part of her was awed by the sheer magnificence of the animal. It was no juvenile. It's sleekly muscled frame moved with an easy, lazy grace. Surely, this one weighed close to two hundred pounds! As it appraised them, its tail twitched hypnotically to and fro, and it continued to emit menacing growls. Tess was close enough to actually *feel* the vibrations, reminding her of the rumbling she'd experienced in her chest as a little girl when a marching band passed by on a parade route – how the bass drums had echoed inside her chest long after the band had moved on.

The big cat continued to assess them, circling cautiously as if wary at the intrusion of two such unexpected creatures in its nightly domain. Tess glanced down at her captor, wishing she could 'will' him to consciousness so he could be of help. It was in that moment, seeing him totally and utterly defenceless, she understood she could not, in good conscience, abandon another human being, even one such as him, to such a cruel fate. And so, not taking her eyes off the cougar, praying that it was only curious, she cautiously bent down and slid her arms underneath her captor's shoulders, muttering up a blue streak as she did so. With a burst of seemingly inhuman strength, she almost lifted him off the ground, so desperate was she to get over to the car. She did not realize until it was too late that her own heroic actions actually sealed their fate. Undoubtedly, she looked smaller and less threatening hunched over as she was, and because of this, the cougar attacked.

It shot toward them, covering the distance between them in mere seconds with a speed that took Tess' breath away. All she had time to take note of was a streak rushing toward them and an ear-splitting snarl. The next thing she knew, it had a hold of her captor's legs, intent obviously on dragging him off. She'd like to say she made a conscious decision to fight back, but if truth be told, instinct simply took over. She hung onto to her captor's shoulders and pulled with all her might so that it became a tug of war. The cougar would pull in short powerful jerks, so powerful she was afraid it would rip one of her captor's legs off. The irony of her situation was not lost on her even in the heat of the moment – but she wasn't fighting to save a serial killer, she was simply fighting to save another human being.

Only then did she finally remember the tire iron, and with this realization, she pulled it out of her waistband and scrambled over her captor's torso towards the big cat. It could not lunge at her without relinquishing its grip, and once committed on a victim, a cougar rarely let go. She was unaware of this, of course, and such knowledge would have brought her cold comfort anyway. Raising the weapon high above her head, she brought it down with all the strength she could muster on the big cat's powerful shoulders. Although it appeared momentarily stunned from the blow, it did not release its grip. She raised the tire iron again, this time aiming it directly at its eye. She struck it there in a powerful jabbing motion, and it reared back howling in agony, its eye gouged and bloodied. She did not waste her advantage, but beat at it mercilessly even as it recoiled. It quickly turned tail and skittered off, swallowed up in mere seconds by the forest. Tess sat on her haunches, bellowing after it in triumph, brandishing her bloodied weapon.

Struggling to stand up, her legs shook so violently, she had to grip the tire iron with both hands for fear of dropping it altogether. Her knees threatened to buckle as she waved her weapon menacingly a last time at the place where the big cat had disappeared.

Not wasting any time, she quickly abandoned all thought of trying to lift her captor up into the trunk of the car. Although he wasn't a big man, she realized there was simply no way she could manage him by herself. That meant he would have to ride *inside* the car with her. That is, *if* she could hoist him into the back seat. She prayed he would not regain consciousness inside the car, knowing she would simply have to take her chances. The fact of the matter was she had no strength or time to do anything else. Whatever the risk, she was determined to free herself from him this night and that meant bringing him with her.

Turning her attention to her captor, she noted the degree of injury to his legs. His jeans were shredded and bloodied, and she could make out several deep puncture wounds around one of his knees. She was not about to tend to him, however, with the injured cougar still lurking out there somewhere, so she concentrated instead on getting him over to the car. Afraid to put away the tire iron, she kept it in one hand as she looped her arms under her captor's shoulders as before. Constantly scanning the treeline, her heart in her throat, she managed to get her burden over to the car. Thankfully, it was unlocked, so she quickly opened one of the rear passenger doors and pushed aside the duffel bag and a duvet onto the floorboard. Hoisting her captor again by the shoulders, she crawled backwards into the back seat, pulling him along after her. In doing so, she discovered that dragging him along level ground was one thing; it was quite another to actually get him up *into* the car. The term 'dead weight' took on new meaning as she yanked and tugged, working up a sweat in the process. As she finally managed to load the body, she quickly reached over and slammed the rear passenger door shut. Only then did she slip the tire iron back into her waistband. Just as she did so, she heard a soft purring sound and felt a movement along her arm, causing her to jerk back so violently, she clunked her head on the interior roof of the car. Winifred meowed an indignant protest at the all the commotion, and then settled herself on her master's chest, purring loudly and rubbing her face against his chin.

"Geez, you scared me half to death!" Tess muttered as she reached out to stroke the tabby cat. In spite of being annoyed, she was actually glad of the company. True, she had just been terrified by her encounter with a 'big cat', but the one purring contentedly before her seemed harmless enough. Winnifred obviously held no grudge against Tess for injuring her master.

Too afraid to get out of the car in order to get into the driver's seat, Tess scrambled over the front seat to settle herself behind the steering wheel. Only then was she able to experience any sense of relief. Pausing only a few seconds to calm her frayed nerves, she dug into her jean pocket for the car keys, determined to get to safety as quickly as possible.

Her stomach dropped – the keys weren't there! She frantically checked both pockets, but it was true – the keys were gone!

Tess collapsed back in her seat, tears of frustration welling up in her eyes. '*Think*, Tess*! Think*!' she berated herself. 'What would you have *done* with them?'

She wracked her brain and painstakingly went over the sequence of events leading up to the cougar attack. She remembered she'd been holding the keys in her hand when she'd heard the cougar...That meant the keys were out *there*. It was the only explanation. She must have dropped them! She felt sick with fear at the thought of going back out there, but what choice did she have? She couldn't very well just sit there when her captor could regain consciousness at any moment. And who knows how long it would be before anyone came along the logging road? *If* anyone came along at all.

She knew she could attempt to hotwire the car using the tire iron to access the ignition wires. Although this idea was tempting, she was aware she would be in big trouble if she only succeeded in damaging the ignition cover. Knowing the keys were out there only steps from the car, she made the decision to search for them. If all else failed, then she could always try her hand at hotwiring.

Steeling herself, she opened the car door cautiously and stepped out onto the gravel road, her heart slamming violently against her chest as she did so. With deliberate care, she reached behind her back and pulled the tire iron out of her waistband just in case. Noting the cougar's blood on one end, she wiped it off as best she could on her jeans. She needed to have a firm grasp – her life could depend on it.

Shielded by the car door, she paused and scanned the place where the cougar had disappeared into the treeline in a desperate attempt to see into the shadows. Nothing. She strained to hear any movement. Nothing.

Not wanting to trigger a hunting instinct if the cougar was indeed still lurking out there, she knew she must not run. As she turned to step away from the car, she realized she had a death grip on the door. At first, she thought of closing it, but if the cougar attacked again, she would at least be able to make a dive for the interior and not waste precious seconds having to swing the door open. Peering into the interior of the car, she wanted to make sure Winnifred was not following her. She needn't have worried. Seemingly content with her master now accounted for, the tabby had settled herself on the rear window ledge. The look she gave Tess was one of typical disinterest like she had no comprehension whatsoever of the seriousness of the situation. Lucky girl.

Tess inched away from her place of refuge and began to walk with painstaking care, always mindful of her position relative to the car. The open door beckoned, and she looked longingly back at it. She would have given *anything* in that moment to trade places with Winnifred or even with *him*, to be ignorant of the dangers facing them, to have someone else assume all the risk, to be spared the pure terror coursing through her.

It seemed to take forever to regain the ground to the point at which she had first seen the cougar. When she was sure she was relatively close, she began to scour the ground in earnest for any sign of the keys. Thank goodness there was a full moon, for with it, she hoped to be able to spy the distinctive metallic key chain, thankful she had made note of it, however briefly. Just as her eye fell on the object she sought, she caught a movement in her peripheral vision. She made a grab for the keys anyway and straightened just as a mother racoon and her family scurried across the road in front of her. They never made a sound, just eyed her warily as if annoyed at her presence in their nightly realm. The relief washing over her was so intense, Tess couldn't help but giggle. Shaking her head, she turned and headed back towards the car, tire iron in one hand, keys in the other.

'OK. Don't jinx it, Tess,' she warned herself.

When she was within a few feet of the car, she lost her composure completely and made a mad dash for the open door, literally launching herself inside, after which she slammed the door shut with a resounding thud. Dropping the tire iron with a thump onto the floorboard, she buried her face in her hands and wept.

It was several minutes before she was capable of collecting herself, but after a quick check in the back seat for both her captor and Winnifred, Tess took a deep, laboured breath and slipped the key into the ignition. As she did so, she threw a quick thank you heavenward, crediting her guardian for watching over her. When the engine mercifully started, she watched with impatience bordering on desperation as the gas gauge slowly rose. Just under half a tank. She prayed it would be enough to get back out onto the highway. Without wasting another second, she swung the car around and headed out, following the tire tracks she assumed were theirs.

Forty minutes later, having reached the highway, she flagged down another motorist – a young couple who were on a camping trip. Tess immediately asked to use their cell phone, concentrating in earnest to remember the correct number, relying on her photographic memory despite her scattered wits. By the fourth ring, she was keenly disappointed at the prospect of reaching voicemail. On the fifth ring, he picked up. Her heart leapt into her throat.

"McLean," her voice broke with his name as she tried to swallow past the huge lump in her throat. Her voice softened, "Hey, where's a cop when you need one?"

Waiting for the police and ambulance, Tess could not shake an uneasy feeling of dread. What if her captor regained consciousness before help arrived? If so, would he be able to get out of the car with his leg injuries? Was she or the young couple she'd flagged down in any danger?

'Be rational, Tess. How far would he get with those injuries?' her inner voice assured her. She tried to calm down but ended up pacing back and forth along the roadside, seemingly oblivious to the light drizzle of rain.

The young man whose cell phone she had borrowed stood with his umbrella watching her. "Hey, are you OK?" he asked.

"Yeah, I'm fine," she answered vaguely.

"Are you hurt?"

"Huh?" She followed his gaze and noted for the first time the blood on her clothing. "No, not me," she replied distractedly. Nodding her head toward the car, she indicated – "Him."

When the young man headed toward the car, she ran after him, grabbing him by the arm. "Hey, stay back. He's dangerous."

"Who?"

"The guy in that car. He just tried to kill me in the woods."

"What? You're joking, right?"

"No, I'm *not* joking. He may be injured and unconscious, but he's really dangerous."

All of a sudden, the strangest feeling came over Tess, and despite her misgivings, she gave in to it. "Stay here," she instructed the young man as she walked cautiously back towards her captor's vehicle, all the while her inner voice was screaming at her to wait for the police. She shook her head to silence it.

As she approached the car, she stopped short several feet away, afraid to go any closer. She tried to peer into the dark interior in search of her captor's prostrate form. Unable to do so, she finally walked up to the rear passenger door and leaned over to cup her hands against the window, but the night was so black, she simply couldn't make anything out. Sensing the young man's presence behind her, mildly annoyed he had followed her despite her warning, she held out her hand, "I need your cell phone again."

"Sure," the young man replied as he dug his hand in his pocket. "But it's almost dead. I have to charge it," he cautioned her.

With phone in hand, Tess reached out and opened the car door, tentatively at first, before swinging it wide. The soft light from the phone illuminated her captor's prone body slumped along the back seats.

"Jesus, what happened to him?" the young man gasped as he took in the bloody clothing.

"Cougar."

"Holy Christ!"

Winifred rose from the rear window ledge as if to inquire why they had both been abandoned. With a graceful leap, she landed on her master and circled his chest as before, but instead of settling there, she merely stretched her legs and moved languidly to rub her back against the front seat. Scooping her up, Tess bent to grab the duvet she'd swept off the back seat earlier, pushing aside the young man as she straightened. Closing the car door, she returned his phone.

Cradling the cat in her arms, she wrapped herself in the duvet to ward off the rain, declining the young man's offer to wait in his car. Assuring him she was fine, she watched as he returned to the shelter of his vehicle to wait for the police. Winnifred's soft purring gradually served to calm her, and she burrowed deeper into the warmth of the duvet. As the minutes passed, the ordeal of the last four days began to take its toll. Her eyelids fluttered…

As exhaustion claimed her and she closed her eyes, awareness came to her slowly as though swimming up from a great depth. At first, the fragrance was barely there, the merest whisper of a scent. As awareness dawned, however, it grew stronger, permeating her nostrils – a sickly sweet, clingy smell. It reminded her of the pungent smell of lilies. It reminded her of *his* shampoo…

Numbly, she made her way over to the young couple's car and rapped on the driver's side window. When the young man rolled down the window, she asked him distractedly, "Have you got a pocket knife?"

"No, I don't carry one. Sorry. Why?"

"Do you have anything in your car? Scissors? Anything sharp?"

The young man's companion began to root through her purse, turning on the overhead light in order to aid her search. After several seconds, she produced rather sheepishly a metal nail file. Leaning over to offer it up, she remarked, "Will this do?"

Tess took hold of it with her free hand and passed the cat to the young man. Hesitating only briefly, she removed the duvet from her shoulders and grabbing one end, she plunged the nail file into it.

The young couple watched her, fascinated. "What are you doing?" the young man asked cautiously as if he didn't really want to know.

Using the hole created by the nail file, Tess ripped apart one pocket and reached inside. Unable to comprehend what it was her fingers were telling her, she frowned. Frustrated at the pitch blackness in which she stood, she threw a cautious glance back toward her captor's car before ducking quickly into the back seat of the young couple's vehicle. Manoeuvring so as not to block the overhead light, her eye fell on the pocket's contents and her stomach turned over. Winnifred, who had been sitting contentedly on the young man's lap, suddenly arched her back and hissed as though equally appalled at the macabre sight within. Despite her revulsion and disbelief, Tess reached out once again to touch the soft, dark filling material, raising a handful of it in front of her face, as if bringing it closer into view could somehow dispel the reality of it.

It was human hair.

"What the hell is *that?*" the young man asked incredulously.

"His masterpiece," she replied numbly.

JULY

It was a beautiful, sunny day in early July, eleven months after Katie Bishop's murder when Tess returned the glass angel ornament to her family. As she drove up the peninsula with the box on the seat beside her, she couldn't help but recall her frame of mind during her visit last fall. She had dreaded the prospect of meeting Katie's parents, knowing she likely wouldn't be able to help them. Katie's mother had been a wreck back then, a fragile, devastated woman who had apparently broken down completely not long afterward. It had been heart wrenching to witness her suffering, and so Tess had asked for something of Katie's with which to channel. She remembered feeling like a fraud in doing so. And as the weeks and months passed, she only grew more despondent and dejected with her failure to produce any leads.

But it was over. It was all over now and Katie's family could at last focus on healing. Tess had been anxious to return the glass angel after having kept it for so long, so it was only a week after Roy Lange's capture when she phoned the Bishops.

It felt strange to know his name – to actually associate a name with *him* and such an ordinary one at that. She had her doubts it was actually his *real* name, of course, as she was certain he probably used numerous aliases. Undoubtedly, it would take a while to figure out who he really was.

A woman's voice had answered her phone call, a voice resonating warmth and sincerity. Tess was surprised at its strength, something that was in sharp contrast with her previous perception of Katie's mother. And so, she'd made arrangements to return the glass angel on the weekend. Parking her car in front of the barn on the Bishop's property as she had done on her previous visit, Tess made her way over to the front of the house. Upon coming into view of the garden, she gasped with pleasure, pausing to take in the full effect of the sight before her. She remembered how it had looked last fall, how she had thought at the time it had all the markings of a true gardener's garden although it had been understandably neglected. As she stood before it today, she marvelled at the transformation. Neat rows of geraniums bordered the front fence line and the walkway leading up to the house. A stately weeping willow dominated one side of the yard, its gently sweeping limbs draped protectively over the garden bed beneath it, a riot of colour emanating from the dozens and dozens of begonias planted there.

The other side of the yard was dedicated to a rose garden not yet in full bloom that encircled a small arbour complete with garden bench. Groupings of Shasta daisies and sunflowers grew in proliferation, their large heads stretched out at this time of day to greet the sun. As if the garden wasn't lovely enough, the entire length of the front porch was lined with hanging baskets.

Sensing Tess' presence, Mrs. Bishop looked up from her weeding and rose quickly, shedding her gardening gloves in the process. She extended her hand warmly in greeting as she approached. "Ah, Miss Walker. Good afternoon. Thank you for coming all this way."

"No problem." Tess shook her hand and smiled shyly. Contrary to her previous impression of Katie's mother, Tess barely recognized the woman who stood before her. For one thing, she looked much younger. Tess surmised that intense grief must age a person, at least temporarily. Now in a better

311

place, the air with which Katie's mother carried herself was full of purpose and confidence.

Tess could easily spot the resemblance to Katie. Both mother and daughter had the same head of thick auburn hair and both were slight of build. Tess had to wince how those very qualities would have attracted Roy's notice. She shoved this thought aside and added, "Please call me Tess."

"Of course, and please, it's Sandra. Only my students call me Mrs. Bishop," she grimaced and rolled her eyes.

"You're a teacher?"

"Yes, kindergarten. They're a handful at that age, but I love it." She stopped short as if to examine Tess more closely. Finally, she nodded her head in approval. "I like your hair. You've cut it."

To put it mildly, Tess was surprised by her comment, for she didn't think Mrs. Bishop had been capable of taking much notice of anything during her previous visit. Still mourning the loss of her hair, Tess ran her hands self-consciously over her cropped locks and answered, "Thanks. It's kind of a drastic change."

"It suits you. Honestly. I never lie about things like that," she said smiling warmly. "I'm *so* glad to finally get a chance to meet you properly. I'm afraid I must apologize for my state of mind at our previous meeting."

Tess nodded her understanding, not quite knowing what to say to this woman who was so refreshingly frank.

Sandra lowered her voice, "I'm afraid I had a really hard time with everything back then. It was such a shock. But I'm better now. When you have three other children dependent on you, you can't wallow in your own misery for too long. Come, let's sit in the shade, shall we?" she suggested as she pointed to the arbour. As she led the way up into the small structure and took a seat on the bench within, she remarked, "I love warm days like this, but it's nice to get out of the heat for a while."

As Tess settled herself on the bench beside Katie's mother, she surveyed the garden and sighed, "You have *such* a lovely garden. It must be a lot of work."

"Ah, yes it is, but it's my passion. George likes to tinker with his cars." With this, she nodded toward the barn. "But give me a spade and a shovel any day. I don't know what I'd do without my garden. It's been my saving grace."

Tess understood implicitly and nodded. Suddenly remembering the box in her hand, she awkwardly handed it to Sandra. "I've been meaning to get this back to you."

A sad smile passed over the woman's face, and for a moment she appeared to be lost in a distant memory. Tess held her breath as Sandra proceeded to open the box and gently take hold of the string, lifting the delicate glass angel into view. As it twirled, it caught the sunlight, and in doing so, it appeared to glow.

"It was so long ago now, but I remember picking this out for her at a market on Salt Spring Island. She was only four months old that first Christmas, and being our first child, we were enamoured with her," she explained in a voice full of emotion.

Tess sat in awkward silence, fearful such a memory might be too painful.

Without taking her eyes off the delicate ornament in front of her, Sandra suddenly announced, "Did you know she was killed the day after her birthday?"

Tess gasped and her hand flew to her mouth in an attempt to stifle her reaction. "No, I didn't. I'm so sorry."

"Her 16th birthday. She'd been begging us for months for a horse; swore she'd take care of it. I told George it was better than her bugging us for a car. So we made her take lessons first, and she volunteered at a boarding farm mucking out stalls and helping with the grooming. If we thought she'd be put off by the work involved, we were wrong. By last summer, she'd found the horse she wanted and that was that.

We bought it as her birthday present. We figured what trouble could she get into out here? Half our neighbours have horses. And there are trails all over the place. If she'd only stuck to those and not ridden along the road. They found her horse along Walman Road." Sandra closed her eyes and took a deep, cleansing breath. Exhaling slowly as if to release the pain of such thoughts, she continued, "I miss her physical presence like crazy, but her essence is still with me." Opening her eyes, she lovingly surveyed her garden. "All I have to do is come out into my garden and close my eyes, and I can call her to mind." She smiled knowingly after which she carefully returned the precious ornament to its box.

Tess reached up and gently laid a hand on Sandra's shoulder.

In response, Sandra laid her own hand over Tess' and confessed, "I was so angry for such a long time, and there wasn't even anyone to be angry with, you know? Just some nameless, faceless monster. But now I can let it all go. I don't want to spend the rest of my life angry. Katie wouldn't have wanted that." Turning to look directly at Tess, Sandra said, "You've brought us such peace of mind, Tess. We're so thankful he won't be able to do this to any other family. And we're so glad *you're* OK." All of a sudden, she embraced her fiercely. Such a gesture would normally have made Tess uncomfortable, but under the circumstances, it felt totally appropriate.

Over Sandra's shoulder, Tess spied George heading toward them with a tray of lemonade accompanied by his three children, little Brett skipping along happily beside him. She smiled a warm greeting.

AUGUST

As Tess and Leah exited the Science building on campus
on a hot summer afternoon, they spied McLean in the
parking lot leaning against his car, arms folded across his
chest, an affectionate smile on his face.

"Afternoon, ladies," he drawled as they approached.

Tess ran her hand through her cropped mane self-consciously. "Geez, I look like a bloody boy with this haircut. I
guess I should be thankful I'm even addressed as a lady."
Frowning, she stopped in front of him. Reaching out, he
playfully pulled her toward him, and wrapping his arms
around her, he tilted her face up to his.

"Alright, you two," Leah reprimanded them as she
brushed past. "Cut it out," she sighed disgustedly. "You guys
are *so* embarrassing."

Ignoring her good naturedly, McLean assured Tess,
"Hey, I think you look adorable." He then proceeded
to nuzzle her neck where he placed a tender kiss.

Tess pulled away from him with an annoyed huff. "Gee,
thanks. 'Adorable'. That does wonders for a woman's ego,"
she muttered dryly.

"Hey, I'd take adorable right about now," Leah piped
up as she waited impatiently for McLean to unlock the car.
"Consider yourself lucky."

"Hey, I'm serious. Not a lot of women look good in short
hair." McLean was back pedalling and he knew it and they
knew it. That lightened the mood and they all laughed.

As they seated themselves in the car, Leah made an
attempt to catch Tess' eye, and when she finally did so,

she gestured at her friend as if to prompt her. Catching sight of the gesture, McLean eyed them both quizzically but said nothing. The atmosphere took on a strained edge as they got underway because it was obvious something was up. Finally, Tess broke the silence. Attempting to sound casual, she confessed, "I had a phone call today from Roy's lawyer."

"About what?" McLean frowned.

"Apparently, he wants to see me," she sighed heavily.

"Who? The lawyer or Roy?" he asked, his tone guarded.

"Roy."

After a moment's hesitation, McLean asked, "And how do you feel about that?"

"I don't know. I thought with his capture, I'd feel a sense of closure; I thought I would feel free of him, you know? But there's something still there. Something I can't quite put my finger on. Maybe I just need to face him?" Tess fidgeted with her hands in her lap. "Leah thinks I'm nuts."

"I did not say that," Leah replied calmly. "All I said is there's absolutely no reason to see him. For God's sake, Tess – just let the bugger rot." She folded her arms across her chest, distaste written all over her face.

"You know, you'll get no thank you from him," McLean gently advised.

Tess nodded her head solemnly. "I know."

"The charges he's facing in your case alone will put him behind bars for a very long time, Tess. And who knows? Maybe we'll be able to tie him to Katie Bishop at some point or even to the case in Manitoba." McLean paused and then exhaled slowly. "I'm not sure what going to see him now will accomplish."

"I don't know either, but I feel like there are still loose ends to tie up," she sighed wearily.

"I just don't want him playing with your head, Tess. Guys like him get off on manipulating other people." The look he gave her when he glanced over at her was etched with concern.

Tess placed her hand on his arm reassuringly. "I promise. I'll think carefully about it first." She flashed him a weak smile.

In the back seat, Leah rolled her eyes and shook her head disapprovingly, prompting a worried look from the young detective's face in the rear view mirror.

EPILOGUE

Tess was unbelievably nervous as the prison guard led her down a long hallway into the drab visitor's room. Their footsteps reverberated off the concrete walls and echoed deafeningly in her ears. She was more than nervous – she was quite literally sick to her stomach. Thankfully, she hadn't been able to force down any breakfast, so at least she wouldn't humiliate herself by throwing up. She'd had a hard time deciding what to wear; after all, how does one dress to meet with a serial killer? She'd felt a strong desire to cover herself up, as if to leave any skin exposed would be to invite his eyes upon her, and although she knew he had no sexual interest in her, she would still feel…unclean. And so, she wore a black turtleneck and jeans. No jewellery, no makeup.

She took the seat she was directed to and listened distractedly as the guard gave her instructions as to what would happen. She was inordinately thankful she would only have to see Roy through the plexiglas partition and speak with him via the phone hanging on the wall beside her. Having that degree of separation gave her *some* peace of mind. As she waited, she ran through in her mind what he could possibly have to say to her. She knew McLean was right. He would not thank her for saving his life. And certainly, he would not apologize. She knew without a doubt he wasn't capable of feeling any remorse for what he'd done to her or to any of his victims. People like him didn't have the ability to feel anything other than their own desires. So why would he summon her? To torture her further? To 'play with her head' as McLean had put it? To 'have the last word', so to speak? He was the one sitting in a jail cell and she was free, but did he still feel the need to have some measure of control over her? She didn't know what to expect from him, and that uncertainty combined with her very real fear of him, left her sorely conflicted.

As she waited apprehensively, she became aware of her thirst, her dry tongue literally feeling two sizes too large for her mouth. She worried it would render her incapable of uttering a word. Part of her simply wanted to flee, to turn around and run back down the corridor and out into the fresh air, to forget all this and simply live her life. And yet something kept her rooted in her chair. Some sick part of her *wanted* to hear what he had to say. She didn't have long to wait, for at that moment a loud buzzer sounded and Roy was ushered in.

The second she heard the door, she dropped her eyes, loathing herself all the while for her cowardice. She knew he was taking the seat in front of her in a very unhurried fashion, as though he had all the time in the world. It was only when she knew he was seated that she willed herself to look up.

He sat across from her with a huge grin plastered on his face as though delighted at the prospect of chatting with an old friend. Without breaking eye contact, he reached over and picked up his phone. When she did not do the same, he cocked his head and arched an eyebrow at her.

She had come this far she reasoned; she would not back down now. Reaching out to lift her phone, she prayed her hand would not fail her. She had to steel herself to hear his voice, willing herself not to flinch, for she did not want to grant him that power over her.

"Ah, Tess. It's so *good* to see you." His voice ran over her like water, and she momentarily closed her eyes as if in a vain attempt to seal him out. When she did not reply, he continued, "I'm *so* glad you came." To anyone who did not know him, he radiated charm and sincerity, but she knew what he was capable of. She knew it all too well.

Opening her eyes, she worried her lower lip and finally spoke in a voice she hoped did not reveal her uneasiness, "What do you want, Roy?"

"Why, your company is enough in itself, my dear," he chuckled and sat back in his chair scrutinizing her, his keen eyes taking in every detail of her appearance.

For a brief instant, she was dismayed this was all it was going to be.

Sensing her disappointment, he gestured – "I love what you've done with your hair." The look he gave her was a conspiratorial one and he smirked. "Of course, I prefer it... long."

Tess had to resist the urge to bash the phone against his thick skull despite the pane of plexiglas between them. She was actually glad of the anger coursing through her though because it gave her courage, but she knew she must not display her temper. He was baiting her, and she would not give him the satisfaction of rattling her cage.

"I actually *like* it short," she remarked nonchalantly, running a hand flippantly over her cropped locks. "It's so much easier to keep this way."

That stole his thunder, leaving him at a momentary loss for words. He recovered his composure quickly, however, and leaned towards her, making a point of his ability to intimidate her. "That's the great thing about hair though, isn't it? You can always grow it out." He winked at her. "That is, if you *live* to grow it out, I suppose..." He took delight in her shocked expression. "Do you know human hair grows at a rate of half an inch a month? Sometimes even faster if

one's diet is right. Sadly, it's not my best attribute, I know."
He ran a hand over the stubble on his shaved head and grimaced self-deprecatingly.

When Tess gave him a sour look, he sat back in his chair
and stretched lazily. "Oh, don't worry. You won't hurt my
feelings to agree. It's the truth, after all. I may have a lot of
other failings, but vanity isn't one of them; I can assure you,"
he chuckled.

An awkward moment passed as he studied her with a
look full of speculation. "I'm just wondering Tess – Why?"

"Why what?" she tried to play for time, annoyed with
herself for not having prepared a suitable answer. She had to
admit she did not think he would actually ask the question.

"You know why," his tone was coy.

Tess broke eye contact and dropped her gaze to her lap.

"Why didn't you just leave me, Tess? You could have so
easily." He leaned forward with his elbows resting on the
edge of the counter in front of him, eager for her response.

Why hadn't she? In all frankness, he was a blight on
society – a miserable, horrible excuse for a human being;
one who had caused nothing but pain and misery. Why then
had she been unable to simply leave him to his fate? A fate
he richly deserved? She closed her eyes and sighed heavily,
wishing she was anywhere but here in this confined little
room with him. But she had come of her own free will, and
she was determined to see this through. Maybe then, she
could achieve some closure.

"I think you know why, Roy," she answered softly.
"Despite what you are, I didn't want that on my conscience."

He nodded his head ever so slightly and slowly stroked
the stubble of beard on his chin as if deep in thought. "And
to think I thought you actually cared." he sighed wistfully.
Having gotten his question out of the way, he sat back in his

chair and quickly switched gears. "Now Tess, you must tell me how you've been keeping."

"That's none of your business, Roy," she replied tersely.

"Oh, but it *is* my business." The lightness of his mood was gone now, and he spoke in a flat, controlled voice. "You know, I don't often know the names of my…*subjects*, at least not beforehand, so you can imagine my surprise when I learned yours – Walker. You see, your surname meant something to me. And as I did a little sleuthing, you can imagine my surprise when I found a skeleton in *your* closet." When he levelled his gaze at her, she could not look away. Witnessing her confusion, he grinned, obviously pleased he had regained the upper hand.

Tess frowned as a slow sense of dread crept over her and a seed of doubt sprouted deep in her belly. She tried to shake it off.

"A skeleton by the name of Eddison Walker."

Her jaw slackened and fell open. Without thinking, she raised a hand to her mouth too late to stifle the strangled gasp that tumbled from it.

Roy paused to enjoy the full effect of her reaction. "He was your father, wasn't he? And he was an English professor, wasn't he?" Not waiting for or even expecting her acknowledgement, he continued, "You see, I never knew *my* father. I was raised with my mother's maiden name, which I'm sure by now you know isn't Lange." He winked at her. "It wasn't until my dear mother passed away this spring that I had a chance to sort through her paperwork, and when I did, I came across my birth certificate. Well, you can imagine *my* surprise to discover my birth father's name after all these years. All I ever knew about him was he was a professor at McGill. Your father taught there in the late sixties did he not?"

Tess sat in speechless silence.

"You see, I've been able to put two and two together, and I've come up with…*me.*" He grinned like a Cheshire cat while he waited for the full repercussion of his news to register with her.

Her eyes flew open and a shocked, horrified expression washed over her face. She felt like she was sliding into an abyss.

"Oh, I'm sure he never knew he'd impregnated one of his students," he assured her with a wave of his hand. "Knowing my mother, she would never have told him. As for me, they say you don't miss what you don't know, and I suppose that's true. I was happy enough with just my mother and me in the beginning. And then she met *him*," he said with contempt as if the actual word left a bitter taste in his mouth. "And they married and had their darling little girl. You remember; the one who had the… accident."

The room began to spin, and his voice took on a hollow quality as though she was hearing it from the end of a long tunnel.

"Our father's untimely death was unfortunate indeed, for I never got the chance to meet him," he speculated. "Although, I suppose," he paused with a dramatic flourish, "he wouldn't *exactly* be proud of my…accomplishments, now would he?" Upon seeing the look of utter revulsion on her face, he continued, "Ah, no matter. I have *you* now. What's the old saying – 'blood is thicker than water'?"

Tess fought desperately for control of her wildly spinning world.

"Intriguing to think of the odds of us finding each another, isn't' it? I wouldn't even want to hazard a guess. Although, can you imagine my chagrin to be bested by my own…*flesh and blood?*" He chuckled and shook his head.

"Kind of ironic, isn't it?" He leaned in toward the glass and searched her face, locking onto her eyes.

"I...I don't believe you. You're sick," Tess finally stammered, wishing she could tear her gaze away from his, knowing she could not, that she was trapped.

"Now, now. Let's not resort to name calling, shall we? Don't just take my word for it," he grinned. "Check it out for yourself." He sat back in his chair, clearly savouring the moment.

Tess struggled with the full horror of his news. How could she possibly be *related* to this monster? How could the same blood flow through his veins? And then comprehension dawned. "You *knew*! You knew and that's why you kept me alive. But you would have killed me anyway?" she cried in dismay.

"Regrettable, yes. But I think we both know I'm not the best big brother," he frowned. "And besides, you were a complication I'm afraid I simply could not afford. But it kind of explains the shared ability, doesn't it?" He appeared suddenly thoughtful. "And our mutual fascination with one another, of course."

Sensing she would flee, he was quick to assure her, "Now, now. Don't worry, Tess. I won't tell a soul. It will be *our* little secret. But I hope you'll stick by your big brother despite what you may learn along the way about my, how shall we say...*colourful* past." He leaned toward the glass again at that point, his eyes gleaming, his face split in a wide grin. "After all – we're *family*."

The phone slipped from her hand to swing wildly to and fro on its cord as if dancing to his maniacal laughter. As Tess attempted to stand, her legs buckled and mercifully the blackness reached out to envelope her. In truth, she gave in to it readily, for it was her only means of escape.

⚜ ⚜ ⚜

Author's Note

A note of thanks to fellow author, Anne Gafiuk, for graciously editing the very first draft of my manuscript and for being my sounding board; to Erinne Sevigny Adachi of Blue Pencil Consult for her editorial services that gave my book a direction to take; and to my literary agent, Romily Withington of Georgina Capel Associates Ltd. for all her guidance and support.

Finally, my sincere appreciation goes to my family and friends who never failed to encourage me.